A CROWN OF CURSED LOVE

J L ROBINSON

J L Robinson

For those who wish to dream.

J L Robinson

PROLOGUE

In the beginning, there was only chaos. Before the forming of the world, there existed only two primordial deities, Gaia, the mother and creator of all life, and Ouranos, her consort and personification of the skies, seas and lands.

Together in their joining, they created twelve beings - The Titans.

Whilst Gaia loved her children more than anything else she had created, Ouranos grew worried that one day the most powerful of his children would overthrow him.

Gaia was not a fool to Ouranos' paranoia and grew suspicious he may try to one day eradicate them. So Gaia, in order to protect her children, secretly forged three objects made from her own primal matter, shadow ore, a deep bronze substance that held the power of Gaia within its metallic matter.

Now weakened, she gave the three strongest of her children each their own relic that would allow them the power to protect themselves should the day come when their father turned against them.

To Cronus, she gave a tall golden staff decorated with intricate images detailing the creation of the Earth.

To Hyperion, she gave a gold sword with an iridescent blade and a golden roped guard finely decorated with the sun symbol along the grip.

And to Theia, she gave a diadem decorated with fine curls of gold wisps, framing a single scarlet eye in the middle.

Each relic contained a fragment of Gaia's power which granted the ability to control life or time itself.

Ouranos grew darker each day with paranoia and an overwhelming greed for power. With Gaia's source diminishing and her power depleting over time, Ouranos with his growing hunger for ultimate control took it upon himself to do what Gaia feared most all along.

Theia knew their father was coming to kill them for the diadem gave her the gift of foresight. Warning her brothers, Cronus and Hyperion, of his intentions gave them time to escape to the only safe place, Tartarus, a one-way prison realm of another world.

But Theia stayed behind to protect her remaining siblings. She got them all out before Ouranos brought down his primordial power on the home of Titans. He foolishly thought he had killed them all, but he had only killed her.

Using the full might of his power gravely weakened Ouranos. And Theia, although not the strongest of the three but easily the smartest, knew her death was a necessary sacrifice. So whilst getting her younger siblings to safety, she gave the youngest, Aphrodite, her diadem.

Gaia was too weak to go against Ouranos after splitting her source into the relics. But now he was weakened, and although Gaia knew using it would mean an eternal rest she would never wake from, she had just enough left in her to strip his very essence entirely from him.

Gaia made the ultimate sacrifice for her children and in those last moments, before the existence of primordial deities passed into oblivion, she used the last light of her power to free her children from Tartarus.

J L Robinson

.

CHAPTER ONE

My mouth gaped open as a metallic-tasting smoke began snaking its route across my tongue, burning its way down my throat.

My lungs desperately pulled at the hot, dense air around me, but I struggled to draw in a single breath. It was dark, almost too dark to see when the sickly scent of spice and ash filled my nose.

Black, inky tendrils now danced from within the dark mist that surrounded me and began to wrap their way across my limbs like the shadow of an ivy tree, polluting my lungs and scorching my skin.

As I looked down through teary eyes that didn't feel like my own, I saw the body of whomever I possessed, lean forward and reach for a small, old-looking dagger.

Unsheathing the silver blade, I noticed a voice, *my voice*. Sobbing furiously, spilling out words between ragged breaths, words that weren't any language I knew or recognised. *But somehow, I understood.*

A briny taste dampened my lips from the tears tracking their way down my cheeks as I tried to make sense of the haze surrounding me.

I felt as though I was outside of my body, somehow in the space between mine and another - a prisoner held captive within a person and forced to feel everything.

My hollow chest now ached with each heavy inhale. A cavity filled with the dark force of fire and ice that writhed around me like a silent storm.

An inferno blazed across my left palm, now tearing my attention downwards.

As I looked down at the clenched hand I recognised not as my own, I turned it over to see a fault line of molton ruby liquid now pouring endlessly from it.

Suddenly lightning cracked around me as a deep thunder boomed, rattling every bone in the body I was occupying.

Wherever I was, darkened further, the air now as dark as night, felt greasy against my burning skin.

A slim arm adorned with bands of tinkling thin gold bracelets reached out into the darkness, and my hands instantly cooled as I pulled forward a thin slab of smooth black rock.

The stone tablet was a cool relief against the open wound, and I noticed the polished face was inscribed with markings. Symbols, or some kind of letters, were carved into the rock began to emit a silvery glow.

Blood burned its way out from the open gash as the hand began to swipe the crimson lava across the glowing symbols. For a moment, the pain was replaced with a dark sensual caress that felt as though it travelled from my hand and settled down, deep into my stomach.

My head snapped back violently as my face was forced upwards, towards a raging storm of silver lightning and dense black clouds now coiling above me. My skin pricked as the presence of something dark brushed against my skin. Something wicked, waiting within the darkness, like an asp ready to strike.

The rain lashed down onto my sore face and across my red-hot skin before hitting the barren ground around me and sizzling into steam. My burning eyes clamped shut as the darkness engulfed me.

Ω

The phone chimed its infuriating wake-up jingle that had woken me up so abruptly as I shifted from beneath my cosy quilt cover to turn the alarm off and scroll through my notifications.

With my eyes still staring at the screen and feeling not quite ready to leave the warmth of my bed, I shouted across the hallway, to the room opposite mine.

"Katerina, get your ass out of bed, it's time for school."

There was a text from Xander, as always.

Good morning!

He had never missed a day since we finished school together four years ago. It was quite sweet.

As I scrolled down the rest of my notifications, I was met with emails from energy suppliers and more overdue bills.

I slumped down, back into the safety of my warm bed and sank under my quilt looking for one last-minute bit of refuge.

"I'm ready when you are Elly," Kat replied and as I reluctantly pulled the covers down, I could see her already standing in my doorway. Her gentle face was framed with her golden hair, which was now tied up, except for the few strands that curled away perfectly from her pale blue eyes.

"I'll make you a coffee!" Her head tilted sweetly as she pushed my bedroom door open further, her cue for me to *get my ass out of bed.*

I took in a readying breath, and with my left hand, I pulled the covers off me. My palm suddenly ceased, a sharp pain that violently shot across it, and my hand fisted at the cramp.

"Fuck!" I released the clasp slowly, but when I looked for the cause of the searing ache, it had already gone. *There was nothing there.*

My room was a heap of organised chaos. Its washed-out purple painted walls had been the same colour since I was ten years old and were now covered in the dark grungy art posters I had collected over the years.

Sifting through the clothes bundled on the floor, I picked out a pair of brown washed-out cargos and my ugly yellow work t-shirt.

I wasn't as pretty as my younger sister but I didn't try to be. I pulled the curls of my dull brown hair back into a lifeless knot and threw on the pair of low-waisted cargo trousers.

Make-up wasn't really my thing, but I dusted a small amount of coral blush I'd had for years across the freckles on my face and licked a few coats of brown mascara over my lashes. I'd once watched a youtube video that had said anyone with light brown eyes, with splinters of gold or honey through them, should stick to brown mascara and who was I to question. So, I've worn it ever since.

The creased work t-shirt I wore almost every day, made me cringe every time I dared to look at myself in the mirror. It was a god-awful shade of mustard with a grumpy-looking cartoon cup of coffee plastered on the front, the logo almost as bad as the coffee I was paid to serve.

When I eventually headed downstairs into the kitchen-living room, I was already five minutes late and Kat was sitting, waiting patiently with a flask of coffee, the smell of fresh toast in the air.

"We can't have you drinking that stuff you sell down at Joey's, can we?" My mother croaked in an attempt to be funny as she plated up some toast, and I felt my eyes roll.

Dagina had always dressed weirdly, and ageing never changed that. Her usually bright and downright offensive clothing, which consisted of severely mismatched patterns, was a daily outfit choice Dagina seemed to make. Typically paired with a tonne of jewellery, equally as gaudy.

One particular necklace that I had never seen her without, had always freaked me out, ever since I was a kid. It was a dark tarnished gold medallion, with a simple red stone in its centre. The metal had distorted over time and lapped over the stone like an eyelid covering its ruby iris. *Seriously creepy.*

Dagina waddled over to the kitchen and put a plate of barely-warm bread down on the mahogany dining table.

But as I clenched my mouth closed, I could still feel the bite in the back of my throat that wanted to berate her pathetic attempts at being motherly.

"I don't have time for-" I started, my voice firm.

"Lana you need to eat, especially when you're at work all day," she said, as she pushed the plate towards me. Heat rose to the back of my neck.

"I said, I don't have time for it." I snapped back as I pushed the plate back towards her disappointed face and shrugged off the anger that already threatened to ruin my day.

From the corner of my eye, I watched Kat as she sank a little lower in her seat, each arm held within the other, and my stomach dropped. I would do anything for my sister, but no matter how much it made me feel like a total piece of shit in her eyes, I just couldn't bring myself to *play nice* with my energy vampire of a mother.

"Kat, let's go, we're going to be late," I said as I swung my backpack onto my shoulders. Already walking towards the door, I didn't bother looking at my mother as I left the house and headed to my car, but I heard Kat talking to her sweetly before saying goodbye.

I waited for my sister on the driveway, as she gracefully walked over, the smile that beamed on her face instantly putting out any of my lingering tempers. In her hand, she held the flask which I had forgotten in my need to get out of the house, to get away from my mother and I started up the car.

The engine scratched as I turned the key of an old banged-up red *Mini Cooper* that used to be my mother's, for a time before she decided she *couldn't drive anymore*. The mere thought of her triggered my irritation.

Kat delicately sat into the passenger side, locked her seat belt in place and set the flask of hot coffee into the cup holders between us.

As we rolled off the drive, I noticed Dagina was hobbling herself to the doorway to wave us off, and I had to press my mouth shut, grinding down against my jaw. Kat beamed a smile back, waving at her whilst I maintained both eyes ahead of me, willing the busted motor to move quicker.

Kat was looking at me, I could sense her stare as if she weighed up on whether or not to say something to me. I glanced over to her and gave her a look that told her, *come on, out with it.*

She always understood my non-verbal cues, but as she looked away from me, down into the footwell in front of her, her eyes avoided mine.

"Why do you speak to mum like that?" She asked, whilst wringing her delicate hands.

A deep sigh left me, hating the feeling I had upset my sister, but there were some things I couldn't see past. *Not even for her.*

"We just...we just don't see things the same way Kat, it's different for you." I tried my best to soften my tone.

"What do you mean it's different for me? Mum loves you just as much." Her innocent sky-blue eyes surely believed her own words and she was trying to make me believe them too.

Involuntarily I scoffed at the response, it wasn't her fault, she was too young to remember what had happened following our dad's death and I wasn't about to remind her. Instead, I passed it off as a cough and cleared my throat as I schooled my lips into a false smile.

Beckenham School was a large, brown-bricked building that looked like a bunch of stodgy boxes stacked on top of each other. With it being only a few miles away from our house, the journey usually took less than 15 minutes, even during rush hour.

As we pulled up across from the drop-off bay, I looked out through Kat's window to the groups of young teenagers all gathered in the school's courtyard. Crowds of kids dressed in the same dull uniform, consisting of grey suit bottoms, white shirts and that god-awful blazer I hated wearing years ago. All now forming their groups and cliques, ready to take on another day of fighting for social status.

I never really partook in any of that high school bullshit, I was the type of kid that got on with everyone whilst keeping no one close. Though, there was a part of me that wished I was that softer, girly girl that had a huge group of friends to go shopping with and talk about boys with - it just wasn't me. I was independent and learnt very quickly not to lean on people for anything. That kind of made me a shitty friend at times I guess.

There wasn't a place for me in any of the groups at school, but one thing I learnt about the ecosystem of schools and their cliques, was not to disrupt the equilibrium they brought. So I fell into place, an unattached *friend* to everyone because having no real connections meant I couldn't be let down. *Until I met Xander.*

Kat kissed my cheek suddenly and I re-focused my attention on my little sister, who, whilst wearing my hand-me-down uniform, looked better in it than I ever did.

"Say hey to Xan for me!" She smiled, and as she slipped out of the car, I leaned forward and pressed my best encouraging smile, back at her.

I waited on the curbside as I watched my sister find her little group of grey-fashioned friends, throwing each of her dainty arms around a couple of them as they now sauntered into the boxy building.

Kat was part of the clique that everyone loved, that group of effortlessly gorgeous, social creatures that always knew how to say the right thing to fit in with everyone. Her best friends included a petite girl with long raven hair down to her waist, who she had been close with for a while, but always seemed a little shy to me. And another, taller with short bright pink hair and a strong handsome face. *I'm pretty sure even I would have been accepted by them.*

A horn blared from behind me and caused me to almost jump out of my skin. I turned back to curse out the impatient school mum, and slammed my hand against my own horn before gesturing something I'm glad Kat wasn't in the car to see. My hand responded agonisingly as my palm cramped again, this time so painful that it pulled my breath straight from my chest. With my hand clenched, I closed my watering eyes, not daring to release the fist, and everything became darker.

The light faded from beneath my lids, as though out of my sight, morning had turned to evening. The day swallowed away before it had even started. The pain was excruciating and my fingernails pressed into my palm as my jaw clamped down a scream.

Suddenly, my phone rang, the loud vibrating chime made me jump in my seat and take in a sharp breath I was holding and the pain went almost as quickly as it came. My eyes still watered when I quickly reached for my phone. *Shit, I was late.*

CHAPTER TWO

Walking into Joey's Cafe was like being stuck in some weird time loop, where every day seemed the same. I'd fling through the doors, usually late and be greeted by Joey, the balding, overweight owner who loved to tell me how replaceable I was. And I thought of anywhere I would rather be right now as I walked towards yet another mind-numbing day of making shit coffee and serving over-fried food.

"You're late, again." Joey complained, thick wiry eyebrows raised.

I pulled back my sleeve and sarcastically glanced at my nonexistent watch.

"Oh yeah, don't you know I can't tell the time?" I retorted, a smile tugging at my mouth when I heard a snickering sound from behind the counter. His greasy eyes roamed their way across my body and lingered at my chest as his slug of a tongue pulled his fat lower lip into his mouth, before looking through narrowed eyes at me.

"Thin ice Lana." Joey rolled his dark eyes and shouted as he puffed his chest and lurched towards the back kitchen where his office was.

He was always the same, all mouth - but we both knew no one was exactly cueing up to work here, so he'd put up with my bite. Still, Joey was a nightmare to work for, when he wasn't telling me how replaceable I was or how I was on thin ice for the hundredth time, he was ogling my boobs or any part of my skin he might be able to scan his eyes over. This was the reason I wore an oversized men's top every day.

Every time he looked at me, I wanted to claw his eyes out but I needed this job, with my useless mother no longer working and Kat at school I could barely afford to pay the bills, never mind think about saving. But luckily for me, Joey wasn't there often.

I shook off the feeling of his lingering eyes as I walked behind the counter and picked up a grey, faded apron. Wrapping it around me twice, and finishing in a tight knot across the front.

"Well good morning to you too." A deep voice snickered sarcastically.

Xander stood tall next to me, a gentle giant with dark curly hair, now banged ground coffee out of the porter filter, and grinned roguishly down at me.

Xander was never late, in fact, I'm pretty sure he arrived early every shift. Only to clean out the coffee machines and make the regular set of crones in the corner, *which we liked to call the OLG (old lady gang)*, their bitter-tasting coffees.

I swear the older women come in here just for him, because it can't be for the coffee they're drinking, it's god damn awful.

Xander's kind eyes were fractured emeralds. His large build, covered in flawless bronzed skin that I know Dorris, our resident milky coffee drinker and agony aunt, would love to get an eyeful of.

"Soooo, what happened to you last night?" He asked, full brows raised above his eyes.

A flash of blood falling from a hand splintered across my memory, followed by the phantom taste of metal in my throat. I swallowed hard as though to push the memory down, the taste already fading.

"L?" Xan asked as he rested a large hand on my shoulder, his head tilted lower to face mine. I must have zoned out because the next thing I saw was Xander's green eyes pinched, now searching my own.

"Morning! Sorry, I'm-" I shook my head and looked down at my hand. Cautiously, I turned my palm over, *no blood.* "I'm a bit out of it today, I didn't sleep well." I managed, still feeling a little hazy.

"Here." His large, tanned hand pushed over a coffee that was sitting behind the counter, presumably someone's order. "Drink this." His mouth pinched to one side and my stomach warmed as a sweet dimple appeared on his cheek.

I took a deep gulp of the bitter-tasting, black liquid whilst he returned to work. The coffee machine clanked and gurgled as he looked back over his shoulder with a sweet smile that beamed across his face.

Xander had been my best friend since we were twelve years old, we were both a little quiet and neither of us fit in with any of the other kids - so we found each other.

It seems only a moment had passed since I saw a scrawny boy with shaggy black hair and innocent green eyes, had himself pressed against a brick wall by Josh Ackett. Beckenham High's local bully had pinned him against the PE block.

So, having always been a confrontational type, I ran up behind Josh, whipped my backpack off my shoulders, and swatted him across his head as hard and fast as my little arms would allow.

I remembered that when I had grabbed Xander's hand and pulled him from the floor he had landed on, it was super gross and clammy. Regardless, I pulled him and we ran and ran. By the end of it, we were in fits of laughter *and I finally had a friend.*

Luckily for me, Josh didn't pick on girls and must have decided he couldn't be bothered to chase us. Instead, when we saw him the next day, he'd already moved on to the next scrawny kid that looked at him the wrong way.

I must have laughed, as Xander turned to face me with his brows raised, and the small towel he used to clean off the coffee filter now hung over his forearm.

"What's so funny?" A single brow raised higher as his dimple pinched at his cheek.

My mouth curled a smile as I looked back at those stunning green eyes, which now looked a lot older and maybe a little less innocent.

"Josh Ackett."

Xander's eyes widened as he twisted the dry dish towel in both hands. Letting out a boyish laugh, as he clipped my outer thigh with a whip of the towel gently.

"Now come on, get to work." He smirked and I picked up a towel hung close by, tilting my head.

"Don't play games you can't win." I taunted as I wrung out the towel with my hands.

"You two! We have customers!" Joey spat through his fat lips. He would have been watching us over the CCTV. The pervert was hardly even here during the day, but when he was, he was typically slumped in his office chair with his shoeless feet splayed across the desk. Probably watching the CCTV in hopes of any fresh meat walking in.

I dropped the towel, and Xander turned away from me, now chuckling and making himself look occupied with his duties. *Goodie two shoes.* I looked back to where the pig was standing.

"Yes sir! Of course sir!" And I bowed mockingly to Joey who grunted and turned away from me. I knew I was testing his patience, but sometimes I couldn't help myself and I'd been winding him up like this for the past four years.

The cafe wasn't exactly a place people were queuing up to work at, and the coffee was as shit as the food. The decor was eighties American-diner inspired, checkerboard tiles with pink and white quilted leather booths, cracked from years of wear - just like Dorris from the OLG. All surrounded by a ghastly New York streetscape wallpaper, ugly yellow cabs and all.

The cafe was usually pretty empty in the morning, except for the few regulars that would nurse one drink for hours on end, but today seemed busier than most. But by mid-afternoon it had quieted down and I began cleaning the tables, taking the coffee-stained cups and crumb-covered plates into the back kitchen where I could clean them.

The old taps spat as they filled a sink that looked too old, and too dirty to be able to truly clean anything. Before squirting the bottle of dish soap into the water, the smell of it reminded me more of something that belonged in a hospital, and not a food and drink establishment.

One by one, I swilled the coffee out, sponged on sudsy water and washed away the day's gossiping lips that were stuck like scarlet wax on the rims of mugs.

As I reached for a plate to submerge, it slipped out of my soapy hand and cracked on the floor right in front of my now soaking-wet black converse. *For fucks sake.*

Annoyed, I groaned and leaned down to pick up the shards of broken ceramic that would *no doubt* be coming out of my next payslip before heading over to the back door, where the bins are.

I already worked every hour I could get, sometimes even covering the kitchen staff if need be and being the only earner in the house was tough. But, even though I despised working here, and hated the ogre I worked for, we really needed a stable income.

With the broken plate in my hand, I ripped open the bin lid and slammed the ceramic shards into the pit of the bin. The shattering sound felt so cathartic.

Something burned my hand and I winced. *Fuck!*

I bit my lip from crying out as I looked down at my palm and saw crimson streams of fresh blood pouring from a single ragged slice across my palm. I clasped my hand into a fist and forced my eyes wide open as my head felt swimmy.

It was strange how I could watch any number of true crime documentaries, with harrowing details and horrendous reconstructions and come out completely unphased - but real blood made me feel sick and usually very light-headed.

With my hand raised, I walked back to the kitchen, trying to slow the flow of blood to it. Xander stood in the doorway, his eyes shot to the red-speckled droplets that covered the floor around my feet and then tracked back up to my face, which had felt pale.

The kitchen around me began to warp through my obscured vision, ringing echoed around my ear throbbing painfully against my skull. My eyes caught a glimpse of Xander, who ran towards me just as my legs buckled and everything went dark.

$$\Omega$$

A blood-curdling scream echoed around my pounding head, making my entire body shudder in response. My eyes felt sore as I looked around me, searching for Xander but the air was thick, dark and hazy.

My arms felt heavy as I tried to heave them upwards, but they wouldn't budge as something heavy pinned them in place. My eyes refocused through the darkness and I saw something large lying across my lap. Suddenly, hot air violently plunged into my lungs and I gasped in horror.

I was gaping down at a pale, limp body, cold in my arms.

His lifeless face was hollow and hanging backwards, hinged only by his flaccid neck. The skin that hung from his face, darkened and drained, framed his wide cloudy eyes.

A high-pitched wail shot from my lungs, burning its way out as my head swung forward into the man's sunken corpse with tears streaming down my face. As I tried to move my arms I realised I wasn't in control. Needing desperately to shift this death off me but I was a paralysed mind inside a foreign body.

I saw the slender arm I occupied, trembling, as it tried to pull the limp, dead man upright. The hand gently caressed his head of thick black hair, shaking as it travelled down to his face and swept over his deep moss eyes, closing them softly. The quivering hand reached up to my soaking face, and in a split second I made out the outline of a scar slicing across the palm before it pressed into my eye and wiped away the streams of tears.

Ω

This will work.

The window will only stay open for thirty days. You know this my lord.

Thirty days is enough, she will remember Cerb, she has to.

You know better than anyone my lord, when a soul is snatched away and born anew, gone are the memories of their past lives.

She will remember me.

Her soul is re-bound. This is a clear act of war, he did this.

Cerb, I know, but we do not have time as we did before. This has to work.

The whisper of strange voices faded from my dizzy head as I lifted my heavy lids. Blinking slowly, I could just make out the grease-stained ceilings of Joey's kitchen before my vision focused on Xander. His warm arms now supported my head upright but I still felt limp in his impressive hold. A shiver danced through my body like an electric shock and with the jolt, my head cleared.

I sat up as quickly as my body would allow and felt my face flush with colour as my gaze fixed on a broad, toned chest exposed by a tight white t-shirt. Allowing my eyes to roam upwards to his face, I made out the stranger's high cheekbones and hard lines that beautifully graced his perfectly-unblemished, tanned skin.

Luscious curls of dark blonde hair that looked good enough to run your fingers through fell casually over his forehead, and looking deep into my own eyes were two sparkling grey-blue eyes, seductively narrowed by a thick row of lashes. *Well, shit.*

The stranger, who looked no older than twenty-seven and might have been the most beautiful man I had ever seen, was on his knees in front of me, his perfectly shaven face inches from mine.

The lowest part of my stomach tightened as the smell of his cologne hit me immediately. It was a familiar mix of spice and wood that reminded me of Autumn. *Delicious.*

His angular brows furrowed and with a hint of concern, I watched him pull out a small silver flashlight and flickered the bright light across my pupils. Involuntarily I squinted at the harsh light and went to move his hand out of my face just as the handsome stranger laughed, low and coarse before standing back up.

"She looks okay to me. She probably just passed out with the sight of blood."

I looked down at my hand, which was now bandaged up neatly before quickly becoming aware that I was still pressed intimately against Xander's front. The man looked down to where I sat between Xander's legs and I could swear for a moment I saw his grey eyes pinch.

"You did a great job at sorting that hand out young man," he said with a nod towards the bandage, his eyes never leaving mine.

"Thank you so much for your help doctor, your coffee's on the house," Xander replied, worry still staining his voice.

The sparkling grey eyes fell over me, travelling to my hand and across my body. I watched the movement with heat whorling in my core as he smirked before his eyes drifted back up to meet mine.

"It was no bother at all, I'm just glad I could be of use." The corners of his mouth curled into a feline smile.

Joey scoffed from behind the tall man, looking disapprovingly towards Xander before grunting and waddling back towards his little office. "Enough dramatics, back to work." *Prick.*

CHAPTER THREE

Xander made his way through the series of locks that secured the cafe up for the night, whilst I waited for him to finish the job that required two hands. The smell of fresh rain was still in the air and feeling slightly chilly, I pulled out an old hoodie that was stuffed into my backpack and wrapped it around me.

The vision of those lifeless eyes still flashed across my mind as my head began to thrum painfully and the throbbing in my hand grew deeper.

"So, I know I shouldn't ask, but any plans for next month?" Xander asked, pulling down the final shutter on the cafe front and avoiding my eyes.

Next month? I mentally combed over any upcoming events but before I could question what he meant, I remembered. My twenty-first birthday was in a month - *shit*. I hated my birthdays, mainly because I stopped having them as a kid. Birthdays weren't a luxury I had - especially not growing up with a mother who was either always drunk, or in bed.

"Just the usual, it's just another day to me, you know that." I eventually replied.

Every year Xander had tried to make a fuss of my birthday, last year even going as far as booking a trip for me, him, and Kat to go down to Cornwall. Of course, I told him he shouldn't have bothered and that next time he shouldn't just book something without telling me first.

It wasn't like I didn't know that he meant well, because he always did, but I've not celebrated a birthday since I was ten so why would I start again now?

Kat knew about the trip because she didn't speak to me for two days when I told her we weren't going. I had always made sure to still celebrate Kat's birthday, so she couldn't understand why I didn't my own.

Being a kid myself meant I couldn't exactly go out and buy presents, but that didn't matter to us, I'd scoop up every bed sheet in the house, throw them over the sofa, the dining chairs, and anything else I could drape them from to make a fortress in the living room.

In the week leading up to Kat's birthday, I would always save up my snacks from my school dinners, packets of crisps, and sometimes even a cake bar and pile them in the fortress for her to come down to. It wasn't much, but I did what I could to make sure that day meant something to her.

"We could always-" Xander started, but I cut him off with a raised eyebrow and narrowed eyes, the same stern look he had grown to understand as *leave it*.

"How's the hand?" He pivoted.

I looked down at the bandage that covered my throbbing hand and smiled to myself as he really had done a great job of it.

"All good, it stings a little but nothing Nurse Xan can't fix." I smiled through low eyes and as he looked to the floor I swore I saw him flush a little.

"I've never seen you faint before, you actually scared me for a second." His green eyes darkened, looking down at me.

Xander was tall, he always had been, he was one of those kids that seemed to get all of their height as soon as puberty hit. Being 6'4, with golden tanned skin, emerald green eyes and dark curly hair that annoyingly always fell perfectly, you'd think he'd be a lady killer, but for as long as I'd known him he'd never been interested in women.

"Well-" I started as I nudged his arm a little with my shoulder "you shouldn't be such a big baby." I laughed as his eyes widened and the flecks of gold glinted through the green.

"Me?! You're the one who passed out after grazing yourself! Tell me how I'm the baby again," he said with a smile tugging at the corners of his mouth.

"Well, you sure looked worried for *just a graze,* and you wrapped it up pretty damn tight too!" I poked back and the sparkle in his eyes seemed to fade, as though for a moment, his mind had taken him somewhere else.

"Hey," I said, punching him gently in his bicep.

"Yeah well, just don't do it again." He shook his head and forced a smile.

As we walked back to our cars, I caught him glancing down at my bandaged hand and he flinched a little, pinching his brow.

"I'm okay you know, it really is just a graze." The cut actually stung like hell, but my hand cramps earlier had been just as painful and moaning wouldn't make it better - so I wouldn't bother. I figured he must have noticed me rubbing my palm earlier, before the accident, and I was now doing it again, without even noticing.

"What's happened anyway? You've been doing that all day." He looked towards my hand. "I'm not sure you get carpal tunnel from making coffee L. Or lack of in your case anyways." A small dimple appeared on his cheek and the sparkle in his eyes returned.

I smiled, *there he was.*

"Honestly I've no idea what I've done but it's happened a couple of times today and I'm not joking - it fucking kills!"

Xander let out a low laugh and playfully nudged me with his large arm.

"Who's the big baby now?" He jutted out his full, lower lip and widened his eyes mockingly. *God, he was gorgeous.*

CHAPTER FOUR

Rain wasn't unusual for October in England and I felt particularly grateful for the banged-up motor that comfortably shielded me from the onslaught that now crashed down around me.

As I waited for Kat outside my old school, the rain seemed to fall heavier and dark clouds rolled in on the harsh autumn wind.

The kids spilt out of the main campus, running for cover to their rides or under the shelter of a bus stop. As my eyes scanned the sea of blazers, I spotted Kat, her golden hair glowed against the dull background of grey downpours and drab uniforms. Her merry smile never faded from her face, even though the rain was heavy enough to wash it away - she just laughed and jogged nonchalantly towards the car.

As I twisted the key and pressed my clutch down to start the engine, I was answered with a deep gurgle. That definitely didn't sound good.

"Oh come on!" I moaned, as I wiggled the key and plunged the clutch down again. Another deep sound bubbled back in response, before a sudden *pop!*

Metal groaned as steam billowed from the crimson hood of my car and I could have screamed. The horn belted loud enough to make me jump as my hand slammed into the steering wheel's centre with frustration.

"Fucking great!" I growled, before covering my face with my hands.

I heard a light tap on the passenger side window, *shit!* Kat stood smiling outside the door, looking like the most elegant drowned rat I'd ever seen, waiting for me to unlock the car.

I quickly fumbled for the unlock button beside the steering wheel, and she flung open the passenger door the moment it clicked open.

Guilt filled me as I scanned over her uniform and noticed it was completely soaked. But before I could say anything, she pointed behind me and as my gaze followed her finger I almost jumped out of my skin. Standing right outside my window was a mass of muscle and grace.

As he bent down, the slate-grey-coloured eyes smiling back at me seemed familiar. My features must have contorted with confusion as the stunning man dipped his head a little lower so our faces were now in line with one another before knocking on my window.

For a moment I was lost in his diamond eyes, before quickly pulling myself together and reaching awkwardly for the window crank. As I began to manually wind down the window, which was painfully slow and equally as embarrassing, the wide-eyed, blonde-haired and quite frankly, devastatingly handsome man, stood watching every pump of my arm.

As the window cracked, the intoxicating scent of wood and spice wafted into the car, warming my senses.

"Hey you." A feline smile crept across his face as the window finally opened far enough for him to peer in.

"Need a hand?" The man's deep, slow voice asked as he looked towards the hood of the car which was now fully engulfed in grey smoke. His dripping wet face suddenly sparked a memory and heat rushed to my face as I realised it was the doctor from earlier at Joey's.

Standing in the same white t-shirt as earlier, except now it was soaked and clinging to him, exposing every inch of his broad chest and impressive body underneath.

My mouth fumbled to form any response as I practically gawked at the towering male and my eyes lingered on his chest far longer than was appropriate. He waited with those kind eyes focused on mine for an answer, and the only response I could muster was a pathetic nod, dipping my head maybe a few times more than necessary. He threw a smirk back as he strode to the front of my car. With a quick flick under the bonnet, he lifted the hood and latched it open.

Kat's face was wry, her sweet smile had turned to something more amused as she raised a single eyebrow and jutted her chin towards the open bonnet - towards the doctor that stood behind it.

I bit down my smirk and hit her thigh with the back of my hand softly in response to her ogling, but I still couldn't help but laugh a little at her telling face.

A few moments later, the hood of the motor came down under the controlled strength of the doctor's flexing arms, and I couldn't help but admire them - they were clearly well-trained in the gym. His long, thick legs sauntered back over to my window and he bent down next to my open window. His eyes narrowed lazily.

"You're all wet." The deep vibration of his voice thrummed sensually against my raw senses and his eyes now dipped down over my body. Immediately I felt the pink flush of heat, blooming across my face like a rose's petals opening for the sun.

"Maybe you should have closed the window." His brow raised and a smirk curled his mouth upwards.

In all honesty, I'd totally forgotten the window was open at all and the rain had poured into the car, where my ugly mustard shirt was now soaked up one side.

"Oh, it's fine." I awkwardly laughed and my face burned with embarrassment as I pulled my wet shirt from where it clung to my stomach. "We're on our way home so it's no big deal."

"Not in this you're not, the gaskets completely gone," he replied as his chin jerked over to the hood of the car.

So not only was this man a doctor but he's also a mechanic now? A gorgeous man, in fact, *a gorgeous man that's clearly good with his hands.*

"I...we don't actually live far." I turned to Kat, "we're going to have to walk it."

Before she could open her mouth, the doctor leant forwards with his hands on the ledge of my open window, and he was close enough that I could now smell the scent of fresh mint on his breath.

"I can drop you off if you need, it's no problem." *Kind handsome man that's good with his hands.*

I was just about to object but Kat had beat me to it, instead, nodding her head and shouting across me.

"That would be great!" She sent a playful side-eye in my direction.

As I bundled my backpack into the doctor's silver Mercedes that was parked in front of us, I jumped as a white-haired, young girl smiled at me from the backseat of the car.

"Hi!" She spoke confidently, gently kicking one leg in front of the other. Her round face was sweet and her sparkling grey eyes looked up to where I was standing still in shock.

"Oh hi!" I replied in the softest voice I could muster, but it cracked, exposing my sudden confusion. The girl must have only been five, but she was wearing the same uniform as Kat, young enough to be his daughter I thought to myself.

"We can all fit. Lana, you can sit up front if you like?" The doctor called over to me as he towered over the car's roof, with my head still half stuck in the door, staring at the beautiful little girl.

I retreated from the back seat and peered over the roof to where he stood and Kat jumped in, nudging me out of the way and already chatting away with the young girl.

It had stopped raining and the dull sky was already clearing up so we could have walked, but at this point, Kat seemed comfy and I was too tired after a full day at work to change my mind now.

I slid into the front passenger side as smoothly as my awkward limbs would allow and closed the door behind me. The doctor followed, dropping down into the driver's side as his sizable weight shifted the car.

As he started the engine, it struck me that he knew my name, but I didn't know his. And although I felt completely safe, I had just gotten in a car with a complete stranger *and* brought my kid sister along.

Reading my concern as though it was said out loud, he looked over to me and outreached a large hand, whilst the other pressed a button that started the engine up.

"Sorry, I never properly introduced myself, Aide." My hand reached for his instinctively and an electric shock passed between us as he wrapped his fingers around my palm.

"Lana, but you already knew that." I smirked.

"Your friend Xander, he basically gave me your entire medical history whilst you were passed out on the floor," Aide said, as I tried to hide my embarrassment and wondered what else Xander may have said whilst I was blacked out on the kitchen floor.

"How's the hand?" He said looking down at the cotton bandage which had now started to unravel.

"It's fine really, thank you." I pulled the wrap around my wrist, tightening the damp fabric before looking back to the road in front of us.

As Aide drove steadily back through the main roads directed by Kat, I couldn't help but steal a few discreet glances at his impressive arms, and down over the wet t-shirt to his thick thighs that pressed against his trousers.

"Just your next left," Kat called from the back seat as we began to turn onto our road and I felt slightly silly for accepting the lift when we really should have just walked.

Still, as the vehicle slowed to a stop outside our house that Kat had pointed out moments before, part of me didn't want to leave the warmth of the car. Aide looked over to my hand again and then unbuckled his seat belt.

"Let's just quickly get that rewrapped up." He lifted himself out of the driver's side and walked to the rear of the car. The boot opened itself with a wave of his foot, below what I'm assuming were sensors in the rear bumper.

"Thanks for the lift Aideeee!" Kat drew out his name and smiled fiendishly as she walked towards our front door, suggestively raising her eyebrows at me.

"No worries at all," he called back and smiled as I reached where he was standing. The boot of his car was now open with him sitting on the ledge of it whilst his large hands rummaged inside a black duffle bag.

He pulled out a roll of cotton bandages, a silver pair of scissors and some antiseptic wipes. He gestured to the space next to him, offering me a seat before gently taking my hand and unwrapping the bandage.

The sharp smell of antiseptic filled the air as he wiped over the open cut on my palm and it burned instantly, causing me to pull my hand back. But Aide held my wrist firm and his touch felt caring and reassuring somehow.

The cut had stopped bleeding now and didn't look half as bad as it did earlier - which only added to the further embarrassment that this whole fuss and attention the graze demanded.

Yet, Aide didn't seem to mind, in fact he seemed to enjoy what he was doing and that made the lower part of my stomach pool with warmth. In a moment that felt unusually intimate, he wrapped up my palm, a little tighter than before and snipped off the excess cotton.

"Thank you-" I managed to start, "for dropping us off, and for this." I lifted my freshly wrapped hand.

"It's no bother, any time."

A moment passed before I jumped off the boots ledge, and with another wave of his foot, the door closed behind us.

As I walked back towards the front to get my backpack, I noticed the young girl with white hair and striking eyes looking at me from the window. She waved a small hand at me as her soft face pulled a polite smile and I waved back.

"I guess it's lucky that I just happened to be off work today for uncle duties." Aide said with a wink as he ducked back into the driver's seat.

CHAPTER FIVE

My skin felt rosy and I couldn't help but smile a little to myself as I walked through the front door to our house. *How could someone that hot, also be so kind?*

My daydreaming came to an abrupt halt the moment I entered my house, as simply passing through the doorway into our morbid home could drain any morsel of happiness I clung onto.

Passing through the living room the air felt heavy as a strange scent I couldn't recognise, made my nose twitch uncomfortably. My eyes rolled as I saw my energy vampire of a mother, lying on the sofa doing absolutely nothing as usual, and anger froze my stomach.

No matter how many times I saw her like this, my body reacted the same way - my fight or flight, a rush of anger and anxiety freezing me as I forced my eyes to look away.

When a child, having just lost her father, is practically abandoned, she must become tough, and learn quickly not to depend on anyone other than herself, no matter how shitty that feels.

Besides the bathtub, my chaotic bedroom was the one place of solace I had within this house, the only place I could truly relax. Slumped on my bed with a favourite smutty book I was rereading for the third time, I couldn't stop my mind from wandering to the doctor again.

Aide's perfectly muscled arms and large hands that gripped his gear stick. Those ashen eyes seemed to see right through me, roaming every inch of me through heavy lids, setting my skin on fire with his lower lip pulled between his teeth. His other arm riding the steering wheel as he sat low in his seat, leaning back as if almost inviting me to come sit—

"Lana?" I heard Kat call on the other side of my bedroom door as I straightened up and shook off the daydream that now heated my entire body.

"Do you want to come eat with us tonight?" She asked softly as she entered my room.

With the delicious heat now fully drained from me, I took in a large breath and lowered my book.

"I'm not really in the mood for playing happy families Kat. You know this," I replied as gently as I could and her facial expression dropped with disappointment.

"I just thought, you know, as she's not well it might be nice if you both-" She began and I felt a rise of frustration now scratching at the surface of my skin.

"Not well? That woman hasn't been *well* for years and I'm tired of trying Kat." I tampered the irritation in my tone down as my sister's face pinched. "I know it's different for you - you didn't have to go through what I went through. And I'm glad you didn't, but please just, stop."

Sickness filled my stomach when I saw her sombre eyes gloss over with the tears that formed against her lower lash line, before turning her back from me, closing the door behind her - not saying a word.

Few things chipped at my soul more than seeing Kat silently upset, because it almost felt worse. There was a part of me that wanted her to slam the door or tell me to stop being a bitch or *anything* - because it was in the silence that I knew she was hurting the most.

Katerina was not like me, she wasn't angry or ruined, she was perfect in every way - but most of all she was kind and completely forgiving. So although I hated to upset her, I knew she wouldn't push me on this.

I sighed as I tucked myself under the safety of a fluffy blanket and continued with my book but the words on the page became hazy through my dampening eyes. I swallowed down the rising guilt that snaked its way up my throat and leaned further into the comfort of my bed.

Ω

Blinking my eyes open I realised I must have fallen asleep, but as I turned I didn't recognise the comfort of my bed, instead, I felt a hard, smooth surface beneath my body. My eyes took a moment to readjust in the dark, and my body stilled in fear as my vision focused on the inside of a huge room I didn't recognise.

The high walls around me looked as though they were carved straight from rock but I couldn't make out anything other than shapes in the room as the atmosphere was red and hazy.

The air felt thick and breathing felt like an enormous weight, the oxygen like lead in my lungs. As I peeled my tongue from the roof of my mouth the taste of iron shot sharply across it, shocking my airways open and making it a little easier to breathe.

I pushed my body up off the floor, noticing the small golden squares that covered the ground around me as I sat upright. Where the hell was I? Was I still dreaming? *I had to be dreaming.*

My body froze as a woman sauntered in, and walked straight past where I was slumped on the floor.

Her long, curly brown hair flowed down her back, with strands pinned half up, and she was wearing a long slip dress the colour of ripe plums, that fell faultlessly along her curved body.

She was beautiful, well, through the haze I couldn't quite see her face, but with the way she walked, I could tell.

"Excuse me?" I asked, but my words choked on the air. Syllables stuck in my mouth like a silent echo.

The woman didn't so much as flinch as I shifted and tried again, but still, no words came out. Stumbling to my feet, I walked toward her with an arm reaching outwards. But as my hand fell to the woman's shoulder, it sank straight through it and her body distorted like mist between my fingers.

Startled, I stumbled back, losing my balance. I fell onto the hard golden floor and my head swung backwards. *Crack.*

Just as my vision began to fade through the haze now darkening my sight, I saw the form of a huge man walk into the room. Iron filled my senses as my vision blurred and a high-pitched noise rattled in my ears.

Ω

My shivering body bolted upright as I awoke abruptly from the nightmare and I felt damp with the sweat now dripping down my chest. I slowed my shallow breaths before forcing in a large inhale. *It wasn't real.*

This was the second weird dream I had had in the past twenty-four hours and although this one wasn't quite as terrifying as the other, there was something strangely familiar about it, something visceral.

The book I was reading had fallen to the floor and closed itself shut. *Great, now I've lost my chapter.*

CHAPTER SIX

I didn't know what time it was or how long I'd even been asleep, but I could still hear Kat and my mother talking downstairs. Rolling my eyes, I let out an exasperated breath before pulling the fluffy blanket off my bed and trailing it with me like a cape of armour as I padded downstairs.

As much as I actively tried to avoid my mother, this headache felt as though it wasn't going anywhere and with the drug cupboard being in the kitchen, I had no choice.

Our house was pretty small and the first floor was completely open, the stairs I descended led right into the kitchen-living room - which made sneaking down and avoiding anyone completely impossible.

For as long as I could remember, the house had been a brick away from falling apart. Ugly-patterned, threadbare curtains fell from rails that looked a light tug away from falling straight out of the wall whilst the papered walls peeled away in every corner - something dad would have fixed easily.

A green leather sofa faced away from the tired-looking kitchen, its worn skin sunken in on itself like a pumpkin long past its prime. All tied unceremoniously with my mother's god awful art.

What used to be brightly coloured, abstract paintings that covered every corner of the living room had dulled and become drab just like the woman herself.

Before my dad had passed she was pretty good at this stuff, *eccentric* sure, but good. But during the nine years since he'd passed, which now seemed like a lifetime ago, she had become an entirely different person.

My mother had once been stunning, with unruly dark curly hair and beautifully sharp features. Now, just like this home, she was dull, energy-drained and a brick away from a full meltdown.

"Oh hey! I thought you weren't hungry?" Kat's face beamed over at me the moment my foot hit the last step.

"I'm not, I just have a headache that's all," I replied as I reached into the top cupboard and pulled out a tray filled with drugs and prescriptions. *I'd never noticed this many pill packets before.* I filed through them and fished out the paracetamol.

"What time is it anyway?" I asked, with the thumb and forefinger of my hand rubbing the ache that now pounded against my forehead.

"Erm, just turned seven," Kat replied as she forked a mouthful of what looked like moussaka into her mouth and my mouth watered.

I thought I'd been asleep for hours but it had barely been minutes.

"Why don't you join us? We made your favourite," crackled a wisp voice from beside me, anxiety now dried out my mouth with a bitter taste.

I turned to my mother, who looked towards me with hopeful, hollow eyes and my stomach turned.

"You made my favourite?" I mocked. "How would you know what my favourite is? I can't remember the last time you cooked for me and Kat. Oh wait, that's it. I remember—" My voice dripping in contempt.

"Lana please." Katerina began but I held a hand up to stop her from interrupting the venom I had waited far too long to spew.

"The last time you cooked for us, I ended up going to the hospital with third-degree oil burns because you had decided it would be a good idea to use a deep fryer, whilst being out of your mind drunk!" I didn't need to lift my shirt to show my mother the angry-red scar that stretched across my stomach - she knew what lay underneath it.

"Lana, I—" Dagina's voice trembled but I wasn't about to stand around and listen to her make excuses about why she was a terrible mother.

I looked over to Katerina whose soft face was now flushed red with streams of tears falling down her cheeks.

"This-" My shaking hands gestured to where my mother was sitting, "is why I don't do dinner, so will you now stop asking." I seethed. Avoiding Kat's puffy eyes I stomped out of the room, ran up the stairs and slammed my bedroom door behind me.

A couple of days passed after my outburst and Kat still hadn't spoken to me. I'd be lying if I said the guilt wasn't eating me alive.

Dagina somehow always managed to do that, to make me the one who feels like the piece of shit in this family and maybe I was. Maybe I was just like *her*.

Kat chose to walk to school for the days that followed the argument, with me trailing behind her like some creep just to make sure she arrived safely.

The school was only around the corner if you took the alleys that passed through the housing estates, but I would never have forgiven myself if anything happened to her. So I would persist with my stalkerish behaviour until the car was out of the garage and she was sitting in the passenger seat again.

Katerina didn't usually get mad and I was even beginning to think it was an emotion she wasn't capable of. But when there were no *good morning* knocks on my doors, no attempts to get me down for breakfast or dinner, I knew that I'd really hurt her.

My mood was already sour when I arrived for my shift at Joey's, but when I swung open the front door of the worst coffee joint in the town and looked over to Xander serving a tanned young woman, my hopes of a better morning were shattered.

With almost every inch of her glowing skin showing between a denim mini skirt and a white crop top, it was no surprise that Xander didn't notice me as I walked in.

I wrapped an apron around my ugly mustard uniform as I walked behind the counter and scoffed as I overheard the young woman tell Xander how his eyes reminded her of her necklace.

I glanced over as she played with a gold chain necklace that sat atop of her impressively large chest with a green stone falling just above the crease of her breasts - something I'm sure Xander didn't miss.

Grudgingly, I coughed and Xander turned around as I quickly busied myself, polishing out some already clean mugs that had Joey's grumpy logo across the front.

The ping that sounded from the till told me her transaction had gone through and as Xander said something politely finishing in *have a nice day*, I rolled my eyes. Because girls like that must always have a nice day, life must just be easier for them. Tell a guy his eyes are nice and the next thing you know he doesn't even notice his best friend walking in.

"Morning!" Xander nudged the arm which was sulkily polishing a cup and I inhaled sharply as the cut on my hand stung. "Shit! Sorry!" His eyes widened as he gently took the cup and cloth out of my hand. "How's it looking?"

The cut seemed to have healed up pretty quickly since Aide had rewrapped it, which made me think it probably didn't require a bandage and maybe a plaster would have sufficed. But, when a handsome doctor with diamond eyes and a jawline you could cut yourself on, wants to give you his time, who was I to decline?

In the days that had passed since my awkward run-ins with the stunning man I now knew as Aide, I hadn't stopped thinking about those intense eyes, warm aura and those *very large* hands since.

"It's pretty much healed, I can just feel it sometimes, aching a little. I'm sure it will be fine after another couple of days." I looked up to Xander whose brows furrowed with concern, clouding his green eyes.

"Seriously, it's fine." I reassured him and nudged him playfully.

"You don't have to do that you know," he said as he walked back towards the counter.

"Do what?"

"That thing where you downplay everything. You know you can just, not be okay sometimes don't you?" He said before continuing, "the world isn't going to collapse around you if you open up a little."
This wasn't about the cut.

"Kat texted me about what happened the other day." He walked towards me as his voice lowered, his tone softening. "I know you don't talk much about your mum, but I think you forget how long I've known you all."

I wanted to stop him in his tracks, but the concerned look in his eyes told me that he needed me to listen.

"I know things between your mum and you haven't been great since, well pretty much forever. But Kat told me about how ill she's getting and I didn't know if...well, I didn't know if you would want to try and talk about it?"

His eyes flicked from my own, then down to my mouth as he waited for a response.

An exasperated sigh escaped me as I tried my hardest to not roll my eyes.

"She's not ill Xan she's just being dramatic as usual. This is what she does. One minute she's *trying her best*," I said, gesturing quotation marks, "and the next, she's depressed, drunk or on a comedown. She's not actually ill." I pulled the small towel back from his hands, turned away and began to pick up another cup to polish.

"My mum has seen her in and out of The Clinic a lot recently though L, she said she's really not looking great."

Xander's Mum Joanne, worked at The Clinic - our local medical practice - so she knew more about everyone's business than she should, and with the way I've heard the receptionists gossip before, Dagina Defixio-Jones would surely be an entertaining topic for them.

Joanne Flynne was a soft woman, gentle just like Xander. She and my mother actually used to be quite close before Dagina became a total recluse in her darkness. We would often be invited around for dinner in the early days after my dad died and I think Joanne felt sorry for us in all honesty.

There were times when she even taught me how to make simple meals, like pasta bake and beans on toast so that I could cook for myself and Kat. At our toughest times, she went as far as buying us freezer meals to make sure there was always something in the house to eat whilst my mother was passed out drunk on the couch.

"My mum mentioned it was pretty serious L and I just wanted to -"

"Xander." I cut him off dead. He knew my limits and he'd crept too close to the line.

My mother had been trying for years to mend our relationship, but those years after my Dad died were the worst years of my life - she left me, alone, a kid fending not only for herself but having to look after a toddler too.

I had just turned eleven years old when my dad died suddenly. With little to no warning, an illness swept over him, decaying him from the inside out.

I tried not to think of those last weeks before he died, but sometimes they plague me in the dark moments that still sometimes consume me.

Kat was five and wasn't entirely aware of what was going on, but I knew. I knew he was leaving us and he wasn't ready.

He'd lost so much weight that his skin had become transparent - speckled with blue blotches that looked as if his blood had escaped his veins and risen to the surface of his skin.

He was a kind man, and he was so patient. He'd actually taught himself how to braid my hair, and then he taught me so I could do Kats. Sometimes we would sit on the floor, one in front of the other in a braid train watching TV, seeing who could finish the braid fastest - extra points for neatness.

My mum would even sit behind dad and pretend she was doing his too, making a mess of his brown, curly hair that would have us all in stitches - mum bowing at her masterpiece. Sometimes we would even let her win.

I wasn't completely heartless, part of me did understand how my mother fell into the hole of despair she tried too little to crawl back out of.

She had lost her mother weeks before my dad fell ill and within a month she had lost both.

Xander stood in front of me, patient as ever and I knew if I did want to talk about those times that I had filed so far away, then he would be there to listen to every word.

"So, who was the chick with the boobs?" I changed the subject and felt a jealous flush of warmth heat my face.

"Chick with the boobs?" Xander parroted, seemingly confused.

"You know Miss 'oh Xander, your eyes are as green as the oceans, fractured emeralds of Atlantis' with the boobs." I mocked her sickly sweet voice.

"I believe she said Jade, not emeralds. But if you wanted to compliment my eyes Lana you could just say you think they are as stunning as the...what was it again?" His mouth curled upwards and a single dimple appeared. "Emeralds of Atlantis." He finished and my entire face felt like it was on fire. *God, I hope I wasn't a walking beetroot.*

"Don't flatter yourself Xan, they're a murky shade of snot at the best of times." I brushed him off but immediately felt a little guilt as the smile in his eyes dropped at my rebuff.

I had a habit of that, keeping people at arm's length. Always knowing just the right thing to say that would push people away. It was like a knee-jerk reaction most of the time, my lips thoughtlessly spilling words out before I could contemplate how it would make someone feel.

Most of the time it was to save me from embarrassment, and sometimes it was to save me from pain. But every time I shot Xander down, a part of me felt gutted from the inside out.

J L Robinson

CHAPTER SEVEN

Perched on a stone garden wall across from Beckenham school, I patiently waited for Kat, but after I checked my watch, it told me she should have been out half an hour ago.

She was definitely still pissed off as the past couple of days she had just walked right past me, barely even lifting her head to acknowledge me before she walked home - so I wouldn't be surprised if I'd somehow missed her.

Digging my phone out from my back pocket, I checked my notifications and noticed there were no texts from Kat, but there was an unknown missed call - probably just someone asking me if I'd been in an accident for the 100th time.

I locked my phone and shifted myself off the wall, aiming to head back home when the smell of spice hit me, along with a huge body that now almost knocked me over.

Before I could fall face-first onto the floor, my arms outstretched bracing for a collision with the concrete, two large tanned hands clasped the sides of my waist and held me firm.

A heated mixture of embarrassment and pure anger flushed to my face as the musky scent of sweet spice and sandalwood became fragrant in the air around me.

With a colourful curse on the tip of my tongue, I was seething, but the anger fell as quickly as it had risen and was replaced by a calm warmth that soothed my body.

I brushed myself off, still feeling a little confused when I looked up. I was met with familiar sparkling grey eyes, now framed below furrowed, worried eyebrows.

Any lingering embarrassment dissipated from me as though it would be impossible to feel such a thing whilst looking at such a perfect, beautiful face and my tense muscles relaxed.

Aide's full lips were moving, but I was too busy looking up at the way his hair, now slightly darker and wet, fell over his face. His sun-kissed skin still glowing with perspiration.

I took in every line of his face before my gaze fell back to his mouth, which was still perfect and *still moving*. *Shit*.

"Lana?" He clasped again at my arms with those goddamn perfect hands. "Lana? Are you okay?" His voice was louder as he lowered his head lower so our faces were now in line. "I'm so sorry, I didn't see you. I can get a little lost in my own world when I'm running sometimes."

The words stumbled before they fell from my mouth as I just hoped I wasn't about to make myself sound like a complete idiot.

"No, no I'm sorry, I shouldn't...I should have looked where I was going, it's not your-" I stuttered.

Aide grinned, his mouth tugging so slightly to the left that somehow made him look even sexier. The grey top he was wearing clung to his muscled chest, with a darker patch right between his magnificent pecs.

My eyes took a moment too long scaling down the length of his body and back up to the curve of his lips.

"Hey." Aide said in that sultry voice that dripped with confidence. He had the kind of voice that sounded hot without trying and it matched the size of him.

Whilst it felt like I might combust around him, there was also something inherently sedative about his aura - like, for a moment, the world around us stilled.

A second before, I was ready to tear whoever had slammed into me, a new one, but a split second later and a flash of an immaculate smile, I was already forgetting what I was embarrassed about and apologising instead.

"It's a little late for a school pick-up." He said as he checked his watch which looked like it was worth more than I'd earn in a year.

"Well, I was waiting for Kat, but I think I must have missed her," I replied and as I dug my hand into my pocket for my phone, I noticed it was gone.

With dread, my eyes shot towards the ground around me, it had to have fallen out of my hand when that god-of-a-man came tunnelling into me. *Fuck.* I spotted it, facedown on the concrete pavement.

I held my breath as I leant down to pick it up, knowing before I'd even turned it over in my hand, that the screen would be shattered. It's just my luck and it seems phones these days were made to break - a simple fumble would see you a hundred-pound down just for a new screen. *Money I definitely didn't have.*

"Oh for fucks sake." I sighed before standing back up to where Aide towered, still watching me and the smile on his face dropped as he noticed the shattered phone in my hands.

"Shit Lana! I'm sorry," he said as he clasped his warm hands around mine. *Good god, his hands were huge.*

"Honestly it's fine-"

"No, here." He took out his phone from the back pocket of his black running shorts and pulled out a card from behind the case.

"Here are my details." He passed over a crisp white card. "Let me pay for the repairs."

"No it's-"

"Lana, I will not be taking no for an answer." He said boldly before I could object.

I turned the card over in my hand and saw the address of The Clinic Joanne worked at along with his *personal* details.

Dr Aide Vasiliás
Emergency Medicine
+447435667932

"Thank you." I pressed a shy smile back at those intense eyes before pocketing the card. I don't know why being around him turned me into such an awkward mess, but I knew it was a feeling I didn't hate.

Our eyes seemed to be lost in one another's for a minute before a cough came from behind me, and I followed Aide's eye line, glancing over my shoulder.

Standing there in her drab grey uniform, Kat was clearly trying her best not to laugh but her eyes gave her away as the corners of her mouth twitched upwards.

"Interrupting something am I?" She asked, barely holding in a giggle as she looked between Aide and I. *God, it was nice to see her smiling again.*

Aide returned the smirk kindly.

"Don't forget to call me, I owe you," he said, popping his ear-phones back in one by one and carrying on with his run. As he ran into the distance, I couldn't help but admire his long, tanned legs, corded with muscle, hitting the ground hard with each large stride.

Apparently, neither could Kat as I turned towards her to find her gawking at his backside too.

Wait, why had she only just finished school?

"Why are you so late out?" I asked with a brow raised.

"No reason, I just stayed late to get some...stuff done." She was lying. She had a tell, a finger now curled a lock of hair from the underside of her head.

"Now tell me the real reason," I remarked, slipping into mum mode.

"I may have gotten detention." She lowered her head, and my mouth dropped open before looking back at her beautiful blue eyes now widened, feigning the image of innocence.

"Detention?! Since when have you ever done anything to make detention?" I was legitimately shocked, Kat was the sweetest student.

The parent's evenings had been my responsibility since I was sixteen and they never had a bad word to say about her. In fact, they had always said quite the opposite and admitted to wishing more students could be as engaging as her.

"What happened?" I lifted her chin gently to face me.

"Some guy made a comment about mum. He was saying he overheard his parents talking about her and how her illness was karma. How she deserved to be sick," she said as tears gathered above her lower lashes. *I didn't know what to say.*

"So I threw my book at him." She continued, "I didn't exactly mean to hit him directly in the face but one nosebleed later and I was given after-school detention." There was a hint of pride in her voice that I couldn't help but admire.

Maybe I should have probably been more annoyed that she was in detention, but between us not speaking for days and her eyes still glossy with tears, I felt relieved and pulled her into my arms.

After a long moment in our embrace, sharing each other's warmth, things finally felt right again.

"Soooo..." Kat drawled out, a smirk tugging at her face again. "Tell me why the handsome Doctor owes you something?"

I pulled my phone out of my pocket and pressed the unlock button, the cracks now distorted the list of notifications that lit up the screen.

"Fuck!" Kat gasped.

"Kat!" I said shocked, mum mode back in full force. She just laughed and right now, I'd let her off anything with that smile.

"So are you going to call him?" She probed as we walked back home. A girlish giddiness warmed my fluttering stomach.

"I'm thinking about it." I smirked back at her and she giggled in response, seemingly just as excited as I was as she hooked her arm in mine.

My mother wasn't home when we breezed through the door still full of laughter, and I'd be lying if I didn't say I was happy she wasn't.

Recently, I noticed she had been out a few evenings during the week but god knows where she was going, probably some bar. I didn't bother pissing myself off thinking about it, at least it meant Kat and I could have dinner together without aggravating conversations and poor attempts to be *motherly*.

After cooking our favourite dinner, we both sat around the TV and rewatched a couple of episodes of *The Gilmore girls.*

It was around seven o'clock when I heard Dagina trying to unlock the front door, which was earlier than I expected but presumably no less drunk still.

Not wanting her to put a damper on an otherwise great day, I kissed Kat on the head before making my way upstairs to run a bath.

Our bathroom was falling apart, like the rest of the house, but I had treated myself to some expensive bubble bath that always made it feel a little luxurious.

As I sunk into the hot, soapy water that soothed my bones, I let out a deep breath and opened my book, thumbing for the chapter I'd left off at.

Just as I had settled, my phone buzzed loudly on the cabinet which was barely just within reaching distance from the bath. It buzzed again. *For fucks sake.*

My wet body half slithered out like some kind of swamp monster, as my outstretched arms ungracefully reached for the phone. After a few attempts that now waved the bath water, I managed to finally grab it and through the cracks, I could see it was a text from Xander.

Xander: Hey, hope you're okay. My mum said your mum has been in again today and she's really not well. I know you

don't want to talk about it L, but if / when you do, I'm here, you know.

I rolled my eyes and didn't even bother texting back.

But as I went to put my phone down and pick up my book again, I remembered that at some point between cooking the moussaka and eating it, I had added Aide's number to my phone.

A blank message box opened up beneath my tapping fingers and I searched for the contact with a doctor emoji next to the flames symbol.

Though, feeling apprehensive I just looked at the blank screen for a moment, gently swishing back and forth in the bath as I considered what to type.

I was pretty sure he was flirting with me but I didn't want to be *that girl* when he might have just been trying to be a decent person.

Before I could form a single word I immediately tapped the backspace and deleted the draft. I had no idea what to say. *What was wrong with me?*

Lana: Heyi how tyit?

I typed quickly and pressed send before my treacherous fingers could delete it, not noticing the message was basically illegible from the damn broken screen.

Three dots appeared and I froze. *Damn, that was quick, was he waiting for me to text him?* The three dots disappeared, then shot back up just as I was about to put my phone down.

Aide: Who's this?

Swallow the ground and eat me whole. Right now. I was ready to submerge myself in the tub. How many times does this man go around just bumping into people and smashing their phones? I should have known when he gave me the flashy business card.

My phone pinged.

Aide: I'm joking.

Lana: Very funny.

The words at least spelt correctly but I still felt like I had texted back a little too quickly. *Too eagerly.* But three dots appeared again instantly.

Aide: The phones not doing too well then I guess?

Lana: It's doing better than me, I'm having to have a hot bath just to soak these bruises. ● Did no one tell you you're too big to be running into people?

I was being obvious but I knew that mentioning the bath was a sure way to get him to picture me naked.

Three dots appeared. Then disappeared again - this happened twice. He was readying to shoot this conversation down. Figuring that he was probably going to ghost me, I locked my phone and picked up my book.

My phone started buzzing loudly, making me almost jump out of my naked skin. Quickly, I tried to pick up the phone that began shuddering itself off the bath ledge and almost into the water with me.

It fell between my slick hands and fumbled from one to the other and as I tried to save it from the water, I noticed I had answered a call. *FUCK*

"Did I hurt you?" Asked a panicked, deep voice on the other end.

"What?" I asked, still confused and flustered.

"Did I hurt you Lana?" The voice repeated as I looked down through the cracks and I saw it was *Doctor Flames.*

Aide had called me.

"Oh no, I was just joking," I said and played it off cool but my insides recoiled with embarrassment.

"You had me a little worried there." The worry in his voice had softened and he sounded genuine.

"Nothing to worry about here, other than the fact I almost dropped this phone in the bath and finished off the job you started. I'm all good," I joked.

"That phone is not having the best of days, is it?" He replied and I could hear the smile in his voice, instantly making the low part of my stomach tighten.

"So when will I see you next?" He asked abruptly.

"See me next?" I repeated, a little confused. *Was he asking me out?*

"Yeah, we've got to go fix that phone right? I told you I wouldn't be taking no for an answer." His voice was like an assertive purr.

My lips pressed into a thin line as I shook my head at my phone in frustration, annoyed that yet again I had fooled myself into thinking he was being anything but courteous.

"Well, I'm free most days after six?" I replied. Realising I had just made myself sound like a complete loser - I might as well have outright admitted that I had pretty much no social life.

"I'll pick you up tomorrow at six then." He replied in that kind but forceful tone that was sexy as hell.

"Okay, great! See you tomorrow then." I attempted cooly. "Do you remember where I am?" I asked.

"Of course. Enjoy your bath Lana," he said and I could hear the smirk in his voice. *God this man could undo me.*

CHAPTER EIGHT

The smell of metal singed the skin on the inside of my nose and with every inhale, I could taste it. I was sitting on a cold golden tiled floor, barely able to see a few feet in front of me.

It was as dark as the dead of night and I couldn't make out my surroundings as my vision was distorted by the inky haze now rising from the floor beneath me.

Coils of dark mist began to swirl and warp as the darkness thickened and the shadowy smog began entwining against itself.

The mist turned oilier, I could feel it lick against my skin sending shivers along my body as it flexed and curved around me like a darkening shadow forging itself into being.

I couldn't tear my horrified eyes away as it became denser, and darker, forming what looked like a huge male body, hiding within its darkness.

I tried to scream, but when I opened my mouth not a single sound would come out.

The balmy air around me was already stifling, like a choking smoke now searing the stone underneath me, it was unbearable.

Quickly shifting now onto my feet, I tried not to stumble back as I saw a colossal form within the shadows, writhe.

A huge torso, tanned and corded in muscles now cleared through the veil of darkness. The shadows seemed to dance around him. Like he was made of them and them of him.

I tried to run but my feet wouldn't move. Now pulling at each leg, I tried desperately to pry each foot from the floor, but they had sunk into the stone beneath me. The gold tiles were molten but somehow not burning me.

A silent scream still ached in my lungs and my entire body stilled in complete terror. My petrified gaze reluctantly observed the being of dancing shadows, form and step out from within the darkness.

A huge male, with long silver hair that shined like the sun, flowing across tanned, tattooed shoulders, now towered above me. Heat flashed across me as I noticed there wasn't a single thread of clothing on him - he was completely naked except for the silver-blue flames that shrouded him modestly.

The air thrummed in anticipation, as though the very atmosphere awaited his instruction and the ground began to tremble as a deep, dark voice spoke.

"I've been waiting for you." Said a voice dripping in dominance. The vibration of each syllable coiled against my skin as every hair on my body now rose with a primal fear.

I could hear myself screaming now but it was still muffled as I stared on in muted horror. My lungs felt on fire.

"Come back to me." The deep voice purred. My body pulled towards the voice, recognising it, *obeying it.*

Fighting against my trembling bones, I could hear a faint voice shouting my name, somewhere in the distance. A warm voice that became louder, cutting through the darkness still rippling around me. I struggled from where I was sitting, still unable to move my treacherous body as a bright golden light shone through the mist.

"LANA! Lana wake up!"

Ω

Kat's hands gripped my shoulders, shaking me from my bed. Her face was pinched with worry.

"What happened?!" I panted, Kat's eyes still fixated on me.

"You were screaming, I was trying to wake you up, but you wouldn't Lana." Her voice was shaking.

I was dreaming again. This was starting to freak me out - I've had nightmares before but the past few felt so real, I could smell and taste the world around me just as I could now. I could feel my body, but it was like walking in another's.

"I-" *What was I supposed to tell her?* "I keep having these strange dreams." I caved. I knew of all people, Kat wouldn't think I was crazy even if I told her the wildest of things.

"Every time I'm somewhere different but I can just sense-" I looked at her to see if she was assessing my state, but she wasn't. Her blue eyes were wide, attentively listening to every word.

"I can just sense it's the same place. It smells the same." I said as I remembered the feel of the air around me.

"What does it look like?" Kat asked as she sat down on the edge of the bed and I shifted up, sitting against the headboard.

"Honestly, not much, kind of like a cave. But it's really hot wherever it is and all around there's an odd black mist that seems to be...alive." I replied with a grimace.

"Alive?" Her voice inclined, those eyes now pinched in a mixture of concern and amusement.

"Yes, alive. Like a man," I said, knowing full well how mad I sounded.

"So the mist is a man?"

"Kind of, well I think so," I said as I tried to recall what I actually saw.

"And...you're in a cave with this misty man?" She said, her mouth twitching.

"Well, I'm not sure if it's me, or if it's someone else that I'm kind of, seeing though." *Now I definitely sounded mad.*

"Is the misty man hot?" She stifled a giggle as her brows raised and I couldn't help but laugh. *I sounded ridiculous, didn't I? And it did sound kind of funny.*

"It sounds like you've been reading too many of those dirty books of yours," Kat said as she picked up the cartoon-covered book on my bedside table.

"And how do you know the contents of my books exactly?" I countered with a smirk that broke across my face as I threw my arms over her shoulders, and pulled her down onto the bed next to me.

No matter how I felt Kat always had a way of making me smile. When times were hard and I was really struggling with everything going on with Mum, having her around meant I had a reason to keep going. If it wasn't for her, I would have left a long time ago but I would never leave her.

She was everything good, sweet and yet somehow still unjaded from the shitty cards we were dealt in life. She grew up never really knowing our dad and in a way not really having a mother, well not a *real* one anyways.

She was still always so forgiving towards her, she would tell me time and time again 'you can't expect someone to lose their husband and their mother in the space of a month and not be a little depressed.'

Whilst I knew where she was coming from and I was even slightly jealous of her outlook on it, she didn't see the worst of it - because I wouldn't have let her.

CHAPTER NINE

After another long day of serving wannabe writers, students and the gaggle of old people the same shit coffee I couldn't force myself to drink anymore, I and Xander were getting ready to close up shop.

I polished off the cups and cleaned down the old coffee machines that sounded as close to breaking down as me most Mondays before I glanced at my watch. It was almost five.

We were open later than usual for a Saturday, but as long as I would have time to get home, shower this cocktail of grease and burnt coffee off my skin, before Aide picked me up I didn't mind getting the extra hours in.

"Fancy the cinema later L?" Xander asked, as he finished closing the till off. "There's a new marvel film out that looks pretty decent if you're up for it?" He said as I pulled my phone out of my back pocket, and checked to see if I had any messages from Aide.

"I'd love to but I'm busy this evening Xan," I replied, my fingers scrolling over the broken glass.

"Nice. What are you up to?" He asked as he took off his apron, revealing the yellow t-shirt that somehow looked amazing on him, but always made me look as though I was starting a shift at *Ikea*.

The fit of his was just tight enough around his arms and chest to show that he filled out pretty impressively underneath it.

"I've got a date with the Doctor," I said, smiling a little smugly.

"Oh, remind me again who's the Doctor?" He asked as he looked back towards the till.

"You know, that big handsome blonde that came to the rescue when *poor little me* took a turn in the kitchen last week," I said, nudging his arm as the corners of my mouth turned upwards.

Xander didn't respond to my nudge for a moment before he turned to face me, his hands leaned back onto the counter and those green eyes splintered with gold now shaded below his narrowed brows.

"Oh, of course, *that* Doctor. For a moment there you had me thinking some dude in a blue telephone box was about to teleport my best friend away to a different planet, and I might have had a problem with that." He pushed away from the counter and closed the space between us before planting a kiss on my head.

I ignored the way it made my stomach flutter like it always did when Xander was tactile with me.

"Well, it's not technically a date," I admitted.

"It's not?" Xander's mouth turned up at the corners and gave away our unspoken secret.

During the past couple of years, I'd be lying if I said I haven't noticed Xander, he was impossibly good looking and I'm not exactly blind. But it wasn't going to happen because he deserved someone far less fucked up than me.

Still, more often than I'd like to admit I thought of him whilst reading the moments in books where the guy's head is buried between the woman's legs, thinking what a sight it is - to look down and see that head of dark soft curls and those green eyes framed in dark lashes looking back up at me.

"He's taking me to fix my phone." I pulled out the phone from my pocket now, turning it over in my hand to show him the shattered screen.

"Shit, how'd that happen?" He frowned, taking the phone from my hand to inspect it.

"I was waiting for Kat outside school, which apparently is on his jogging route and long story short, he ran into me and I dropped my phone." I had already romanticised the moment in my head like it was a scene from some early noughties romcom. "And he's offered to fix it for me, so that's what we're doing." I finished.

Xander let out a breath between a smile. "It doesn't sound much like a date to me."

The phone in his hand lit up, chiming and I snatched it from his hands before he could even look down.

I could make out a message notification from Doctor Flames. The time was five-fifteen - he was picking me up in forty-five minutes.

"You're gonna have to close up Xan, I've got a date to get to!" I quickly untied my apron from around my waist and pulled it off over my head, before pushing it into Xander's hard body.

"It's not a date." He called out laughing, as I ran through the cafe and out through the glass front door.

I burst through the front door of our house, practically having run home. I was dripping in sweat. I looked down at my watch - five-thirty.

My legs darted up the stairs heading for the bathroom, passing Kat and Dagina who were sitting together in the living room watching something on the TV.

There was no time to wash my hair, but I stripped off my clothes, and turned on the shower dial - a body wash would have to do.

I bunched up my hair in a curly knot at the back of my head, securing it with a purple claw clip and jumped in the steaming shower.

I squeezed out a glug of my favourite honey-almond shower gel that made my skin smell amazing and soaped down my body.

My body had always been fuller than that of the women I'd seen in magazines and TV, but I couldn't care less. I liked the way my hips were wider, cute dimples dipping in at the sides and whilst my boobs weren't exactly huge they were definitely still a good handful.

I tested them in my hands as I brought the honey almond suds upwards around them. *Yep, a bloody good handful if I do say so myself.*

Careful not to get my hair wet, I quickly rinsed myself off and stepped out of the shower.

Now wrapped in a towel, I picked up my phone and headed to my room. I had completely forgotten that Aide had texted me in my mad rush to get home. I unlocked my phone and tapped open the message.

Aide: Still on for 6pm?

It was now a quarter too. I wiped my hands on the towel wrapped around me and began typing out a reply.

Lana: Hey, sorry I've just seen this. All good for me if it is for you? ●

For a moment I thought he may have changed his mind. Three dots appeared on the screen.

Aide: All good for me Lana. I'm outside whenever you're ready.

I crept towards my bedroom window, which faced the front of the house, and looked down to the curbside where Aide's silver Mercedes was parked.

A tanned muscular arm hung outside the open window and my gaze traced upwards to his shoulders, covered in a tight black t-shirt. *God, I loved a black t-shirt.* As my eyes flickered up higher I saw his perfectly chiselled jaw and tanned face now wearing oversized classic squared Ray-Bans, staring back at me. A wry grin cracked his perfect face and I jumped back from the window as my phone pinged in my hand.

Aide: No rush ● *I'm happy to wait as long as you need.*

So he definitely saw that. For fucks sake.

Lana: I'll be down in 5!

I quickly tapped back as though I wasn't completely mortified. How long had I been gawking at him before he'd noticed?

Although it was Autumn, the weather was still pretty warm today, so I pulled out a sage-coloured summer dress that made my boobs look great, from my wardrobe.

It was tight around the chest, with cute capped sleeves. The lower part flowed outwards from the waist to just above my knees.

I pulled a few stray curls from the claw clip to frame my face and added a little gloss to my lips. Adjusting my boobs one by one with each hand, and smoothing down the skirt, I had one last glance in the mirror. *I felt kind of pretty.*

I grabbed a little bag I could pop my gloss and phone into, and headed downstairs.

"Erm, where are you going?" Kat called out as I ran downstairs which led into both the kitchen and living room.

"Out with the Doctor - he owes me remember!" I shouted back and as I toed my converse and swung open the front door, I heard her giggle.

"Have a great time!" She yelled over to me as I closed the front door.

Aide was standing waiting for me when I stepped out of the house, leaning casually against the side of his car. With one relaxed leg crossed over the other, he was wearing straight-fitted charcoal trousers and a black T-shirt tucked in loosely at the waist. The dark fabric clung tightly to his muscle-bound chest with his capped sleeves rolled up once, now exposing an extra inch of his thick, lean biceps.

His hair was slightly curly but looked styled effortlessly as a single stray honey curl fell over his sunglasses.

"Hey." Aide pulled off his sunglasses, his diamond eyes taking in the length of me as he raked a hand through his hair.

"Hey," I replied, feeling a little shy under his gaze yet loving every moment of it.

"Let's go get that phone of yours sorted," he said as he strode around to the passenger side of the car and opened the door for me.

My eyes widened, taking full advantage of the view that those charcoal trousers gave me of his backside, looking away quickly before he faced me.

Nothing about being around Aide felt awkward. In fact, it felt intensely the opposite.

The inside of his Mercedes smelt like him and was impossibly clean, but that didn't surprise me one bit, he was a doctor after all. What did surprise me though was his choice of music.

He really didn't strike me as a swifty, but the songs that he flicked through apparently confirmed he had the same taste in music as me. A smile unintentionally hit my face as he flicked the new song *Anti-Hero*, and cooling sitting back deep into his seat.

He pressed his palm into the gear stick and wrapped his fingers around it, pushing into first whilst my mind now made something so uneventful, feel so beautifully inappropriate.

With the windows slightly open, I watched those perfectly kept curls bob as the early autumn breeze ran through his hair. My gaze followed the lines of his chiselled profile. *Absolute perfection.*

He turned to me with his head slightly dipped, so his slate eyes could look over the frame of his Ray-Bans, our eyes locked and he flashed a smile. He was the picture of pure confidence.

I was still looking at him when he turned back to face the road - watching the muscles in his arms flex as he upped the gears.

"Do you like it fast?" Aide glanced over to me again with a smirk.

I clenched my legs together under his gaze.

"Really fast." I smirked back in response, dipping my eyes low.

The pull of the car was almost instant as he pressed his foot to the floor, his lower lip gripped under his teeth, holding in a smirk.

A laugh escaped me as the sheer speed of the vehicle forced my body back into my seat and pinned me in place.

The wind whipped at my legs lifting my dress, and nearly exposing me, but I quickly clasped my hands down - preventing my very own *Marilyn Monroe* moment.

I caught Aide's eyes on my legs before his low carnal laugh broke from his lips.

When we finally arrived at the mall, Aide reversed the car expertly into a spot right outside the doors and unclipped his belt.

As I reached down for my own, I was met with his own large hand's unclipping mine too.

"I've got you," he said before pushing down the release button.

The back of his hand grazed the side of my hip and the contact sent a shiver of heat down me, making me involuntarily press my thighs together.

I would have thanked him, but I wasn't confident the words wouldn't come out as an over-excited, stuttering mess.

A moment passed before I composed myself, climbed out and walked over to where Aide was waiting for me.

He seemed to know exactly where to go as he made a bee-line for a small kiosk in the middle of the mall, right next to the escalators.

"So how many phones have you broken exactly?" I laughed, jutting my chin towards the kiosk we were approaching.

"Exactly one, but I wanted to make sure it would be done properly so I checked this place out before." He reached into the pocket of his charcoal trousers and pulled out a black leather wallet.

"Turns out-" he continued, "this was the only place that could fit us at the last minute."

"Oh really?"

"Apparently screen repairs are a busy business when the majority of phones manufactured these days are designed to break." He smirked.

"I guess with all of these wild men running around, not looking where they're going, no phone is safe." I jibed.

"I guess not." He laughed as he gestured his open hand to me.

I pulled out my sorry-looking phone from my little bag and handed it over to him.

"I'll be one moment, you good?" He asked and I nodded. He walked up to the counter of the Kiosk and spoke to a man with greasy long hair. Handing down the phone to the man, who was probably an average height, I couldn't help but notice, everyone looked tiny next to Aide.

After a few words and a fistful of notes, Aide walked back over to where I was standing.

"Do you want the good news or bad news first?"

"Good news?" My stomach felt unsettled.

"The good news is, they said your phone is totally repairable. The bad news is, it's going to take 3 hours to fix it."

"Oh that's okay, I can just get the bus back, no need for you to wait around too." I tried, feeling slightly gutted that this was it.

"So, are you hungry?" He smiled down at me.

"I'm starving." The corners of my mouth pulled into a grin I didn't try to hide. *IT WAS A DATE.*

Sat opposite Aide in the mall's food court, after having a quick scan of what each of the food outlets had to offer, we had both decided on Five Guys.

A burger each and fries to share because apparently, they're huge.

Here was this impossibly good-looking man, sitting finishing off a Five Guys 'all the way' burger, now pushing the brown paper bag filled with the nicest fries I'd ever eaten, towards me in a moment that felt strangely intimate.

"Any good?" Aide asked as he nodded towards the empty foil wrapper.

"Soooo good! I feel like I could eat four!" I said, still chomping down on a mouthful of the tastiest burger I'd ever eaten.

Aide reached into his pocket pulling out his leather wallet.

"Go get another," He said, pulling out a twenty-pound note that looked like it was fresh off the print, and handed it over to me across the table.

"We're in no rush." He smiled reassuringly.

"Oh no-" I swallowed and let out a laugh. "I was just joking."

"Well only if you're sure you've had enough?" His brows raised attentive eyes.

He was checking up on me and it felt amazing.

There were few people in my life I felt I could trust just enough for me to rely on, one being my best friend, *obviously*. But with the way being around Aide made me feel sure and safe, I could easily see myself feeling the same with him.

Before I could think of the consequences, I looked up, across to Aide whose lips were now wrapped around a straw and mid-pull on his strawberry milkshake.

"Is this a date?" I blurted, immediately regretting it.

He looked at me and the straw dropped from his parted mouth.

"I know it *wasn't* a date-" I continued, "but like, now we're sitting here, together, eating? It kind of feels like a date." I squirmed, trying to play it off.

The corners of his mouth turned upwards and I was about to backtrack, my mind telling me *to retreat!* When his low voice replied.

"Lana, do you want this to be a date?" His mouth smiled widely enough to see his immaculate teeth.

I was not one to back down easily and already feeling as though I'd committed to my humiliation, I kept going.

"It wouldn't be the worst thing in the world if a hotshot doctor wanted to take me out I guess." My eyes could barely meet his as I took a sip of my milkshake.

He practically purred at my response before leaning across the table, closing the space between us.

"And I guess it wouldn't be the worst thing if the clumsy girl with the amber eyes and perfect legs-" His eyes roamed down over me.

"Would want to go on a date with me," he continued. "But, this is not a date." Aide said, and my stomach dropped.

"Because when you let me take you out on a *real* date and I get to have you by myself-" He looked around at the people sitting in the food hall around us. "I won't feel the need to hold back quite as much." One corner of his mouth curled upwards as he pushed his knees against the inside of mine under the table. The contact slightly parted them, and I did my best not to gasp.

"So, is that you asking me?" *I wanted him to ask me so badly.*

"I would love nothing-" Aide was cut off mid-sentence, as a tray clashed down on our table.

I shifted up in my seat and pressed my legs together as I peered up at who was holding the tray.

Xander stood looking over us, his hands still gripping the tray. But he wasn't alone, he was standing with a girl wearing a familiar pair of assets, big eyes and a Jade necklace.

This was the first time I have ever seen Xander with someone and it felt like he had just punched me right in the gut. *I should be happy for him, right? I'm on a date, he's on a date. This was fine.*

But this was not fine. I don't know why seeing him with someone made me feel like this but I couldn't help but look at her absolutely stacked chest and down to my own little handfuls and feel a little gutted.

Of course, he would go out with her, *damn* I'd go out with her if she asked, she's absolutely gorgeous and has the whole, totally-effortless pretty girl thing going on that I'd spend hours just trying to mimic.

"Well if it isn't my assistant." Aide stood up, towering over Xander. *Holy shit how tall was he?* Aide presented Xander his large opened hand and Xander, now releasing the tray, clasped his hand into a shake.

"If I remember correctly, Doctor. I did most of the work." Xander joked, lifting his other hand and propping it on Aide's shoulder.

Aide looked at me, and down at my, now healed, hand.

"Oh, of course, that will be why it needed rewrapping when I dropped her off at home." Aide joked back.

They were both laughing but the energy was tense - like watching two lions, each of their lips curling in a warning growl, guarding their hunt as though the other would snatch the food from under them. *Was I the food? I can't say the idea of being eaten by any of them sounds that bad to me.*

My legs shifted across in my seat and now feeling slightly nosey about the girl Xander was with, I tapped the seat next to me.

"Join us if you like, we were just finishing up but trying to find a table in here that isn't filthy or sat opposite a bunch of eight-year-olds at a McDonald's party is harder than you would think." I laughed, peering around Xander, doing my best to smile at his date, but deep down wanting to tip her upside down.

The testosterone in the air must have eased off as Aide sat back down, now shifting himself further across to make room for Xander.

"Of course, and help yourself to the fries guys, we were struggling." He pushed the brown paper bag into the middle of the table.

Being sat opposite both Xander and Aide felt weird and exciting at the same time. The thought of them both had my mind wandering shamelessly.

They were opposites in many ways, but there was no denying they were equally, possibly the most beautiful men I had ever seen.

"Sorry I know I recognise your face-" *or your boobs* "but I don't think I caught your name? I'm Lana." An awkward attempt at cutting the lingering tension.

"It's Holly." She said bluntly, quickly followed by a saccharine smile, before looking away from me and back to

Xander. My temper stoked beneath my skin but I swallowed and choked it down.

"Holly, this is Aide." I forced through gritted teeth. Her eyes flicked to Aide and stared a little too long for my liking.

I felt Aide's knees brush against mine under the table as he politely smiled at her before immediately refocusing his attention back on me. The feel of him soothed me.

I caught Xander watching me, his chest rose seemingly to draw in a large breath.

"So what are you guys up to?" I said, trying to break the uneasiness.

"We're going to the cinema," Xander bit out. "To watch that new Marvel film I was telling you about." He continued and I felt he was having a slight jab at me. *It's not exactly my fault I was busy, but I did tell him I was going on a 'not date' that turned into an actual date.*

"Oh yeah? It looks good!" I looked towards Holly and attempted to bring her into the conversation but she was too busy immersed in editing a selfie on her phone.

"So we better get off actually, the film starts soon," Xander pressed his lips together in a poor attempt at a smile and stood up from the table - the food on his tray still untouched.

"Holly?" Xander interrupted her scrolling. "Shall we get off?" *More of a demand than a question.*

"Oh absolutely!" She said, eagerly lifting from her seat whilst her eyes were still fixed on her phone.

"So I guess I'll see you on Monday?" I said as Xander prepared to walk off.

"See you Monday L," Xander replied, before he turned and walked away, his sombre tone made my stomach wrench a little.

"Nice to meet you, Holly!" I called out after her, my tone overly sweet, but she didn't so much as turn around and I rolled my eyes.

I faced back towards Aide, whose grey eyes were still fixed on me and I pulled a face that summed up what I was thinking. *What the fuck.*

We both burst out laughing.

J L Robinson

CHAPTER TEN

My phone was as good as brand new, and as I lay there on my bed, I couldn't stop replaying the night in my mind.

It was only the fourth time I'd been around him, but I was completely intoxicated by the idea of having him and his mouth on my bare skin.

I cannot remember the last time someone had a hold over me like this.

When Aide dropped me off I had hoped he was going to ask to see me again, but when he said nothing I just thanked him again for the food and sorting my phone before I tried to get out of the car without flashing my ass.

Disappointment weighed me down like a sack of rocks. Maybe I had read the situation wrong.

The next morning, like muscle memory, the first thing I did was reach for my phone.

As I unlocked it, I was able to actually see my screen saver again - an old picture of Kat and me as kids with Dad. I'd taken a photo of the physical print that I kept in my bottom drawer.

There was a text from Xander, but no text from *Doctor Flames.*

Xander: So how was last night?

Lana: Good morning to you too! It wasn't much, but at least I got my phone fixed and a free burger. ● How was the film with Holly?

I hit send and pulled the covers from me, readying myself to get up out of bed.

My bed was so cosy I could have stayed in it all morning, it was one of those days where I woke up extra comfy - it was also the first in a few where I hadn't woken up sweating from a nightmare.

Through the wall on the far side of my room, I heard the shower flick on, which meant Kat must be up because I knew damn well it wouldn't be my mother awake at this time on a Sunday.

Dagina was already blacked out on the sofa when I got in last night, lying in the dark with a blanket over her. It didn't look as though she'd even bothered trying to get to bed properly.

I threw on an oversized, overwashed t-shirt and loose-fitting pyjama bottoms, before heading over to the landing.

My fist knocked on the door of the bathroom.

"I'll just be a minute," Kat yelled from the shower.

"No rush, we still on for today?" I shouted back at the door.

"Yep! I've asked Isha, she's coming too if that's okay?" Kat replied.

"Perfect, it will be nice to properly meet her!"

Isha was Kat's girlfriend, not that she had told me that yet but she's my younger sister and I know her better than she gives me credit for.

I could tell with the way her voice goes up an octave whenever she mentions her, and the sparkle in her already sky-blue eyes that gave her away.

Nothing made my heart warmer with love then seeing my sister happy, so as long as Isha didn't hurt her, she'd be just fine in my books.

I padded back to my room and googled the name of the mechanics my car was at. It was due to pick up today, but I hadn't heard from them and I was hoping I wouldn't have to force Kat and her date to get a bus.

The search pulled up three local garages, and I recognised the second one from the top. A click on the link opened up the company's details, including their workshop number.

After a couple of rings, it went to an automated message.

"Hi, you've reached Clay Motor Works, we are currently closed for the weekend and will be open again Monday at eight am. Please leave a message after the tone."

Just my fucking luck.

My phone pinged loudly against my face, almost bursting my eardrum.

Xander: The film was good, though I don't think Holly would agree. She never took her eyes off her phone the entire time.

Lana: ⬤⬤ I wasn't gonna say, but I think she was more interested in her own Instagram feed than anything else.

Xander: Lol. I didn't even ask her out, she invited herself. I was shutting up shop and she walked by, asked what I was doing and basically came along. Weird. ⬤

Lana: Very weird.

I heard the groan of water pipes indicating the shower being turned off and began to undress.

Xander: So what are you doing today?

Lana: Well I was supposed to be taking Kat and Isha (her GF) out into town for the day but the bloody garage is closed and my car's still there. Wbu?

My trousers dropped to a heap on the floor and using my foot, I tossed them to a corner pile of clothes I'd get round to sorting soon.

I lifted my t-shirt off and pulled it over my head when my phone rang. My arms got caught in a knot as I tried to free them from the sleeves and reached for my phone. Finally freeing a hand, I grabbed my phone and pressed the green icon to answer.

"So she's finally told you then? About Isha?" Xander chuckled on the other end.

"What do you mean you finally told me? She's told you?!" It didn't surprise me, Kat had always trusted Xander, he had been like an older brother to her.

"Of course, she told me L, Kat tells me everything, you know this." I could still hear the smile down the phone and my heart warmed.

"Well, she might not want me to meet her when I tell her we have to get the bus into town later." I rolled my eyes as I paced butt-naked around my room, using my feet to shove the piles of books and clothes out of my path.

"Well I'm not up to much, I can come take you guys if you need?" "Are you sure you're not busy with *Boobs*?" I poked, but really I just wanted him to tell me Holly was out of the picture, and I know that made me selfish but she wasn't good enough for him. *No one was.*

"I don't think I'll be seeing *Boobs* again. So, what time shall I pick you girls up?" He asked.

"Well, I'm just about to jump in the shower and Kat should be ready soon too. Shall we say an hour? I'll tell Kat to text Isha."

"Already on it. Right, I'll see you later then!"

My bedroom door swung open as I went to put the phone down.

"Xanders coming with us too?" Kat's face was beaming. *How had he texted her so quickly?*

"Yep. The car's in the garage and apparently, even though I was supposed to collect it this morning, they're closed on weekends." I replied, still standing in the buff.

"Well it's no good standing around in your birthday suit Elly, Xan will be here soon!" She smiled as she turned back, closing the door.

"I'll be downstairs!" She shouted across the hall.

Of course, she was ready exactly five minutes after getting out of the shower. She didn't need makeup, or half an hour trying to tame her hair into something that resembled less like a bird's nest.

I bunched my hair back and held it in place with my favourite purple claw clip before heading to the shower.

It took me almost an hour to get ready and I still looked rushed. I popped on some high-waisted straight-legged jeans, a low-cut t-shirt and my converse - which were probably ready for the bin but I'd get a few more wears out of them.

As I stood at the top of the stairs, I overheard Kat's soft voice.

"She'll come around when she understands."

"My sweet girl. I'm afraid I have pushed Lana too far over the years." Daginas voice crackled quietly. She *almost* sounded sincere.

"She will, I'll talk to her. We will not be out long, but if you need me, if you're struggling at all, please ring me." Kat replied, and she sounded so...grown up.

I made my way down the stairs and coughed loudly to announce my presence.

"Have a good day darling." I saw Dagina, still lying on the sofa, slightly sitting up as Kat brushed a kiss on her head of grey curls.

"Come on Kat, Xanders outside." Headed toward the door.

"Say hello to Xander for me girls." My mother smiled at me but I pretended to not see her as I walked for the door.

Xander was waiting outside in his black Renault Clio - the same car he had had since we finished school - a sixteenth birthday present from his parents.

It was small but it was definitely better than the pile of scrap that I had. Opening the door, I dipped down and pulled the latch on the passenger's seat, pulling it forward to make room for Kat to climb in the back.

"Well, who's Boobs now?" Xander laughed as he mockingly looked away from me, holding a hand up in his sight line.

I looked down to see my shirt had dipped a little lower with me bending over, and the new push-up bra I'd bought recently, was doing its job perfectly.

I blew a stray strand of hair from my face, standing back up and readjusting my t-shirt.

"Well I can't have you forgetting whose number one, can I?" I taunted.

The past few years had been this way, one of us jokingly flirting, the other batting it off. Neither of us had the balls enough to ever step over a line we couldn't fall back behind. So we lingered on the border, never peaking at the possibility of *'what if.'* Besides, I could never make him happy that way, he deserved someone sweeter, someone, softer. Someone more like my sister.

"I'll text Isha to let her know we're on the way," Kat said as she climbed into the back seat of the Clio, and pulled the passenger side seat back down for me to clamber in after her.

The light-grey plastic interior of the Clio seemed archaic in comparison to the spaceship of a car Aide had picked me up in the night before. But the smell of forest pine diffusing from the green leaf-shaped air freshener, along with the pillowy seats, soft from years of wear, made for a much cosier ride.

"My Mum says *Hi*," Kat said as she leant through the gap between the two front seats.

"How's she doing?" Xander asked, throwing her a sympathetic smile, which made me feel both sad and annoyed simultaneously, but I bit my lip.

"She's trying her best but I think the new meds she's on are kicking her ass," Kat replied and I pushed down the scoff that burned in my throat.

"That's really shit Kat. If you ever need a hand, any help with anything, you know I've got you. Don't even feel like you can't ask," He said smiling, nudging her arm affectionately through the gap she still leant through.

"So-" I needed to change the subject before my self-control slipped and I said something that would upset Kat. "You told Xander about Isha but you still haven't technically told me?"

"Oh stop, as if I needed to tell you. Besides, you've been busy yourself with Doctor Flames." The corners of her mouth turned upwards in a mocking grin. For such a sweet, innocent-looking girl, she sure doesn't miss a single thing.

I noticed Xander's hands tighten slightly on the steering wheel at the mention of Aide, and I couldn't help but feel good about the jealousy he so poorly attempted to suppress.

Of course, we were never going to go anywhere romantically, we would always be *just friends* and just friends only, but I couldn't help but feel good about the daydream of him wanting me more.

"Well, Xander had a date last night too, can you believe it?" I said as I slapped my hand down on his thigh through his denim jeans. *Pure, solid muscle.*

"No you did not!" Kat's head spun to Xander as her eyes looked him up and down.

"No I did not. I think the polite way of putting it was harassment." Xander's green eyes flicked to mine as he shifted a little lower in his seat. I realised my hand was still resting on his thigh, only now it had shifted a little further up the inside of his thigh.

"Well-" I pulled my hand back and pushed it between my legs as though to keep it under control. "I think she seemed lovely," I said with a touch of sarcasm and raised brows that both Xander and Kat understood meant the complete opposite.

"So lovely." Xander mimicked me as both turned to me in tandem, and burst out in a fit of laughter so filled with joy, that I couldn't stop myself from joining them.

After ten minutes of turns and dirverting, due to my complete lack of directional awareness following google maps, we finally turned onto Isha's road.

It was a beautiful cul-de-sac, full of houses that were at least three times the size of ours and probably tailor-made for the people that lived inside them.

It couldn't be further from our own home.

I pushed down the shame and embarrassment that began to rise in me. If only I could find a better-paid job, or I could get more hours I could give Kat a better life.

I had done my best over the years to make sure she never felt how I felt growing up - having nothing and no one. Thick skin and a wicked mouth were now part of me, that and a great right hook through years of other kids making comments about our situation.

But I would never let that happen to her. I had saved every penny I had, spent every paycheck on making sure she wouldn't feel that way and I would work myself into the ground if I could just keep her from ever feeling like I did.

My mother never bothered to try to comfort us in those years after Dad died. I quickly learnt how to manage a household, piecing together things I had seen my parents do. She mostly kept herself confined to her room, which she had locked us out of. And during the nights, she wandered the house like a ghost. But it was us that felt invisible.

We pulled up outside a house with a red Range Rover parked on an immaculately paved driveway. A raven-haired young woman stepped outside the front door.

Her perfectly straight hair, swept behind a pearl headband, showcased her soft facial features on a canvas of deeply bronzed skin.

"Well she's a total babe," I said, smirking behind to Kat whose face had lit up. My stomach fluttered at the sweet delight in her eyes.

Isha walked towards the car, looking a little shy like I had remembered her. I jumped out of my seat to allow her to get in. *I loved Xander but I hated his three-seater car right now.*

"Hi." A reserved, softly spoken voice came from Isha as she came closer.

"Hey Isha, Kat's in the back! Let me just-" I leant back in and pulled the seat back as Kat moved over to sit behind Xander. "There you go, hop in!"

We set back off and luckily Isha knew the way into the city centre from hers, saving me the hassle of having to read out the google maps and getting it wrong most of the time.

"Hey," I said, catching Xander's attention over the giggling girls currently chatting away in the back seat.

"Do you fancy doing something together and leaving these two to have some time to themselves?" I nodded to the girls and flashed him a smile.

"I don't think they'll miss us." Xander chuckled. "Sounds good L, I'm in."

We dropped Kat and Isha off in the centre right outside Piccadilly and told them we would pick them up at three - which gave them loads of time to wander about the city.

Although Kat seems and acts a lot older than her age, she is only fourteen and I wouldn't usually let her wander around the city without me or Xander.

Having convinced Xander to come book shopping with me, I was now five shelves deep in the latest cartoon-covered romance books, when I could tell something was on Xander's mind.

His weight rocked from one foot to the other and his mouth pressed together as he bit down on his jaw.

His large shoulders rolled back in his tight red t-shirt that displayed every inch of muscle-bound underneath it.

"What are you looking all broody for?" I threw a book towards him, which he instinctively caught.

"Just a few things on my mind." He flicked through the pages mindlessly.

"Care to share with the class?" I bunched my shoulders up mimicking Miss Letterman, our eighth-grade English teacher who had the posture of a croissant.

"Not particularly." He shrugged as his large hands flipped through the pages of the book I'd thrown at him.

It wasn't like Xander not to want to talk to me about something, in fact, it felt really weird that he wasn't saying exactly what had brought his mood down during the past hour.

"You know what you were saying to me and Kat earlier, about us being able to talk to you about anything?" I stood next to him, closing the space between us.

"The same goes for you." I snatched the open book from his hands looking down at the open page.

My face contorted into a wry smile as I looked at the top line.

'I want you face down ass up so I can eat you like my own
personal banquet'

"My goodness Xander Flynn what is this you are reading?" I mocked, as I flipped to another page.

My feet stepped closer to him and my eyes scanned the deliciously scandalous book that would feel right at home on my bookshelf.

"Well, at least let me know what you think of it once you've finished." I winked as I pushed the book into his chest, with a sly smile.

Xander looked down to the book, presumably at the top line of that particular page. *He is going to die of embarrassment.*

'My cock aches and I have to fight the urge to haul her onto my
lap.'

Instead of turning red, he jutted out his lower lip, raised his eyebrows and tilted his head, those green eyes now fixed on mine.

"Sounds pretty interesting to me."

The muscles in the tops of my thighs clenched.

"But I'll leave the dirty books to you, I have my own way of-" He paused and I didn't know whether or not I could handle the next thing that was about to come out of his perfectly shaped mouth. "Relieving myself."

My heart threw itself at my ribcage as I tried to exhale the breath I had been holding slowly, to not give away that the idea of him *relieving* himself had my mind picturing that exact thing.

I wondered what he might think about it.

"So what do you fancy doing now?" Xander asked, and part of me wanted to reply, '*I fancy doing exactly what that book you're holding describes with you.*'

Instead, I pulled my mind from the gutter and stepped back towards the bookshelf creating the distance between us that my body needed.

"We could grab something to eat?" He pulled his phone from his back pocket, and I watched as his muscles tensed with the twist.

My eyes dipped below his leather belt. He was wearing straight-cut jeans, low riding and fitted just tight enough around his front that you could see his manhood strain against the dark denim.

Xander and I waited in the car outside the same square where we dropped the girls off and a text from Kat had let me know they were on their way back, bubble tea in tow.

I ended up buying that book, along with a couple of other YA books that were definitely not for young adults.

It had felt weirdly tense between us since the bookshop, but we grabbed an iced latte each and a quick bite to eat before heading back into the city.

I discreetly watched Xander's lips purse around the straw of his iced latte, as he sucked up the golden liquid. I had never wanted to be straw, more.

My phone pinged, thankfully interrupting my torturous thoughts and as I turned it over in my hand to check the notification, I caught Xander looking at the screen too. A text from Aide. *It's about time.*

Aide: Hey you.

My stomach fluttered with the giddiness of a girl half my age, which I in no way was ashamed of as I tapped open the message.

"So, do you really like him then?" Xander spoke, his eyes focused entirely on the iced latte he was holding, with one hand mixing the liquid lazily.

Truthfully, I didn't know what to say, but I had accepted that Xander and I were never going to go anywhere romantically because he deserved so much better. And what was I supposed to do? I couldn't just put my life on hold. Besides, I did like him.

"Yeah, he's nice, he's actually really sweet." I shrugged and played it down a little.

"Mm, he seems a little arrogant to me," Xander replied shortly.

"Arrogant? Really?" I played into it.

"Yeah a little. Like he thinks he's just like some hot-shot doctor," Xander continued, his heels fully dug in.

"Well I mean, he kind of is a hot-shot doctor." I laughed and smiled as I searched those big green eyes for a hint of humour.

"Yeah, I just didn't think he was your type." His mouth pressed together in frustration.

Was he upset? He didn't seem like himself but he's been so hot and cold all day, it was not like him at all.

"You have seen all the guys I've dated in my life, what makes you think I have a type." I tried to lighten the mood again. And I had dated a lot of guys, I went through a phase of dating anyone who would take me out for a meal at one point and ordering extra so I'd have enough to take home for Kat.

"I just didn't see this coming I guess and I-" A knock on the window stopped Xander in his tracks.

Isha and Kat were standing outside, both now looking in through the windows of the Clio. Their two sweet faces smiling widely at us, each pair of hands that belonged to them, now carrying a bunch of pink shopping bags.

My eyes flicked back to Xander, whose eyebrows furrowed and his face held a flush of pink now staining his cheeks. I wanted to know what was wrong. *I wanted him to tell me.* But now wasn't the time.

As we set back off to drop Isha off home, the two of them seemed to be on cloud nine. Laughing and giggling, I even heard the shutter noise of pictures being taken on their phones.

"Ishas dad works at the same clinic your Mum works at Xan, did you know that?" Kat's soft voice cut through the remaining tension.

Xander shifted lower in his seat, immediately looking more at ease. Kat tended to have that effect on people.

"Oh trust me, I've heard. Apparently, all of the women calling up for 'urgent appointments'-" He began, throwing a glance over his shoulder, "turn out to be in perfect health."

The girls broke out in laughter in the back. Isha's laugh was the loudest, she had a deep, throaty laughter that was hilarious in itself and caused us all to laugh harder just listening to her.

"Ooo Doctor Ashah, I think it's time for my appointment." Kat mocked, making Isha double over.

Even Xander spit out the burst of laughter he failed to keep in, which made me fall further into my own fit of giggles. *These were the moments I lived for.*

"Well I'm surprised they don't all thirst over your fancy doctor, Elly," Kat said, her face still flushed pink from laughter.

"I bet he would as well." Xander jumped in, but that beautifully traitorous dimple showed the smile he was trying to hide.

"Pack it in you!" - I clipped his thigh with the back of my hand and he pretended to flinch as though it hurt. "Or else I might start thinking you're jealous." I smirked back, with a single eyebrow raised.

We pulled up outside the pristine driveway and I hopped out of the front to let Isha out.

"Thank you so much for the lift," she said, her beautiful dark brown eyes looking at me.

"You are so welcome, next time though, I want in on the bubble tea!" I said with a smile as I leaned into the back seat, where Kat passed over some of the bright pink shopping bags.

"I'll facetime you later Ishh," Kat said waving, with her head dipped through the open door of the car. Isha smiled in reply and nodded before she turned back towards her house.

Before she reached the immaculate white door, it opened to reveal a tall, older man, probably in his fifties with the same deep bronze skin and raven hair, only peppered with grey.

I gave a wave to Isha who had turned back, probably to wave to Kat, before sitting back in my side of the car.

The days were shorter now, it was barely four o'clock by the time we pulled onto our road, but it had already started to grow dark as the autumn sun lingered low in the sky.

Xander pulled up on the curb in front of our house, its brown door flaking with sun scorch and lacking any kind of upkeep.

"Are you coming to hang out for a bit Xander?" Kat asked and dread filled me instantly.

I hated people coming into the house. Me and Kat did our best to keep things tidy but there was no hiding the fact that the house needed more doing to it than we could ever afford on my wage alone.

Not that Xander would care, he's been around before and nothing phases him. He wasn't the type of person to look down on our situation or to make anyone feel embarrassed or ashamed. He accepted me for exactly what I was, and he took Kat on like the younger sister he's never had.

"Yeah of course, but only if you let me kick your ass at a game of Chess." Xander unbuckled his belt and pulled up the stiff handbrake with ease.

"Oh absolutely, you're on." Kat said as she pushed forward the seat I had just got out of, hopped out and skipped towards our house.

"I'll set up!" She called back, as she headed for the front door.

"She will win, you know, she always does." I pulled my bags from the footwell.

Xander closed the door and locked the Clio up. He walked from around the car and threw an arm over my shoulders, instantly making me feel tiny next to him.

"And I'll let her." He smiled down at me.

As we walked through the front door, I saw a heap of shopping bags discarded in the doorway, stationary and clothes spilt out of them.

"Lana!" The spine-chilling wail of Kat's voice cut through every fight or flight sense I owned, and I instinctively ran towards the cry.

CHAPTER ELEVEN

Daginas body lay limp on the living room floor, barely conscious in Kat's arms, whose body was shuddering with sobs, desperately trying to wake our mother up.

Not this, not now. Xander had seen Dagina drunk before, but I had played it down, every time blaming something different. The flu, arthritis medication, basically anything I could think that wasn't the truth, that my mother was an alcoholic that chose getting flat out wasted over the care of her own children.

"Dagina," Xander gasped. Rushing over, he gently slid an arm under her lower back and under her knees as he pulled her up with ease and set her on the sofa.

"Mum! Mum" Kat sobbed.

I felt like my world was about to come crashing down, anger, embarrassment and utter shame rearing up to choke me. Overwhelming my ability to form any words. I stood there watching as Xander and Kat tried to bring her back around.

The air in my lungs was suspended as my entire body froze. I daren't take in a breath as the only thing stopping me from falling apart right here right now, was my stillness.

My throat ached and my eyes stung as I felt emotion trying to bulldoze through the armoured wall I had spent years building.

The sound of their voices was now muffled, and their actions slowed as the panic rose in me.

I tried to repress the spiralling anxiety threatening to overcome me, forcing it down in an attempt to regain some kind of control. I felt for the ground beneath my feet, drawing in the smell of the air around me. I hadn't realised I had closed my eyes until I reopened them.

My mother's eyes were now open and focused on the glass of water she was now drinking, still lying on the sofa where Xander had put her.

"What happened?" Kat asked softly, leaning against the arm of the sofa, and looking down at our mother.

"I, I didn't realise the time, and it was time for-" Dagina took in a deep breath, and I could hear her chest rattle.

"It was time for my medication and I didn't want to bother you whilst you were out." She continued as Kat grabbed her hand, holding it tenderly.

"I thought if I could just make it to the cabinet, I could sit down at the kitchen table." Her voice cracked, and each word sounded painful. I had never heard her sound like that before.

"But, I just couldn't do it, I fell and I tried to get back up I-" Kat's eyes filled with tears now threatening to spill over.

"I'm so sorry mum. I should have known, I should have got them ready for you like usual." Kat replied and I looked across to the kitchen cabinet, piled full of crumpled white paper bags, pill packets spilling out of them across the sides and down onto the floor.

How had I not noticed all of those?

"My darling, I am not your responsibility." Dagina, seeming to have come around a little more, shifted up and Kat slid onto the sofa next to her, burying her head into her chest. Just below a transparent mask, dangling around Dagina's neck from a cord of elastic.

"I know but I've been so in my head with Isha." Kat shook her head as though she was chastising herself.

"I will hear none of it, you are living your life my darling, I am not your burden to bear." Dagina stroked

Kat's hair softly and looked up towards me, her amber eyes were the twin of mine.

My eyes dropped to the mask again and my gaze followed the fine hollow tubing it was attached to down to a small silver-green bottle, with a pressure dial atop it. *I felt so confused.*

My mind scrutinously wandered back, revisiting moments and replaying conversations I had had over the past few weeks, and my chest began to feel heavy.

Xander's voice was a whisper in my mind.

"My mum has seen her in and out of the clinic a lot recently." His green eyes were sympathetic. *"It's pretty serious Lana."*

I glanced over to the kitchen and the ghost of a memory formed as though I was in the room again. *I watch my mother's hands shake, the skin too thin to hide the blue veins as she plates up breakfast that I dismiss, pushing the plate away from myself.*

We are outside of the school, as I look around I see Katerina standing in front of me. "Some guy made a comment about mum. He was saying he overheard his parents talking about her and how her illness was karma. How she deserved to be sick."

I'm back at home, standing watching myself walk through the front door. I come in late, my mother is passed out on the sofa. But then I notice the silver-green tank. I walk closer through my memory, I see the corner of a pillow hanging off the side of the sofa. I see my mother's head, resting, a patchwork quilt over her. A clear mask over her nose and mouth.

As I opened my eyes, I looked at my mother still lying on the sofa with Kat, she was stroking her hair as she did mine when I was small.

Her face - *how had I not seen this?*

Her amber eyes were now sunken, set in deep dark pits on her pale, ashen face. The colourless skin hung gauntly from her cheekbones, hollowing her face and sharpening each feature.

Her eyes caught my own and my throat tightened.

How had I been so blind?

I had been so wrapped up in my own anger, in my own resentment, that I hadn't seen what was happening right before me.

My mother was dying.

It was like the carpet had been pulled from under me, as my eyes burned and welled over and I fell to my knees. I couldn't control my breath as it unsteadily broke from me in shuddering sobs.

I felt Xander behind me, he had knelt on the floor, to support my leaden body as I broke down, devoid of my armour, I allowed myself to see, to *really see* and to feel.

My tears were unconstrained rapids tearing through a newly demolished dam. Through the blur, I saw honey-golden hair.

The warmth of Kat's body pressed into my side, and the force of her arms wrapping around both myself and Xander, anchored my body, soothing my unmanageable emotions.

Xander's arms squeezed as I felt him look towards my mother before nestling his head in the nook of my neck.

"You're ok Lana," Xander breathed softly into my ear. "You're ok." He held me tighter.

I closed my eyes, clamping my lids down and pushing out the overflow of tears, as I breathed in deeply, *intentionally.*

I pulled at the shoulder of my shirt and used the purple satin to wipe my face. I shook my head, more to myself than for any other reason.

I felt so stupid.

Forcing my eyes to look up at her, Dagina was looking back, her hollowed eyes now softened as the tops of her cheeks crinkled around them in a small smile.

I shifted my weight onto my knees feeling like I was somewhat present again in my own body, both Kat and Xander loosened their embrace. Using my hands on the carpeted floors I braced my untrustworthy legs, a foot solid under each before I felt I could stand upright, still looking towards Dagina.

It felt as though time was going slow like someone had pressed pause on a moment in life so important that I must be truly present.

Kat's mouth parted, a small inhale passing her lips as I walked towards the sofa, passed the green tank, and perched on the edge of the worn leather seats.

This was the closest I had been to my mother since I was a child and I felt the prickle of tears in my eyes as I looked at her closely for the first time in years.

The patterned slip dress she was wearing was one I had recognised, though previously it was vibrant and kaleidoscopic, now grey and threadbare. Her arms were now thin enough that they looked as though they may break under little force.

A tarnished gold necklace hosting a dull ruby in its medallion, that same necklace she has worn for as long as I could remember, burdening the delicate neck it hung from.

"Mum I-" My words trembled out. I struggled to think what I could possibly say to her.

"My Lana, my big girl-" Her voice was a wisp, and she struggled to lift her arm as she cupped my face with her slight hand. I felt the coolness of fresh tear tracks before I realised I was crying again.

"I didn't know. I didn't know you were...sick. I am so stupid, so blind." I sobbed into her hand.

"You took care of things long enough Lana. I am not your responsibility, you are mine." She said, her arm failing to hold itself up now falling to her side. I should have felt angry, but this was what I have wanted her to say my entire life.

She left me, I was a child and she chose the bottom of a bottle over me. This was what I needed to hear.

I've picked her up, passed out on the kitchen floor more times than I could remember and cleaned the blood from her split lips and gashes that she would get from hitting the tiles head first after one too many.

Feeling the presence of my scar beneath my shirt, a memory that pained me most slid its way to the front of my mind like smoke through a crack.

"Hey Mum, what are you doing?" I walked into the kitchen.

"I'm cooking you, I'm cooking us, me, you, some food, see." She stumbled over her words while poking at something black-brown bubbling in hot oil.

"Do you want me to do that?" I held out a hand to take the spoon still slick with oil now waving around her head. She stubbed the cigarette out and picked up a short glass, almost empty save for a few dregs of amber liquid swirling in the bottom.

"Here mum, let me do that, I can help." I held my hand out again away from her body, conscious not to let the oil drip on her.

She started swaying to the song on the radio humming to herself mindlessly, her feet unsteady beneath her.

"Please mum...please just let me-" I pleaded.

"LET ME COOK THE FUCKING DINNER!" She spat, leaning down to me and swaying with the shift in weight, she dropped her glass. I shot back as the shards landed almost on top of my feet and she almost fell to the floor, knees inches from the glass before I quickly stepped forwards, sacrificing my own feet to stop her fall, the shards sinking into my heels.

I held back a scream as I tried to support her weight.

She grappled at the kitchen side, trying to regain her balance. Her arms slipped where the oil had dropped from the spoon onto the marble sides and she lost her footing again. I shifted my weight under her, so she could use me as a support, so she could get up.

She pushed a hand down onto my shoulder and the other elbow on the kitchen side.

She finally managed to get to her feet, and her weight released from my shoulder with a grunt, her elbow gave way on the slick side and she fell backwards, arms splayed out in front of her.

I reached to grab her arms, but as I stumbled backwards, my mother's hand, still holding the wooden spoon, knocked the smoking pan of hot oil off the cooker.

There was no time for me to get out of the way before the molten grease hit the side of me, soaking through my school shirt and searing the skin on my stomach beneath it.

I remember screaming in pain, and looking down at my mum for help but with her eyes filmy and unfocused she just dusted off her hands, closed her eyes and laughed. Still splayed out on the kitchen floor as my skin was melting, bobbing her foot to the sound of the radio. She hadn't even heard me scream.

But that wasn't the face that was looking back at me now. Her eyes, though clouded, were present. Her speckled hand rested over mine tenderly.

"I am sorry for everything I put you through Lana. And you, my sweet Katerina." Daginas head turned towards Kat, who was still sitting with Xander, before turning back towards me.

"You deserved a better mother than I could be at that time. When my mother passed away, I was heartbroken, my soul felt chipped. But losing your father only weeks later, well that was the blow my existence could not withstand." Her amber eyes glossed over with tears, her sparse brows pinched together above them. "I should have tried harder, I should have done better. But as each day passed that I didn't leave that bed, our bed, the harder it became to face the thought of a life without him."

Kat came up beside me, carefully scooching into the little space left between us. Tear tracks fell down her unblemished skin. She placed her hand over mine and our mother's.

"My girls, my beautiful girls. You look so similar to your father. Lana, you have my eyes but my dear Katerina, looking into yours I see a part of your father looking back. For you Lana it is the way you walk, it is identical to his, that and this-" She said tapping the tip of my nose softly. I let the tears fall.

"When I looked at you both, I saw him and my heart broke a million times over. I felt I had nothing left of me to give. And Lana, when you started picking up the pieces, I fell further down that hole, drowning in my own despair." Her voice was breathless as she hung her head shaking it side to side. Kat lifted her chin with a soft hand and pulled the clear mask over our mum's mouth. She drew in a deep, rattling breath.

I didn't know what to say, I didn't know if there was anything to be said, so I let the tears roll as I grabbed Kat and my mother in my arms and released a sob that turned into weeping, crumbling the last sediment of resentment I had barricaded around my mother.

I felt her hand on my head as she weakly stroked my hair, and I nestled in further, breathing in her familiar scent, the softness of her strokes calming me like I was four again.

I heard the clink of ceramic and looked upwards to see Xander placing three mugs gently down on the mahogany coffee table. Each cup was brimmed with steaming amber liquid, a labelled thread hanging out over the sides.

"I thought you ladies could do with a drink." Xander smiled.

Shifting in my seat I looked up to Xander, his sweet forest lingering eyes on mine. *I was looking at the kindest man I would ever know.*

He stood, tall but not intimidating, his aura settling and accepting. He has seen the worst of it, he has seen the worst of me, and he didn't baulk, he didn't run. *He made me a cup of tea.*

His smiling eyes flicked over to my mothers, who was looking up towards him, her lids heavy from exhaustion.

"Is there anything I can do for you guys before I get off?" Xander never needed a cue, he always understood what went unsaid, and the look on my mother's drained face told him it was time for her to retire.

I stood, shifting gently from Kat who had drifted off, her head still resting lovingly on my mother's chest, with a frail hand adoringly trailing through her honey-gold locks.

"I think we'll be ok. Thanks, Xan, for everything." My eyes fell to the floor.

Xander hadn't ever done anything to make me feel self-conscious, but I had never let anyone see me like that before, and part of me was ashamed.

I noticed Xander had already picked up the brightly coloured shopping bags that Kat had dropped to the floor. He had placed the clothes and colourful stationary back neatly inside and placed them on the kitchen's white countertops.

"Anytime L, I'll keep telling you, there is nothing you need to hide from me, you are my...you are my best friend and I'll be here for you, through anything." He lifted a hand to my face and I wanted to lean into it, tilting my chin upwards to meet his eyes. "Through everything." His mouth pressed tightly into a smile.

I blinked away the damp prickling my eyes. I wanted to kiss him, I wanted to show him how much he meant to me.

He had no idea how he had saved me over the years, every time I was on the ledge, he had walked me back down. Scaffolded each breakdown, keeping me held together.

I inched closer, our bodies close enough that I could smell the subtle tones of fresh pine and black pepper cologne he always wore.

His hand still held my chin and the skin underneath felt on fire.

My mouth parted and I closed the space between us. My lips were sensitive with longing, as I pressed them against Xander's cheek. His newly surfaced stubble grazed against my skin, making my nerves feel exposed, the contact sending a wave of titillation across my whole body.

He wrapped his large toned arms over me, pulling me in closer. My head fell into his chest and I couldn't help but take in a deep breath of his scent. His arms gave a tight squeeze, his head bowed down to kiss the top of my head and warmth filled me like a cosy blanket on a stormy day.

Xander softly released me from his embrace all too soon, I felt like I could have stayed there, safe in his arms forever. On quiet feet, he walked closer towards the front door while I followed behind. He opened it slowly, a creak sounding out every inch. Our heads darted towards the sofa where both Dagina and Katerina were now sound asleep. We both chuckled silently.

"I'll see you tomorrow Xan, thanks again...for it all." I patted him on the chest as he hovered in the doorway.

"See you tomorrow L."

I closed the door softly behind me, turning the key twice in its stiff lock trying not to wake the two sleeping soundly behind me.

"He's a good man, isn't he?" A voice whispered from the living room.

"He's the best," I replied as I leaned my back against the door, my body still longing for the man who previously stood in its place.

I walked towards my mother, whose eyelids looked heavy, her breath audibly struggling to fill her lungs.

"Shall I take her up to bed?" I looked towards Kat who looked like a princess from a Disney film, her golden hair swept perfectly behind her angelic face.

"Do you love him, Lana?" Dagina asked softly, her voice rattled and the hollows of her eyes tightened. *She looked concerned.*

"We're just friends, of course, I love him, but not 'love him' love him." *I wasn't ready to admit how I felt, not to my mother and not to myself.*

CHAPTER TWELVE

The acrid smell of burning wood, mixed spice, and ash stung my nose. Pressing my hands into the earth beneath me, I could feel, grass. I was lying in a field, surrounded by greenery and tall thin cypress trees. Pushing my hands into the soft ground beneath me, I sat up.

Glancing around, I could see nothing but fields, a chess board of green and yellow crop fields. The sun was beaming down and there wasn't a single cloud in the sky. The smell of fire now fading and mixing with the fresh earthy tones around me. I began looking around, trying to gain my bearings, when I heard a female sobbing something indistinctly. The solemn sound coming from behind a tree closest to me.

On quiet feet, I followed the sounds of the weeping, turning around a tall tree, a woman was on the ground, curled over her knees and dressed in a deep purple tunic. Her head of brown curls pinned up, hanging in her hands, her fuller body trembling with each whimpering breath.

Hearing a noise from afar, I began tracking the distance with my eyes, following the sound of...*laughter?*

Gazing over the luscious fields and crops, through the cypress trees, I found another young woman.

Her blonde wavy hair tumbling down to her slim waist. The stunning woman was wearing an ocean blue dress that flowed from her waist like a waterfall and was tightly knotted around her chest.

Two large tanned arms caressed her, one wrapped around her waist and the other underneath the skirt of her dress, raising her leg up and outwards allowing him closer, shifting between her legs.

The man's tanned skin was on full display, his tunic now falling to the floor with each push of his hips. His head of dark hair burrowed in her neck, before moving downwards towards her chest, devouring every inch of her.

My heart was pounding like a prisoner in its cage, the feeling of anger sweeping over my senses. Looking away, my focus turned back to the woman on the ground sobbing. She was staring directly at me.

Her gold-flecked brown eyes searched mine before trailing across the curves of my body. Her arm, layered with thin metal hoops, moved the stray curls that fell around her face.

I tried to draw air as I scanned the familiar lines of her face. Recognising the dusting of freckles across her face, my gut was struck by the impossibility of it all. My body slackened. Falling to my knees in front of her, my eyes the twin of hers.

My breath was cold air trapped in my lungs as her hand began reaching for my face. My own hand involuntarily reached up towards hers, mirroring her movements exactly.

There was no controlling the movement, each gesture puppeteered by the woman I was looking at, the woman that had our dad's nose, the face that was identical to mine.

Her amber eyes turned black and the taste of metal forced its way through my mouth as a dark smile twisted the face in front of me .

Around us darkness began sweeping in, ash in the wind, blackened my skin. The sound of laughter faded and the woman disappeared back into the darkness. The expansive mist engulfing her face, now whipped against my prickled skin.

Tendrils of ink swirled around my vision, and through the mist I heard a scream, as the shadows began forming the image of hand, bloodied and sweeping across a luminous set of inscriptions along its dark stone face.

A scream rang through the mist, echoing around me as I clawed at the phantom air. The shadows began contorting against themselves, dissolving the image and forming a new one.

Whipping my skin sore, the mist curled in towards itself, growing darker. A tall, thick, inky silhouette formed at its centre shrouded in licks of blue flames dancing along the outline of the veiled being.

Clamping my eyes shut, I began repeating a mantra to myself, that this wasn't real. *This wasn't real.*

The air was pressing against me as the presence grew closer, the crackling sound of flames setting every nerve ending ablaze.

A dark sensual voice, slick with confidence began echoing through the haze as though he was standing right in front of me.

I've been waiting for you.

The air was alive and dripping with electricity.

You made a deal. A smooth, sultry voice reverberated around me.

My breathing became ragged, my fear furiously spilling over - I was losing control. I forced my eyes open to find a dark face inches from my own, silver ignited eyes, staring manically into mine.

Tearing its way from my lungs, a scream ripped itself from inside me as the glowing eyes were violently pulled backwards. Something was dragging it back towards the centre of the mist. My scream ruptured the dark haze that closed in around me as small cracks of golden light splintered through.

My heart was thundering in my chest and with my eyes closed, I released a scream so loud that I felt it fracture the very air around me.

A blinding light flooded through the darkness, coursing its way towards my eyelids and causing me to press my eyes protectively tighter against it.

The air was lighter, as the light dimmed to a soft warm glow. I opened my eyes slowly, and through blurred vision, I looked towards my bedside table. The yellow light from my bedside lamp still illuminating the ceramic mug of tea that I had brought up to bed with me.

I sighed and reached up to switch the light off. My fingers fumbled underneath the beige lampshade, searching for the switch, but I still felt half asleep and my eyes were a little blurred.

I dipped my head underneath so I could see, and looked for the switch. I gasped and breath caught in my horrified throat as I looked at a hand, wrapped in whispering shadows, turning off the light.

Ω

I must have somehow fallen back to sleep, because the next time I opened my eyes was to shut my damn phone up from ringing the whole house awake.

It was October half term for Kat, so she didn't need to be up for anything and I knew my mum would probably still be asleep like most days, when I thought she was just...when I was wrong about her.

I rubbed away the sleep from my eyes and tossed the covers away from me. My hands shot to my mouth covering my scream. My entire body, from my legs, up towards my chest and all along my arms were covered in thick black ash. I clambered out of bed and noticed the soot had already stained my entire bed.

Horrified, I kicked my legs and wiped at my arms, pawing at every part of my skin, but it wouldn't shift. I stumbled over a pile of clothes at the foot of my bed and fell to the floor, my bare ass hitting the ground with a loud thud. *Fuck.*

My door swung open and Kat stood in the doorway. Her hair bunched on top of her head, except for the few strands that finished off the effortless grace she always emitted, as her palm rubbed at her eye.

She looked down half-awake towards the pile of clothing I was now butt naked on top of, with a pair of bright green underwear that had somehow wrapped itself around my foot. *The culprit.*

"What are you doing?" Kat laughed as she padded towards me, and offered me a hand.

I looked down to my skin, *nothing.* It was totally bare, its usual shade of olive, unblemished by the soot I had just felt a second before.

"I tripped." I lifted my foot, still wrapped in the neon underwear. I wasn't exactly going to tell her I woke up with scary mystic ash all over me, from some crazy dream I had of a tall dark demon man with terrifyingly beautiful silver eyes.

"Is mum up? Did I wake her?" It still felt strange the change in how I felt towards a woman I had resented for most of my adult life, but I couldn't bear wasting another minute feeling that way, not for me, not for Kat, and not for the woman whose sand had almost fallen entirely through the hourglass.

"She's not up, the meds she's on for pain relief usually have her out until eleven-am." She said, hoisting me to my feet.

"Is there anything I can do? Before I go to work?"

"I've got this, don't worry Elly, I've been taking care of her meds for a while, just last night-" Guilt shaded her eyes.

"You have been amazing, and you're not doing it alone. I'm right here." Because Katerina had been doing it alone, all these years I thought I was the one holding us up, the strong one, but the truth was that she had always been the more capable one. The one who carried a weight I couldn't bear.

"Are your boobs planning on helping too or are they just out for show?" She scoffed, lightening the mood. *I was still stark naked.* Quickly, I placed an arm over my boobs, crossed my legs, and leant down awkwardly to pick up the lilac top I had thrown off yesterday. I tossed the top at her as she shielded herself with her arms and giggled.

"I'm getting back in bed! I'll see you after work?" I nodded and she turned back towards the hallway, closing the door behind her.

I looked down at my skin again, inspecting it as I turned my palms up, and back down. *What the hell was going on.*

I didn't have time for Joey's snarky comments today so when I turned up on time, his face was just as shocked as mine. Even Xander couldn't help but steal a sneaky glance at his watch when he saw me saunter through the front door with a smile that told everyone just how proud I was of myself.

No customers were in as we weren't opening for another ten minutes, so it would give me time to talk to Xander. I needed to talk to someone about what was going on, someone I'd trust not to send me to a psychiatric ward.

These weird dreams I kept having, they all connected in one way or another and from my little understanding of dreams, they are supposed to be random, meaningless moments jigsawed together from past memories yet these definitely didn't feel meaningless. I was seeing myself, *experiencing myself.*

"Lana Defixio-Jones, I didn't know you'd ever seen the light of day at this time." Xander smirked as he emptied small plastic bags full of coins into the empty till trays.

"I'd love to say it was because I had a great night's sleep, but I didn't." I smiled back and pulled my apron from under the counter, wrapping it twice, tightly around my waist.

"Why? What happened? Is your mum okay?" Xander stopped filling the till and turned to look at me, leaning against the counter front.

"Yeah she's fine, well, as fine as you can be." *For someone who was dying.* "I just keep having these weird dreams." I knotted the apron in a bow at the front and dusted off the front with my hands. "Like, super vivid scary shit." My hand cramped and I looked up towards him. He pushed off the counter with his brows pinched. The corners of his mouth curled as a small, *god damn sexy*, smile made its way across his face.

"Sounds like you could do with a sleeping buddy." That dimple at the side of his mouth deepened and my entire body flooded with heat. My mouth parted, I wanted to say *hell yeah I do*. But the front door swung open, the chime disrupting the tension as Xander turned away and I looked over his shoulder.

A tall muscular body walked in, wearing a perfectly fitted white shirt with the top few buttons open, deliciously exposing his toned chest. Black trousers hugged his hips and fell perfectly ironed down to fresh white sneakers that looked as expensive as a month's wage for me.

His powerful presence filled the room, confident and charming. He lifted a large tanned hand to his handsome face, removing the same square Ray Ban sunglasses I'd seen him in before.

"There you are." His grey eyes looked right at me, almost as though Xander didn't even exist and I was the only other person on earth here with him. "Is everything ok Lana?"

So much was going through my mind and the heat caused by Xander still felt rosy on my skin. Aide radiated sensuality, he was every woman's wet dream completely embodied.

With those intense eyes still focused on me, he trailed the length of me and my body reacted to his gaze as though it recognised him. Each glance caused a wave of heat in its direction. When I finally realised he had asked a question, my answer came out more of a stutter than an actual sentence.

"Oh, morning. Fine yep, fine, are you- how are you?" I managed to say and he smiled, like an animal that liked to play with his food.

That's how I felt around him, completely caught. A willing prey ready to be devoured.

"I'm fine. Morning Xander." His voice deepened as his eyes flicked over to Xander for a second.

"Aide." Xander nodded.

He stalked closer towards the counter, his attention back on me.

"I didn't hear from you." *Oh shit, I never texted him back.*

"Sorry, we were out-" I looked to Xander who avoided my eyes. "And when I got back home. Well...the day just escaped me."

"That's okay." His eyes narrowed with a smile. "Could I grab a coffee?"

"Oh, yeah. Sure, what can I get you?" I asked, feeling a little deflated. I thought he had maybe come in here to see me. Xander hovered around the till, trying his best to look busy and uninterested.

"I'll have a latte please." Aide pulled his leather wallet from his back pocket and his shirt strained against his hard chest.

"No problem." I picked up the portafilter and pressed the double dose button on the coffee machine, which began to loudly grind the beans. The three of us stood there awkwardly as the machine whorled.

I steamed the milk, with my back turned towards both men who were pointedly not saying a single word to each other.

"Do you want it to go or are you staying in?" I asked, glancing over my shoulder. Xander stood ramrod straight, looking up to Aide who stood inches taller across the counter.

"To go, thanks." Aide replied shortly, pulling out a crisp five pound note from the wallet in his hand.

The espresso drained from the machine into a white takeout cup, the grumpy coffee printed on its outside. I cleaned down the steam wand and poured the hot milk into the cup. Swirling the milk twice around the dark liquid, before trying my best to attempt some form of latte art on the top that didn't look like a penis. *I failed - It unarguably looked like a dick with balls, one larger than the other.*

I added the plastic lid, concealing my erotic master peice and popped it on the counter.

"There you are. That will be two-seventy-five please." My mouth twitched upwards. This felt like it should be awkward, but my body was like butter in his presence.

His hand placed the note in mine and the back of his fingers lightly brushed my palm. The contact was electric, a shock passing through us both and if Aide felt it, he didn't show. Instead, he just smiled and picked up his coffee.

"Apparently, you can't taste the coffee, if you can't smell it," he said, removing the lid.

"I'm not sure that's a bad thing. You might want to keep the lid on," I replied and his brows raised. He looked down to take a sip, those perfect lips pursed. I kept my face poker straight as one corner of his mouth turned upwards and his head tilted to admire the dick and balls he was going to sip from.

He looked back towards me, a smile now fully plastered on his stunning face.

"Tastes great," he replied, dragging his lower lip between his teeth to lick off the milky foam. And as I watched his mouth work, I thought to myself, *I bet it fucking does.*

Xander still stood next to me, the back of his hand close enough to mine that I could feel the warmth of it. Aide didn't seem phased in the slightest as he leant over the counter closer to me.

"So, how about that date?" He asked, catching me off guard.

A part of me felt bad that Xander was standing so close, able to hear what was being said. Because if I was honest with myself, I knew he wouldn't like this, but we both had to put up with each other being with different people because neither of us would take the friendship-shattering leap off the cliff of faith.

"I'd like that." I played it cool.

"There's a place in town, Barracuda - it does great sushi and has a bar on the other side if you fancy? We could eat and then stay out for a couple of drinks after?" He'd thought this through and that made me feel giddy.

"Sounds like the perfect *plaice.* Sorry, I couldn't help myself." *A fish pun? Really lana?*

His low laugh rumbled through me, sending a warm shiver across against my skin.

"Is Saturday good for you?"

Saturday was actually perfect for me, I don't work Sundays which meant I could actually have a drink and, *oh shit...*Saturday was my birthday.

"Saturdays great." I said, pressing my lips into a smile as I looked up at Aide who raked a hand through his blonde hair, sweeping it back away from his face.

"Perfect, I'll see you then." He flicked open his sunglasses, placing them back on the bridge of his nose. "Xander." He nodded politely, turned on his heels and walked out through the front door and my limbs released the tension it was holding.

J L Robinson

CHAPTER THIRTEEN

Xander had been quiet again all day, barely speaking a word to me since this morning. We had the regular morning rush and since I was the quicker one on the coffee machine I kept myself busy. We closed late afternoons on a Monday and sometimes stayed an hour later to do a deep clean too, but right now I wasn't thinking about staying any later then I had too.

My Mini was finally ready to pick up and I had made plans to go to the local supermarket and pick up some things for dinner. I still remember my mum's favourite, because dad always used to make it; Pastitsio. Growing up we used to call it the 'Topsy Turvy Lasagne', because it's basically the same thing, and everyones heard of lasagna.

My mother had been on my mind all day, the concern felt weirdly nice. A loving feeling, a stowaway, never in sight but always present. Before this, I'd like to have thought I had pretty good control over my emotions, but shutting down and closing off now seems to suggest quite the opposite. The years I had wasted being viciously angry at her, mournfully squandered.

She never pushed me, she weathered every single one of my storms, as I did hers and she wasn't perfect. She was actually the complete opposite at some points, but she *was* a person.

"Everything okay?" I looked up through blurred eyes, away from the coffee machine I was just cleaning out. A tear welled over the rim of my lower lashes, cooling a single trail down my cheek and I brushed it away with my shoulder. I hadn't realised I was crying.

"Is everything okay with me? How about is everything okay with you?" I shot back as I sniffled up the snot that threatened to fall from my nose. "You have been hot and cold with me the past few days and honestly, I just need my friend right now." I released a sob, dropped the portafilter, and turned towards Xander.

Xanders shoulders dropped, as though he had been holding them tense and his hands slackened from the rigid grip he had been holding them in all day.

The front of my brows, raised and pinched as I looked up towards my best friend, the one person I could trust more than anyone, the one who should trust me too.

"What's going on Xander?" His mouth pinched as he schooled his face into neutrality.

"Nothing Lana, I'm sorry." He hung his head, his dark curls falling beautifully over his full brow. "You've got so much going on right now, I'm fine. I'm completely fine." His warm hand wiped away another tear that fell from my eyes.

"You promise?" I looked up, feeling small under his gaze.

"I promise L." He wrapped his large arms around me and pulled me into his chest. The warmth of him felt like home. He idly stroked my hair as I breathed in his beautiful pine and black pepper fragrance. One arm after the other, I wrapped my arms around his waist, tugging him closer.

I could have stayed safe in his arms forever, a shatterproof shield against everything threatening to pull me apart. But, I had a coffee machine to clean and a cafe to close up.

He loosened his arms around me and I lifted my head up, facing his. With my arms still wrapped slack around his waist, I felt his breath hot on my skin, and if freckles could dance they'd be performing a whole ensemble right now.

"I should probably-" He started, gesturing a hand over his shoulder, thumb pointing towards the till.

"Yep, I should finish this too," I replied, now looking behind my own shoulder I let my arms fall back to my sides.

I returned to cleaning the coffee machine, the grounds were like dust and got everywhere and in everything.

"You fancy coming round for tea tonight?" I polished the tamper I held in my hand.

"I'd love to." A soft smile pulled at his lips.

"Great because we're making Pastitsio and by we're, I mean you, because I actually have no idea how to cook it."

He chuckled.

"I guess I'd better get googling then," he said as he pulled his phone from his pocket and typed. "Ah, so it's a lasagne?"

"It is, but don't go telling my mum that." I laughed back.

I checked my phone, it was four o'clock. I had plenty of time to pick up the car before the garage closed at five and then I could nip to the shops and pick up the things for dinner.

"I'll see you at six?" I asked as Xander closed the shutter over the front door.

"Sounds good to me." He nodded with a smile I reciprioted before heading in the direction of the garage.

It wasn't far from here, less than a ten minute walk through the small square of small businesses and restaurants we liked to call our town centre. We're not far from the city and we're still classified as London, but Beckenham is a far smaller town, with more of a village feel for it.

I've always lived here, it's all I've ever known, but my mum is from the city and my dad was from the north. They both worked at the same restaurant, Meraki, whilst still studying and that's where they met. Mum was studying art, *obviously* and my dad was studying history. I remember he had always said that he wanted to be a curator at The British Museum and before he fell ill, he was working his way up as an archive assistant. They moved up here when mum fell pregnant with me, I'm guessing because it's almost impossible to afford living in central London on an unknown artists and assistants wage and a newborn on the way.

The afternoon air was fresh, the earthy smell of fallen leaves and autumn showers lingered.

As I strolled along the street I passed the quaint shop window fronts, each displaying hoards of handmade items and tokens you'd buy as gifts when you have absolutely no idea what to get someone.

I passed one shop front full of hand-crafted ceramics, beautifully imperfect, vases, crockery and ornaments. You could tell the flaws were intentional, each warped piece held its own beautiful identity.

Another store, filled with all kinds of handmade jewellery. Layer upon layer of silver and gold necklaces, earrings and rings. A candy store of coloured crystals set beautifully within them. My eyes zeroed in on a plain silver cuff bracelet, the metal oxidised and darkened - in its centre, a small iridescent opal stone, fractured hues of turquoise and marine blue sparkled in the low autumn sun. It was absolutely stunning.

I'd never been the type to wear much jewellery, mainly because it's not something I chose to spend the little money I earnt on. But it was my twenty-first birthday coming up, and I had the perfect top that this would go with. Besides, I never treat myself much beyond a new book every now and then, so I'd consider it a birthday gift from me to me.

The store was closed, as were most shops in town after four so I'd have to come back another day - I'd be a little gutted if it sold before then.

It took me less than ten minutes to actually arrive at the garage and I saw my sorry looking car parked up outside the unit's half-closed shutter. I dipped my head under it and spotted a man that looked as though he could be Joey's twin. His gut tested the zip's strength on his overalls and his shiny head was holding on to a thread of hair, swept to the side as though it might help grow more back atop his barren scalp.

"Hi, I'm here to pick up the Mini. How much do I owe you?" I swung my backpack around to my front, unzipping the smallest compartment on the front where I kept my purse.

"One-fifty for the labour and four-hundred for the parts sweetheart." My breath hitched. *That's two weeks worth of wages.* I schooled my face into a tight smile and pulled my debit card from my purse.

"Do you take cards?" I asked politely, when I really wanted to say 'the fucking car isnt even worth five-fifty itself, *sweetheart.*' I guess that bracelets off the cards too.

When I arrived home after nipping into the local supermarket, Xander was already there. A dish towel thrown over his thick shoulders, wearing a tight black t-shirt and a casual pair of grey shorts. *God help me.*

Mum and Kat were sitting at the table, digging through a worn box full to the brim with old photos. Snapshots of our life, before our dad passed away and before things turned sour.

I felt my gut somersault, I'm not sure I was ready to replay my childhood just yet and I hadn't looked at any of these since I was much younger, the sight was just too painful.

"Hey, you're eager aren't you?" I placed the shopping bags on the kitchen side and began pulling out the ingredients Xander had sent.

"I thought I'd get a headstart on the lasagne." A smirk curled his lips as he looked over his shoulder towards my mum who was audibly unimpressed but laughed before rolling her eyes back at him. Kat laughed at their exchange. My gut settled like a storm that had passed.

"Well, if you've got this-" I finished emptying the shopping bags onto the kitchen counters, "then I guess I'll leave you to it." I flashed a grin, lowering my lashes through slightly squinted eyes.

I turned to the kitchen table, only a few feet away from where Xander had now glugged a load of olive oil into a warming pan and pulled out a chair to sit with Kat and my mum.

She looked a little better than yesterday, a slight touch of colour dappled her hollow face. The muscles in her cheeks twitched as she strained a sweet smile towards me.

"We were just looking through old photos, look-" Kat flicked through a few of the pictures, some stuck together through years of disregard. She passed over a picture of a young girl, unruly brown hair that curled in every direction and large light brown eyes, sitting on the shoulders of a large man wearing a denim shirt and matching denim jeans. His sky blue eyes were identical to Kats, and that nose, the twin of mine.

I must have been six, I remember being so happy when I was on my fathers shoulders. To me, he was a giant, so I felt on top of the world when I was on his shoulders, my little feet tapping on his chest as we walked the world together. Tears pricked the back of my eyes and I pressed together a smile as Kat handed me another photo.

"Look Elly, my very first selfie." She passed over another photo, one of my mother, her dark hair thick with tight chocolate curls, she wore a long floating tie dye dress, her gold necklace with the red stone casted a sun strand across the lense and one hand, covered in rings, held her lower stomach. The other hand held the camera, and three faces beamed towards it, huge smiles plastered across each face, including my own little one. I choked back a breath, it was beautiful. Our perfect family. I had forgotten how happy I was as a child. The years of anger casted a sour shadow over my memories, and I was now working hard to clear it.

"We should frame these." I smiled as I handed the photos back over to Kat and she replaced them with some more.

I looked down to see a picture of my mother, she could have only been my age, and she was dressed in a dungarees completely covered in paint. Beside her was another woman, smaller in stature, wearing a matching painted dungarees. Her face was spotted with age and framed with grey curled hair, a beautiful smile reached her eyes. I recognised my grandmother, even though she was far younger than I'd ever seen her.

I didn't realise we had any photos of her, my mum had fallen out with her own mother when she was younger. We never knew why. But this photo looked like it was taken whilst my mum was still at university, probably around the time she met my dad.

It shocked me, seeing how much I resembled my mum. Seeing her, a young woman, with the light still in her eyes and joy spread across her face, solidified my shame. She was a person, just like me. She had her own life, her own loss and her own trauma and I had punished her for it. My chest tightened and I forced a deep breath in to steady myself. Seven seconds in, seven seconds out.

"You look just like my mother." Dagina spoke softly, her voice retired. She leaned across and pointed a long thin finger, tapping on the photo. "We both have

Cora's untameable hair, although-" She coughed into a handkerchief, "it seems mine isn't as much of a bother nowadays." She smiled as she curled a thinning grey strand around her finger.

"What happened with you and grandma mum?" Kat asked a question we had both never wanted to ask. When my grandmother passed away weeks before my dad, my mother was heartbroken. We had never had a relationship with her, save a few birthday cards and batches of baklava sent for our birthdays. Our grandfather had passed long before we were born, so my mother was left with no one but us.

Dagina coughed into her handkerchief once more and my body recoiled as red droplets stained the fabric. She smiled sweetly at Kat, lowering her head and pressing her lips together.

"She kept a secret from me." She began, her tone solemn. "She told me something that crushed me and I was expected to go on as though she hadn't said a thing." She nodded to herself, but did not lift her gaze from the table.

I didn't want to press the subject but what kind of secret does a mother keep from her own daughter bad enough that it broke them apart?

"Do you miss her?" I asked.

"Every single day." My mother looked up from the table, the flecks of orange now glistened her eyes with the tear that fell from it.

I felt the unspoken regret as I looked at my mother, and then I was certain of one thing. I did not want to repeat the same mistake she had. I wasn't sure how long my mother had, but I wouldn't let her die without knowing I loved her. I looked down at the table, back towards where the photo of my mother who grinned proudly, pregnant with Kat as I sat atop my dad's shoulders. Our faces radiated pure happiness, and though her face was now drained of colour, her cheeks sunken and her hair thinning, that same smile now looked back at me.

The smell of garlic and oregano filled the kitchen as Xander started on the meat filling which fragrantly sizzled away on the stove.

"I'd better go help him," I said as I jutted my chin towards Xander, who now swayed his hips to country songs that played in the background from our old radio. "Before he makes a mess of it." Not that he would, Xander was a far better cook than me, but I struggled to look at any more photos without feeling my throat constrict. I would have to pace myself and do this bit by bit.

Xander jumped as I clasped my hands around his swinging waist and peered my head under and around his large arms.

"Howdy partner, how's the food coming on?" He glanced down towards me with those large green eyes that lit up my body and I shuddered with the closeness.

He clamped his arm down on me holding me close and tight, my face at his waist, inches from his hips and I breathed him in. Through the savoury scents of the food cooking, I could still smell him, fresh pine.

"You want a taste?" He smirked.

He released the arm that was holding me in place, but I didn't move. I stayed low.

"I'd love a taste." I looked up through my lowered lashes at him. His mouth parted, his lower lip pulled underneath his teeth, making my entire body writhe within itself.

Kat coughed from behind me, and I turned to see her smiling, a grin spreading across her face.

"Well come on then, let me try some." Standing up straight I nudged him with an elbow.

Xander tossed the dish towel that was in his hand, back over his shoulder and grabbed a wooden spoon from a grey utensil pot within arms reach. He stirred the ragu and scooped some of the meaty sauce onto the spoon.

He held the spoon up to my face, and I parted my lips eagerly.

"Ah ah ah," He tutted as he pulled away the spoon an inch further away from my open mouth. "Blow first."

Every inch of me burned, and my muscles tightened as I pursed my lips, looked up towards him, blew out a soft breath and then wrapped my mouth around the spoon. I cleaned the spoon entirely, never leaving his gaze and I could have sworn I felt him pull it closer towards him as my mouth pulled away.

I swallowed, the sauce was mouth watering, the tomato sharp but sweet mixed together with the meat and herbs - it was perfect. Using the back of my hand I wiped my lips.

"Delicious."

His eyes widened before he pressed his mouth tight and turned back towards the stove, his cheeks rosy. I bit down a smile, he was my best friend, but there was something so sexy about seeing him squirm.

"So do you need a hand?" I said with a smile, the image of innocence and he choked. I was pushing it now and I could tell his mind was exactly where I was directing it. If he knew it was intentional he didn't let on.

"It's all good, I've got this." He smiled. His gorgeous cheeks still flushed as he continued to stir the sauce.

I cleared the table and Kat helped me set up the placemats and crockery. I can't remember the last time we sat at this table together to eat a meal. It felt like walking back in time, like I was eleven again and my dad was about to walk through that door after a long day commuting from the city.

I placed a plate on each mat, and a trivet in the centre of the table as Xander placed the piping hot Pastitsio on top of it. The smell of molten cheese upon layers of beef and tomato smothered pasta drifted up from it, and I was immediately starving.

My mother, who was still sitting supported by her chair, was taking a few deep inhales from her clear mask, the silver and green tank now rolled up to her side.

"Xander, this smells, well it smells amazing." She said gently, the words breathy.

"Well, I couldn't have done it without this." Xander smiled over his shoulder at my mother as he waved a scrap of paper in his hand.

"What is that?" I asked.

"Your dad's recipe. Kat found it out for me when I came round earlier." He said as he placed another bowl on the table, this one full of fresh tomatoes, red onion and feta cheese.

My gut tugged as though my stomach recognised it, the smell.

"Shoulder rides are only for big strong girls, girls who eat all of their dinner." He poked me and I giggled, shovelling every last mouthful into my face.

"See I finished, look dad." Eyes bright I showed my dad the empty plate.

"That's my Elly." His blue eyes sparkled as he planted a kiss on my head.

"What a man!" Kat said as she side eyed me, a small grin tugged the corners of her mouth. "Can we dig in Xan?"

"You better!" Xan laughed, "Anyone need a drink?" He asked, Kat already shovelling out a hefty portion onto mum's plate, then her own, before piling a slab on both mine and Xanders plates.

"I'll have water please? Mum, do you need anything?" I asked.

"I'll have water too please Xander darling." A rattle audible on each word.

"Make that three," Kat said mid mouthful.

The rich tomato and cheese Pastitsio paired with the freshness of the salad was perfect, I could have eaten it three times over. With a full belly and a warm heart, surrounded by the people I love the most, I felt perfectly content.

My mum was smiling and for a brief moment I saw through the hollow eyes and sunken skin, the vibrant woman I remembered. She laughed animatedly as she told us the stories behind the photos of her and dad together as I watched Kats face light up with every word.

Xander began clearing the table and I looked down to my phone, it was almost nine. We had been sitting for hours and I hadn't even noticed, I had taken in every second, every laugh and drank in the reminiscent feeling of being whole again.

Kat filled up the sink with hot soapy water as I began to dry the pots she had washed before passing them over to Xander who put them away. We were like an efficient factory line clearing away the plates as though we had a target to hit.

"If it's okay with you, I think I'll have a little lay down." My mother said, her voice sounding exhausted.

"Here, let me help you." Xander placed down the plate he was holding and walked over to where my mother was sitting. She stood up from the chair and on unsteady feet, but supported   by Xander, they slowly walked, one foot carefully in front of the other towards the sofa.

"He's something special." Kat said, with her hands still dunked under the water as she cleaned off another plate. My head turned to gaze over my shoulder as Xander helped my mother down slowly to the sofa.

"He is."

"Would you two ever, you know, try being more than friends?" Kat asked casually, keeping her eyes fixed on the pots she was scrubbing.

I didn't like to lie to my sister, she was only fourteen but she was far more mature than I ever was at her age and she would see straight through it.

"I'm not sure. Besides, I have another date with Aide!" I changed the subject and Kat gasped, a huge smile was now gaping across her face.

"Yep, he's taking me to Barracuda on Saturday." I smiled back at her, but her face dropped.

"But Saturday is your birthday?" Her eyebrow raised.

"Yes, but you know I don't like a fuss so it makes no difference whether I'm in or out I guess."

"But it's your 21st Elly, we have to do something!" She was giving me the eyes, those blue, doe eyes as deep as the ocean and she knew I couldn't say no.

"Why don't we do something during the day?" I asked. I couldn't afford to take us out for lunch, but we could go for a nice walk or watch a film.

"I'm up for that!" Xander abruptly appeared beside me again. "We can see about asking Joey about closing up early too? It's never that busy and he'll be happy to keep the hours wage."

I wiped the dish towel which was now sodden, on the inside of a mug, and looked from Kat to Xander who both now looked at me with puppy dog eyes. I really didn't like making a big deal of a day that ultimately, was just another day but saying no to these two, well that's even harder.

"Ok ok." I relented as I rolled my eyes sarcastically. Xander exaggerated a win, with his arms in the air he cheered to a crowd of ceramics that drip dried on the counter top.

"Oh Kat! How about that game of chess after? If you're still up for losing of course."

"Poor Xan-" Kat looked at me, an eyebrow raised and smirked back to Xander. "You actually think you could beat me? You're on." Xander glanced a wink towards me.

"Well I'll get set up then! L, shall I set up in your room?" He looked over his shoulder at my mother who was now sound asleep whilst I had a quick scan in my head of my bedroom floor, *no dirty knickers at least.*

"Yeah you go ahead, we'll not be long," I said quietly.

Kat and Xander had played three rounds of chess, Kat won every time. Xander would play brilliantly and every time it looked like he was going to win, he made a stupid move, ultimately handing Kat the victory.

I was twelve chapters deep in my new book. It was a romance about a student who kisses a professor in order to let her bestfriend date her ex. Talk about complicated, but it worked and I was eating up every word like a greedy school girl.

I looked at my phone and got distracted for a couple of minutes scrolling through social media. I had them all, but I never posted anything myself. I was what people my age called a lurker - which sounded way weirder than what it actually was, I just didn't have much to post, nor did I care for others' need for near constant validation.

A new follow request had come through since that last time I had checked maybe a week ago.

AideVasiliás1

Immediately I clicked the approve button and followed him back, so I could have a quick stalk of his profile in the morning. It was almost midnight and I was mentally and physically shattered.

Part of me felt silly for it, but I was afraid to sleep. Afraid to dream. Those eyes shrouded in flame and shadows haunted me, and it was like every sense came alive in those nightmares making it hard to distinguish the reality from the illusion and it was utterly terrifying.

My phone pinged in my hands.

Aide: Hey you, what are you doing up at this time?

A notification dropped down from the top of my screen. *AideVasiliás1 accepted your follow request. Shit*, I was a total lurker.

Lana: Working off a load of pasta and watching a very boring game of chess

Aide: You're going to have to elaborate...

Lana: It's nothing interesting haha, what are you doing up Dr?

Aide: Well I was... in the middle of something.

Lana: You're going to have to elaborate.

Aide: Well, I'll say this, you were actively on my mind.

My stomach tightened and I slipped down a little further on my bed, pulling my phone closer to my chest.

Lana: You're not regretting asking me out are you because I was kind of looking forward to some free sushi.

Aide: No regrets here.

Lana: So what was on your mind?

Aide: I'm not sure you want the details

Lana: Oh but I love the details

Aide: I was thinking of how your hair would feel in my hands

Lana: My hair?

Aide: Whilst your mouth was occupied, of course.

My body reacted to the thought as though it knew exactly what it would feel like to have him in my mouth. If Kat and Xander were not sitting a metre away from me I would have already been at my bedside table - pulling out something that could help relax the walls of muscle that made me suddenly feel warm between my legs.

"I'm exhausted from kicking your ass and I wouldn't want to embarrass you anymore," Kat said as she folded up the chess board and held it underneath her arm. "Night guys, and Elly-" She looked up to where I was laid casually on my bed. "Thanks for tonight, it meant a lot to me." Her smile could crack my heart wide open.

Kat strolled out of my room, blew a kiss to me, and lifted her arms proudly undefeated at Xander before padding across the landing to her room.

"Shit!" I looked up to Xander who was stood in the centre of my room, every pocket on him now being searched by his large hands.

"What's up?" I sat up and swung my legs off the bed.

"I think I've left my house keys at work." Xander dropped his head back.

"Can't you just call your parents?" I sat on the edge of the quilt.

"And wake them up? Have you met my mother?"

Xander's mother wasn't exactly the scary type but I can't imagine waking up a middle aged woman in the middle of the night would go down well with even the kindest of souls.

"Why don't you just stay here?" The words may have escaped my mouth a little too eagerly. It had been a while since we had had a sleepover, seven years exactly, because according to Joanne Flynne, when puberty takes over it's not appropriate for boy-girl sleepovers. But with the type of sleep I have been getting recently, that being very little, it would be nice not to feel alone.

"You can come through on your offer." I nudged his leg where he stood in front of me.

"My offer?" He asked as his head fell forwards, and his green eyes scanned mine.

"Bed buddy?" I laughed.

"Right." His face turned pink and he looked around him, seemingly trying to get a last glance at the floor where his keys may have fallen from his pockets.

The insecure part of me felt like he was looking for a way out, like he didn't want to be here.

He ran a hand through his dark curls and smiled back at me.

"Bed buddies." The dimple blessed his cheek as an unsettled curl fell over his eyes.

My skincare didn't comprise of much, a simple micellar water would do the trick at erasing the day's paint. I had gone into the bathroom to change into a large grey oversized *Rolling Stones* t-shirt before getting tucked under the covers, slightly shifted to the side to allow room for Xander.

I couldn't remember the last time I saw Xander shirtless but it was obvious, as he pulled off the tight black t-shirt, that he had filled out enormously since then.

His bronzed chest was corded, each tanned pec thick with muscle, sat large above his tapered waist. My eyes followed the thick line that carved its way through the centre of his stomach, cutting through a canyon of abdominal muscles, down further to where the black band of his boxer shorts sat low on his hips.

I tried my best to give him privacy, but it was like being told not to look at a gorgon, and maybe I'd be turned into stone a happy woman if the last thing looking back at me was that magnificent male form.

I turned my head away, not trusting that my own eyes wouldn't scan over him as he pulled down his grey shorts, and stood in the middle of my bedroom practically naked.

The weight of the bed shifted as Xander squeezed in next to me, but when I turned over to face him I was greeted by a large foot in my face.

My eyes trailed the length of the bed to see Xander, clearly far too large for this bed, peeking out over the bottom of the quilt where my own feet lay.

I couldn't help the small giggle that escaped me.

"Top and tail?" I smirked. "I'm not sure which is worse, the nightmares or those things being this close to my face." I gestured towards the huge feet beside my head and laughed down to him as I wiggled my own toes closer to his face.

Xander's head hit the black bed railing at the foot of the bed as he shifted uncomfortably.

"Just come up here, there's plenty of room." Plenty may have been a stretch but we could easily both lie here without being on top of each other.

Xander manoeuvred under the quilts, his head now lost under the rolling pink duvet caused my stomach to tighten. A mound of dark brown curls popped up beside me as Xander mocked gasping for air.

It quickly became apparent he was a lot larger than I thought and his shoulders were snug against mine. I shifted onto my side to face him, allowing more room in the single bed as he did the same, the bed groaned with the extra weight.

An inch of space separated our bodies under the cover, but I could feel the heat rippling from his body roam around mine, a magnetic pull begging my body to close the space between our skin.

"I didn't know you liked sushi." Xander remarked quietly, his face plain and his eyes looked down between us then back up to mine.

It took me a moment to realise he was talking about Barracuda, and my date with the doctor.

"I don't really, but it looks like a nice enough place." I shrugged a little under the quilt. "Plus, it's something to do and apparently, they make one hell of a cocktail."

"If you wanted something to do you could have just asked me." Xanders eyes darkened slightly, his gaze flicked up across my chest and lingered on my mouth before looking into my eyes. Our faces were perfectly parallel, inches apart. I could see the fractures of gold that split between the vivid green iris', the scent of fresh mint on his warm breath.

"You know I'm not one for doing much on my birthday, it's just not my thing." I shuffled a few inches down in bed, further under the cosy covers.

"I know that. But letting someone else take you out-" I looked up to him, my face now slightly lower rested on the pillow. "When I've been trying to get you out every year I've known you...it just feels a little...shitty."

I felt my brows pinch together as I looked at his face, one dark brow softly raised and his smile was pressed to one side, disappointment hung on every feature.

I inched further to him under the cover, and my bare legs touched his for a moment. His skin felt warm as his hair tickled against my skin and I immediately felt sensitive to his heat. My arms bent in front of my chest creating a wall between my breasts and his chest.

"Xan I'm sorry, I didn't even, well I didn't think of it like that." The backs of my arms caught the heat of his chest and my body shivered softly.

I wanted nothing more right now, than to run my hands across the short dark hair that dusted the hollow plain between his pectorals and pull myself closer to the heat.

"I just want you to be happy L." His hand reached underneath my chin, tilting my head up to his eyes as his lips parted. "But don't think you're getting away from the next one. We're talking about big and super embarrassing birthdays from here on." His mouth curled into a grin before he kissed my forehead softly.

I didn't move back from the space he had closed between us, instead I nuzzled slightly further in, the gap between us now minimal, but just enough that we weren't flush.

He leant across me and turned off the lamp, and I thought for the first time in a while, warm, safe and surrounded by the scent of pine and black pepper, that I might just have the best night of sleep I've had in my life.

Ω

My body felt on fire, writhing in pleasure as my hands clenched onto the two large thighs in front of me. My hair cascaded over my face with each circular movement of my hips. The room was dark, the air heavy with sweat and the scent of sweet spices licking against my bare skin.

My hips ached, searching for a release and as I felt the pressure of him deep between my legs, I closed my eyes. Leaning back, I filled myself with him deeper, the ache rising, my muscles tightening around him. Two large hands wrapped around my hips, pushing me down further, rocking me back and forth. Leaning forward, I reached for the front of his calves, I needed to stretch out across him, feel more of him.

His strong hands rocked me still, one now on my lower back pushing my arch deeper. The heat began racing across my soaking skin and my legs began shuddering.

A large arm stretched from behind me, wrapping around my bare breasts and pulling me back onto a hard naked body, hot and flush against my bed. Still inside me, massive, toned arms reached underneath my knees, opening me wider.

His hard hot body tensed and relaxed as he pounded inside me from underneath me, the strength and size of him made me feel small and light as I tightened around him. My back arched against his stomach, with my head resting on his chest, his mouth let out a deep groan sending shivers across my entire body.

Pushing down into each of his thrusts we were perfectly in sync, our breath heavy. Flipping me over with one arm, I was facing down on the bed, with my ass up and his body never leaving mine. I widened my knees, opening myself up more for him and he released whatever restraint it seemed he had and began filling me up. Pounding against my behind, the force of it pushed me further and further into the plush pillows underneath me as something underneath us cracked. The sound of stone breaking.

My legs began quivering and the hands now gripping my hips, lifted the weight of the bed, using my legs, pulling me into each thrust.

Heat began simmering underneath my skin, the aching between my legs pulsed, the feeling of pressure filled me each time my ass hit the front of him.

I couldn't stop the whimper escaping my mouth with each breath, as he went faster and faster. My body was on fire. Moving inside me, we felt like one. The feeling was overwhelming, my body writhed against each push, clenching against him.

I felt him shudder against me, driving inside deeper and deeper. My skin flushed with heat, racing to where he filled me.

My vision brightened as pure pleasure ripped across me, travelling every inch of my red hot skin, taking the breath from me.

Shuddering, still inside me, two large arms fell either side of me, large tanned hands resting either side of my head holding the owner up above my back.

My body was still quivering underneath him. Glancing towards the hands, I saw a faint golden band wrapping around each large wrist before closing my pleasure ridden heavy eyes.

J L Robinson

CHAPTER FOURTEEN

I woke up pressed against Xanders front, my body flush against his. A large arm, draped lazily over my waist and my head a few inches lower than his, I could feel his hot breath against my neck.

The oversized t-shirt that I wore to sleep, had ridden up in the night, leaving my bare backside pressed against his boxers. I shifted gently, so as not to wake him, but his arm pulled me back towards him closer this time, and a groan escaped his sleeping lips. He tucked underneath and around me, and I immediately felt the hardness of him twitch against me.

It took every ounce of self restraint I had to stop myself from pressing back into him.

The early light streamed through the thin curtains, casting a soft glow across my bedroom and I could hear the sounds of pans clattering in the kitchen beneath me.

I lifted his heavy arm and placed my pillow underneath it, shifting off the bed carefully.

Quietly, I padded over to the small set of wooden drawers next to my window, and pulled open the top draw. I pulled out a pink thong before opening the bottom drawer and finding a comfortable pair of loose, red plaid pyjama bottoms.

Xander was still hugging the pillow when I grabbed my phone, and headed downstairs. It was still pretty early, but we both had to be in the cafe in an hour so I thought I'd make us a coffee, seeing as the shit we drink there shouldn't be considered consumable.

Kat was seated next to mum on the sofa when I reached the bottom of the staircase, and I could hear the familiar voices of Rory and Lorelai coming from the TV.

They were sitting snuggled up together, watching our favourite show as my mother stroked her golden hair. I wanted nothing more in that moment than to curl up beside them and have a GG day like we used to as kids, but I had a job to keep and a hot best friend upstairs.

"Morning, does anyone want a drink?" I leant over the edge of the sofa to where they were cosied up.

"Please!" Kat responded, lifting her head a little to look up at me from my mums lap.

"Mum, can I get you anything?" She looked better this morning, her face held a little more colour and the rattle on her breath seemed less harsh.

"I'm ok for now, thank you darling." Her breath was still soft but she definitely seemed better.

There was a sudden loud clambering noise above us, and we all looked to the ceiling in unison.

"Did Xander stay over last night?" Kat lifted her head, eyes narrowed and a small grin crept across her face.

"He didn't have his keys on him and I guess he didn't want to wake his parents," I replied, deadpan.

Kat pressed her lips, trying to hide her smirk before lying back down. I flicked my gaze to my mother who was now looking up to me with her brows gently furrowed.

"So no coffee?" I asked again, feeling a little awkward.

The sound of Xander moving upstairs interrupted me again and I just knew he'd woke up frantic as he'd realised the time.

He hated being late for work - me on the other hand, if I'm on time I'm too early.

I hadn't spoken to Aide all day, but I had been thinking about him, about those texts. There was something so familiar about him. I'd only known him for a few weeks but I was drawn in so quickly. And quite frankly, if it wasn't for Xander, I'd think he was quite literally the single most attractive thing I've ever laid eyes on.

Heat filled me as my mind wandered back to last night's dream. I thought back, combing over the sordid memory of those hands. They were huge, tanned and...they had some strange golden bands around the wrists.

When I got home later that day, Kat and Isha were standing around the stove, mixing something in a large pan. Kat had text earlier to let me know she would be walking home from school with her from now on. I guess having your big sister pick you up from school every day in a banged up little motor, wasn't exactly the coolest thing.

I stomped in, my mustard t-shirt smelling of grease and coffee and hair hanging out of my clip. I kicked off my converse, pushing them to the side of the front door where the other shoes were paired up.

The smell of rich spices drifted to my senses, my mouth immediately watering as I peaked over to see what Kat and Isha were cooking up in the kitchen.

"Damn that smells good," I said, looking over Kats shoulder to the chicken she was stirring, fragrantly browned with spices.

Isha was chopping up onion, using the flat edge of the knife to transfer the fine slices from the chopping board and into the pan.

"It's something my nani taught me how to make." Isha looked back at me with a small smile, but something sad shone in her eyes.

"Well she must be one hell of a cook!"

"She was." Her raven hair turned back to the chopping board, as she concentrated on mincing the garlic clove in front of her.

I looked at Kat, my eyebrows pinched that said *did I say something wrong?*

"Isha's grandmother passed away not too long ago." Kat said, wrapping an arm gently around Isha's waist, pulling her an inch closer.

"Oh, I'm really sorry to hear that." I never really knew what to say in these circumstances, but I softened my tone.

"No, don't be sorry, this is just a way I like to connect with her, I wanted to share it." She glanced over her shoulder to me, with glossy eyes.

"Is there anything I can do?" I placed a hand on each of the girls shoulders, and took in a deep breath through my nose. The rich aroma was intoxicating.

"You can go get changed, you stink." Kat said with her nose wrinkled, before she nudged Isha with an elbow and burst out laughing.

"Charming this one." I looked at Isha whose mouth was now turned up in a shy smile. I could tell she wanted to laugh too, because after a day working at Joeys, I definitely did stink.

I peeked over the sofa to where mum was napping before I headed upstairs. As I entered my room, I found my clothes still pushed into a pile in the corner with the curtains only slightly open, I slumped on my bed for a minute's rest.

The past few days had been a lot, and pairing that with no real sleep, it was beginning to get on top of me. I shifted down further to lay on top of the quilt and unlocked my phone.

Checking the bank app my current balance was *minus two-hundred-pounds* into my overdraft and I wouldn't have another wage until the rest of the bills came out.

I couldn't ask my mother to help, she didn't have money herself and this was the last thing she needed to worry about right now. Besides, it wouldn't be the first time I'd skipped a meal or two to make things stretch a little further, so I guess until the next pay came in, I'd just make out like I wasn't feeling too well.

I took in a large breath, and sunk further into my bed, the smell of pine and black pepper sent a shiver down to my core. Plunging my face into the sheets I took in even more of the delicious scent that Xander had left behind like a calling card to my deepest desires.

A loud ping distracted me from my salacious thoughts, and I looked down to my phone now lit up with a new text notification.

Aide: You're driving me crazy.

The last message above read *'Whilst your mouth was occupied, of course.'*

Lana: Oh I am?

Aide: You are. How was the chess?

Lana: Not as exciting as the night you were proposing.

Three dots appeared immediately, he was so quick to text back and having his full attention made me feel tight and warm between my legs. A smile crept across my face as I waited on his response.

Aide: You have no idea.

Lana: I really don't. Maybe you should help educate me, Dr.

I bit my lip and hoped he'd take the bait. It had been years since I had actually slept with someone, I guess I just got pickier as I got older, but my body ached at the idea of being with both Xander and Aide. Three three dots appeared and my body reacted in anticipation. An animal in heat, ready to take on a challenge.

Aide: I have an idea...

Lana: I'm listening

Aide: On wednesday evenings, I volunteer at the local dog sanctuary, why don't you come with me

This wasn't exactly the type of education I was alluding to, but I can't deny that while the idea of visiting a bunch of little dogs didn't immediately make me giddy - it would also mean seeing him again before our actual date.

I had always loved dogs, some would say I was obsessed in fact. We almost got one as kids, but when we found out Kat was severely allergic (meaning that even coming into contact with one would swell her face up like a puffer fish), we never did.

It didn't stop me cooing and petting any passing dog I could get my own paws on though.

Lana: Dogs? Say no more I'm in.

Aide: 6pm still good for you?

Lana: 6pm is great for me! 🐾 🐾 🐾

The fragrant smell of food had made its way to my room, and like a snake to a flute, I followed the scent downstairs.

Isha, Kat, and my mother were sitting around the table, food piled in front of them. A huge mound of steaming rice, a pot rich yellow sauce with chunks of chicken, and hot bubbled flatbread lay across the centre of the table.

Three plates sat in front of them and a spare plate sat across from an empty chair as they began spooning the food onto their plates.

"Just in time." Kat nodded to the empty space at the end of the table and my mum smiled over to me.

Isha spooned a generous amount of the chicken onto my mothers plate before she served Kats. She made sure everyone's plate had food on it before she served herself a portion of the chicken and rice.

The room smelt sweet, rich with spice and garlic. It took everything in me not to launch myself at the food and consume everything in sight.

As I sat down at the table and looked around at the people sitting with me, my heart felt like it had doubled in size. Kat glanced over to Isha, her mouth curling upwards as she forked in the food. Isha's own beautiful, dark eyes sparkled back at Kat.

My mother, with her green tank pulled up beside her, slowly took small portions on her fork. Her delicate hand strained as she clearly struggled but was doing her best to enjoy the moment too.

We barely said a word as we dolloped more onto our plates and tore apart the warm bread, but the silence was as sweet and rich with love as the food we were eating.

CHAPTER FIFTHTEEN

The weather forecasted sun for the day ahead, so having decided it would be nice to walk back through the town, I left my car at home.

Heading back from the cafe, I took the route back through the quaint little shop fronts, admiring the artistry that each unique piece held.

After passing rows of handmade ceramic stores, I came to the one I really had my eye on.

The low, autumn light glinted off the crystal works in the window, shards of sun splinted technicolour beams as it passed through the multiple pieces of jewellery adorned with vivid crystals and gemstones.

My eyes scanned each piece, passing rings with large iridescent opalites, and embellished necklaces of every colour you could imagine, before landing on the simple, yet beautiful silver cuff bracelet.

There was absolutely no way I could afford it, but I still enjoyed looking at it. Its imperfect polished curves and hammered edges, made me think how crazy it was that someone hadn't already picked it up.

The weather was turning a little chillier as the wind crept up. I tucked my hands into the front pocket of the black hoodie I was wearing, shifted my backpack more comfortably, and turned away from the shop.

By the time I had turned around and made my way to crossing the otherside of the road, the sky had darkened and it had started spotting with rain. *Just my fucking luck.*

If the rain got to my hair I would be a walking frissball in minutes so I pulled up my hood, yanked the straps tight and sped up my pace.

I must have been only five minutes away from the shelter of my home when it started to pour down.

My black hoody offered no barrier to the onslaught of rain that lashed its way across me on the back of a ragged gale, as I began running home.

I turned onto a street and passed my highschool, now looking duller than ever surrounded by dark clouds and the haze of falling rain.

As I ran towards another road leading onto a cul-de-sac, I looked in through the large bay windows with warm lighting, and cosy curtains being pulled to.

The rain pelted against my cold skin and I could barely feel my tongue run across the outside of my lip, tasting the salty downpour.

A horn sounded from behind me, and as I turned towards the noise, I could hardly see through the curtain of rain around me. Two dimmed headlights became larger as the vehicle came closer, I didn't stop running.

The horn sounded again and I heard a voice shouting, unclear through the rain but familiar.

I felt him before I could see him, recognising something I couldn't hear or see.

"Lana! Get in the car!" Aide shouted, his voice a deep vibration cutting through the thrum of rain that battered the floor around me.

I looked over to see his head hanging out of the side of his car, his hair was drenched, before his door swung open and he ran towards me.

Aide had taken off the suit jacket he was wearing, leaving just his white shirt to become transparent with rain and he ran towards me - the Mercedes' engine still purring.

With the jacket lifted above his head, he made his way to me in seconds, the smell of him hitting me before he wrapped the suit jacket over me and shielded me from the rain.

One arm held the collar of the jacket slightly above my head to cover me, and the other wrapped around my waist, bringing me in close to him as we raced underneath the pelting rain back to the car.

He was absolutely soaked by the time he had opened the passengers door for me, and had quickly made his way back around into the drivers side, slamming the door shut behind him.

The blonde hair on his head curled downwards above his brows, and the rain that ran through it now dripped onto his face.

"Are you okay?" He asked, brows furrowed as he brushed back the hair out of his face with a large hand and placed the other on my knee.

His hand was so warm I felt like all I wanted was to be wrapped up in him.

"Well that came out of nowhere!" I laughed as I lifted his jacket from around me, conscious that I must have been soaking his beautiful leather interior.

"Is your car still not fixed? You should have said I could have given you a lift wherever you needed." His hand still hot against my thigh.

"No honestly it's fine, I just fancied a bit of fresh air, you know." I shrugged, smirking at my sodden jumper.

"Here-" Aide reached to his back seat and pulled a large navy zip hoodie from behind the seat I was sitting in. "Pop this on."

I looked over to him, his shirt now failed to conceal his magnificent body as it was practically see-through, except for the seam lines.

My eyes lingered a little too long over his impressive chest before I looked back up to his eyes with a smirk.

"I think you might need that more than me." The corners of my mouth twitching.

He looked down to where his abs were on full display and huffed a laugh.

"Seriously, take it, you'll catch a cold sat in wet clothing." He passed over the hoodie and turned his gaze away from me as to give me privacy.

"Okay doctor." I smiled at the gesture.

I peeled off my own soaked hoodie and threw it on top of my backpack that was now slumped in the footwell, before pulling on the navy hoody. The heady scent of mixed spice and sandalwood warmed me as I zipped up the hoodie and relaxed back into the seat.

"Thank you." I signalled that he was okay to turn back towards me, still sitting in his soaking shirt.

"You never have to thank me Lana." His voice was a sensual, dark comfort that felt like everything I was missing in life.

His hand reached for the gearstick, the key was still in ignition and parked in the middle of the road.

"Let's get you home." He pushed the gear into first and set off.

It was probably quicker to walk home through the back ginnels than drive from here as most roads were cul-de-sacs, but I sunk further into the plush leather seats as Aide pressed a button symbolled with a seat icon.

The heat came through the chair to my lower back, warming my core and the intoxicating scent of his cologne might just be my favourite aroma ever. It reminded me of warmth, the spices rich like an autumn's harvest, the woodiness grounding and homely. It felt like being wrapped up, safe and loved.

I nudged in a little lower, allowing the heat to warm through my bones as I rested my head against the door, savouring the moment. Aide gently rested a hand on my knee and I felt so calm, so relaxed and I closed my eyes.

A woman's whisper, muffled as though speaking quietly through a vast open space, spoke to another, in my ear.

You need to tell her.

I still have time.

You are running out of time, the realms are breaking and the veil is splitting. Without you here, he will shred it apart.

She will come Cerb, I know she will

You cannot risk it, you are endangering the entire shadow realm.

She cannot survive in this form she must remember.

And when she doesn't?

Well, then I will have to make her.

I had forgotten what it must feel like to close your eyes and fall into blissful darkness. I knew stress could manifest itself in many ways, but now I was hearing voices in my head, I couldn't deny that quite frankly I was scared.

They felt so real, like I was there, and I don't know why I kept seeing things that felt like disjointed memories. The woman who looked exactly like me, her haunted amber eyes staring back at mine. The body, cold, and limp slumped on my lap, his cloudy unseeing eyes staring back up at mine. Blood pouring from the agonising deep cut across my palm.

I winced, opening my eyes as my palm ceased and I lifted my head from the side of the door.

"Is your hand still bothering you?" Aide asked and I noticed we had already pulled up outside our house. I didn't know how long I'd been asleep for, but Aide's shirt had seemed to dry out a little.

I turned my palm over in my hand and looked down at the fine white scar that the cut had left behind.

"It's fine, it's just-" I probably shouldn't tell the handsome doctor who would potentially just refer to me to a psychiatric colleague of his then ghost me, about my dreams. But as he looked at me, concern shadowing those diamond eyes and his hand gently stroking my knee, I felt as though there was nothing I couldn't say to him.

"I keep having these dreams, I've seen myself in them, I've seen things my imagination couldnt conjure," I started, surprised at how intently Aide was listening to me. "And sometimes I can feel them. Before I had the accident in the cafe I had a dream. I sliced open my own hand exactly here." I pointed to the fine scar.

"And then I saw a man, I think I've seen him a few times. And another woman." I couldn't believe how much I was telling him, his face concentrated on every word I was saying, no doubt diagnosing me with something or another.

"And what else did you see?" He asked and I felt taken aback. "Was there anyone else?"

"There was someone, or something I don't know. I couldn't see them but it was terrifying."

"Tell me." His brows pinched and his body turned towards me. I took a moment to think through what I was about to say, and how crazy I was about to sound, my eyes fixed on my jeans, flicked up to his slate eyes, now widened.

"There was a man, at least I think it was a man. The darkness danced around him like the shadows were a part of him, and a dark inky mist covered him entirely. I was terrified, but I couldn't scream, until I did." I looked up to him, his eyes narrowed. "And when I did it was like the shadows listened to me, like they knew I was scared and it took him away. When I woke up I was covered in black soot. But then it disappeared." I sighed as my eyes couldn't meet his.

A warm hand reached underneath my chin as he lifted my gaze to his.

"I'm sorry you we're scared Lana." He said as he dipped his head to mine, his hair had dried curlier than I had ever seen it and the boyish charm it gave him, made me smile.

"Well it was just a dream, I don't know. I just want a good night's sleep!" I joked as though I hadn't just made myself look like a complete lunatic. "So I'll see you in-" I pulled my phone from underneath me, "an hour?" I laughed.

"I hope you're ready to be bombarded with over excited dogs." Aide smirked.

"Didn't you know, over-excited dogs might just be my favourite thing." My mouth turned upwards to match his smile, as I opened the door and got out of the car.

The sky had now cleared, though it was still grey, and the ground still wet. Before I closed the door shut behind me, I leant down and smiled again at Aide.

"Thanks again! See you soon!" He smiled back in response and I closed the door, dodged the huge puddles and made my way to my front door.

"I've got this, don't worry. I'll sort us something out." Kat smiled as was getting ready to leave the house an hour later. Mum was fast asleep on the sofa as I pulled on a jacket and from the corner of my eye I saw a silver car roll up through the front window, I checked my watch again, 5.59pm. *Right on time.*

Although Kat assured me she would be fine, I still struggled to accept the fact she had clearly been fine a long time, and didn't need me to mother her. Still, I sat up and went to the kitchen, and checked the cupboards.

"I've got out the penne, it needs six minutes in boiling water, don't forget the salt." I pulled out a jar of pasta sauce from the top shelf. "Then just stir in this sauce for a couple of minutes on the heat, but be careful."

"Got it!" Kat called back as she lifted an arm from the sofa with a thumbs up. "Have a good time!"

My black converse were at the front door where I had left them, still sodden, so I decided on the vans instead and wiggled a foot in at a time.

"See you later and call me if you need me!" Kat's arm shot up again from behind the sofa, thumb in the air.

The last few rays of sunlight were dipping below the row of houses opposite our own, and it reminded me of the one thing I never really liked about the colder seasons. Cosier nights were not the issue, but shorter days meant colder nights and a far more expensive heating bill.

I shrugged off the niggling worry and smiled at Aide who was sitting on the silver bonnet, waiting for me.

He looked more casual then I had ever seen him, tapered navy jogging bottoms and a navy hoody to match. *Shit, I still had his hoodie.*

It took less than twenty minutes to get to the other side of town where the dog shelter was and luckily the weather had held off raining.

"Am I dressed okay?" I asked as I looked down to the jeans and knit combo I had decided on.

"You're perfect." Aide glanced away from the road for a moment to smile back at me. The kind look in his eyes always felt so reassuring like he wouldn't lie to me.

We pulled up through an old wooden fence, and the ground beneath us became bumpy as we drove off track towards a small farm house, surrounded by worn wooden kennels.

A small chipped sign hung from the home with the title 'Thornberrys Dog Sanctuary' spelt across its split wooden face.

"How long have you been helping here?" I asked as we pulled up to the house and the car stopped.

"Actually, I'm pretty new to this." He pressed a button and the engine stopped. "I'm a huge dog person, and I thought I could help. A few courses later, here I am." The seatbelt around me loosened as he clicked it open for me, before undoing his own.

"That's really sweet of you."

"Listen, I get just as much out of it as they do." He laughed as he opened the door, stepped out and I followed. "But the Owens, the couple who run the shelter, do it completely by themselves. They rely on volunteers and donations to keep up and running." He walked around to the boot.

Aide pulled a large black duffle bag and a laptop case before he hovered a foot beneath the rear bumper and the door began to close itself.

As we walked over to the farm house, a chorus of barks became louder and louder as though the dogs sensed visitors. It had always intrigued me how dogs seemed to have a sixth sense, like they knew a person's intent just by the smell of them. I thought to myself of a few awkward situations such a sense may have saved me from, and a few awful dates too.

That's the difference between men and dogs; dogs only ever want to please their owners and they're fiercely loyal. Whilst men are the complete opposite.

I'm not saying I have the sixth sense that dogs do when it comes to judging a person's character, but there was something I had always felt around Aide, from the very first time I saw those eyes staring down at me at Joeys. It was like feeling safe, protected. Like my body recognised that this was a good man and I could trust him. My body also reacted in other, far cruder ways when I thought about him or was in his presence but that was something closer related to a dog in heat.

As we reached the porch of the farm house Aide knocked on the wooden door, the white paint peeled away by the years.

A clank of the lock being turned and unlatched and the door opened to reveal a small elderly couple, tanned, lined faces and spotted with freckles smiled up at us.

The woman shuffled backwards as she opened the door to allow us in, whilst the old man with a grey moustache for a top lip took Aides hand into his, shaking it gently as Aide placed the other free hand on top.

"We're so glad you're here, the pups are coming but she has been bleeding." The man croaked, his wiry brows furrowed as he looked up to Aide who seemed to tower over him.

"How long has she been bleeding?" Aide asked, his tone strong as he walked in through the home and I followed.

"A few hours. Usually the bitches don't bleed before. You've come just in time-" The old man squinted over to me, "and I see you've brought help."

"We need all the hands we can get." The old woman's voice was soft as she smiled at me, handing me something plastic.

"This is Lana, she's great with dogs." Aide looked behind his shoulder to where I was standing and shrugged slightly as I pressed my lips together in response, smiling awkwardly.

"I'm Jerry, and this is Gillian, my wife. Thank you for coming." The old man grabbed my hand and shook it firmer than I was expecting.

"Just through here." I heard Gillian call back through the hallway where she had disappeared to.

The farm seemed cosy, it's dark wooden floors worn, but still polished. Small ornaments sat on top of the lattice radiator covers that lined the hallway through the kitchen.

Aide and I followed Jerry through the kitchen, and out into a conservatory.

Lying, panting on the towels that covered the chequered floor, was a gorgeous black-brown rottweiler, her stomach swollen and blood dripping from her hind legs.

My breath caught, at the sight of her in pain and before I could put on the plastic poncho the couple were now wearing, I rushed to her side.

Jerry and Gillian looked startled, and went to say something, but as I lifted her head and gently rested it flat on my knees, their words were lost.

"Mabel has been snapping all day, neither of us could get near her," Jerry said, his mouth open in disbelief.

"I told you she was good with dogs." Aide smiled proudly down at me, and I smiled back as I stroked the soft ears laid on my lap.

Aide placed the duffle bag on the floor, knelt down to unzip it and pulled a pair of blue latex gloves from a box. He snapped on the gloves one by one and slowly approached the panting dog.

Her soft head lifted from my lap in caution, looked towards Aide and dropped it back down. *He's approved.*

With a gentle touch Aide placed his hands around the rottweiler's lower stomach, feeling for the position of the pups.

I continued to stroke Mabel's soft head, her eyes barely opened and she looked exhausted. Aide began to softly massage her stomach and she winced a couple of times in response.

"We're going to need more towels." Aide smiled up towards where Gillian and Jerry were standing, shock still warped their faces and Gillian scuttled off.

Mabel shifted underneath his touch, turning slightly, lifting a hind leg as though to get in a more comfortable position. The back of her head now rested on my lap and continued to stroke the sides of her face gently.

Blood began pooling from between her legs, and her eyes began blinking slowly.

"Try to keep her awake, we need to keep her awake." Aide nodded to me, his voice straight but calm.

As I leaned over the face of the rottweiler, I could feel her slipping away from beneath me, her eyes blinking one last time before staying closed.

"It's now or never girl." Aide said, taking the fresh towels Gillian handed over, he continued to massage her stomach.

Her head lolled in my hands, I could feel her slipping from consciousness, she had lost so much blood. My head fell to hers, the soft fur warmed my forehead as I whispered.

"Come on girl, you can do this. You can do this."

A whimper came from her mouth, her eyes still closed but her head stiffened as though she was concentrating.

"That's it. I'm here, I've got you." I spoke softly to her as I held her head with one hand whilst the other stroked the side of her face.

Another whimper, a little louder this time and I looked down to where Aide sat, still gently massaging her stomach. He nodded to me and I dipped my head low to Mabels again.

"I've got you." I breathed.

A sharp yelp almost made me jump, but I kept my head low, staring down at her and I continued to comfort her. Her body stiffened and her mouth dropped open as she started to pant. Each breath intentional.

I lifted my head a little to give her space, the touch of my hands never leaving her.

As I looked down to Aide, his latex covered hands were low and my eyes welled up as he lifted up a tiny, whimpering pup.

"This one was causing you some bother hey girl," he said directly to Mabel who seemed to relax a little. "There's a couple more in there, but this little thing was causing the obstruction," he said as his gaze flicked from me to the old couple. "Do you want to take it from here?"

Gillian slowly came down beside Aide and stroked down Mabel's spine, and Jerry took the pup from Aide and brought it up towards where her head rested on my lap.

Mabel began licking the pup immediately, and my heart felt like it could shatter seeing such an innate love.

I looked down to Aide who smiled back up at me, lips pressed into a wide grin, his eyes sparkled.

Mabel gave birth to two more pups and we stuck around a while to make sure the bleeding had stopped.

As Aide packed up his duffle bag and stripped off his pair of gloves, I looked over to the beautiful rottweiler, who was now napping contently as three, pot-bellied puppies suckled on her stomach.

Saying our goodbyes I promised the couple I would be back soon before Aide and I headed back to the car. He dumped the bag in the boot and walked round to the passengers side where he opened my door for me.

Serotonin was still coursing through my veins as I slung my arms around him, barely able to reach his shoulders. I placed my head deep into his warm chest and took in a large breath of his spiced cologne. His huge arms wrapped around me, each hand reaching the opposite side of my waist.

I tucked deeper into his embrace and he responded by pulling me in closer.

"That was amazing!"

I felt Aide's face drop down towards my head as he placed a soft gentle kiss on top of it.

"You were amazing." His deep voice replied, a soft bass that vibrated against where we touched.

We stood embraced in the chill of the autumn evening, and I felt as though every worry, every stress in my life, ceased to exist around him, as though there were only the two of us.

My mind stilled as I rested my head on his warm chest, no thought of anyone or anything other than this moment, us, together. I never thought I would feel this way around any man other than my father or Xander of course, but this was different - more intense.

His pull felt almost magnetic, like my body was an internal compass and he was my true north.

There was no denying the connection we had. That same gravitational pull I felt anytime I'm around him, as though it was against our nature to be apart from one another and I wondered if he felt it too.

A part of me felt ridiculous for having such strong feelings for a man I'd not even known for a week, but they say when you know you know, and he felt like something my body had known forever.

A gentle hand rested on my shoulder as Aide pulled back slowly and smiled down to me.

"Shall we get you home?"

I turned my face and looked up at the kind, slate-grey eyes that waited on a response.

The harsh reality shifted back into place as my mind wandered back to what awaited me at home. Where dread used to reside, I now knew only sorrow. Regret at how much I had missed, at all the things that had gone unnoticed. I thought of Kat cuddling up to my mother, me beside her, the three of us watching *Gilmore Girls* and drinking hot chocolate whilst she stroked the lengths of our hair.

"Will you bring me again?" I asked, as I moved from his embrace.

"I don't think I could stop you if I tried." He laughed and I remembered the look on the old couple's face when I practically launched myself at Mabel.

On the drive home I couldn't help but feel completely content, as Aide rested his hand on my knee between gear shifts.

"Are you looking forward to turning twenty-one?" Aide asked, his eyes focused on the dark road ahead of him.

"I never really do much for birthdays to be honest, it's just another day to me."

"Twenty-one's a big one though, it feels like an age since I turned twenty-one." I realised I had never even asked his age, but he couldn't have been older than twenty-seven, either that or he had an unbelievable skincare routine.

"How old are you exactly?" His eyes flicked to mine, a feline grin crept across his face.

"Old." He replied, eyebrows raised with a smirk.

Surely he wasn't over thirty, there was absolutely no way someone passed that threshold without a few lines here and there.

"I'm twenty-seven." *Bang on.* "Is that a problem for you?" His smirk softened as his eyes widened with a glance towards mine.

"Absolutely not, I might even prefer older men." His eyes slid over me and the wry grin returned.

"So, if you're so young, how long have you worked at The Clinic for?" I wasn't sure how long medical school took but I knew from watching *Scrubs* and *Greys Anatomy* that young, accomplished doctors weren't really a thing.

"I haven't been there long, I transferred from the city hospital when I completed my fellowship."

"So you're a city boy then?" I realised how little I knew about him, not that it changed how I felt but it made me feel warm inside knowing more about his life.

"I wouldn't say I'm a true city boy, but I've definitely adapted to the smog." He laughed.

The car took a turn gently, it was pitch black outside save for the headlights hitting the tarmacked road still wet from the day's downpour.

Time is running out. A feminine voice whispered against my ear and I screamed, jumping forward from my seat.

Aide slammed the brakes and my skin pebbled with goosebumps as the air around us suddenly dropped in temperature.

"What is it?" Aide was staring at me intensely, eyes narrowed beneath pinched eyebrows.

Shivers danced along my skin, like a cold serpent snaking its way down my body.

Aide's hand grabbed my knee, the shocked skin underneath became blistering hot, as I could feel the imprint of his hand beneath my jeans.

Instead of flinching away from him, my body felt drawn to the spot where we connected. Every petrified nerve ending, extinguished.

"Lana what is it?" He asked again.

The whisper was familiar, like a voice I've never heard but have always known.

The dreams, the voice, everything feels connected, it feels the same even though it's different. I couldn't explain what was happening to me and maybe I shouldn't tell a doctor that I was hearing voices anyways.

"It's nothing, I just thought I heard something. It made me jump a little." Aides grey eyes narrowed, and as he searched my face, a single brow lifted.

"Are you sure you're okay?" I shouldn't be okay - I was pretty sure I was losing my mind - but with those eyes sparkling back at me, it was hard to spiral too deeply into concern.

"I'm alright." And with a smile, I sunk back comfortably into the heated seat.

Aide's hand never left my knee the entire way home, even going so far as to use his one free hand to steer and change gears simultaneously. I probably should have allowed him his hand back but with him close to me I felt safe, shielded.

"Thanks again for tonight." I said as we pulled up outside my home. "I guess I'll see you Saturday then?" I didn't want to leave him, I wanted to stay here in his bubble that somehow alleviated all my worries.

"It's a date." Aide smirked, the grin widened and he let out a little laugh.

"Are you sure it's a date?" I poked back.

"I'm sure." He leaned closer, his eyes lit up.

"No holding back this time either?" My chin raised as I watched his jaw work in response. The column of his throat swallowed, before his mouth parted open.

I waited a moment for a response, but Aide's eyes now faced away from me.

My lips parted, but before I could say another word, two large hands cupped my face, forcing my mouth upwards.

My body set on fire as Aide's lips crashed into mine, and I melted under the taste of him. With each pull and push of his lips parting mine open, heat filled every corner of me.

One hand trailed from my jaw and gently wrapped around my neck. I tilted my head back, giving him deeper access to my mouth and he groaned in response - the vibration of it rattled my body and I shifted closer.

With his lips never leaving mine, one hand now on the nape of my neck, he pulled me in closer. His other hand unclipped my seat belt before undoing his own.

His large body shifted forwards and I could feel the heat of him. His scent filled my senses as his lips were hard on mine, his moan undoing me. He tasted sweet and I was starving.

I pulled myself even closer to him, I was halfway across the centre console but I didn't care I needed to feel his body against mine.

He lifted me up and in one easy movement I was on top of him, my legs straddled the sides of his body.

The centre of my legs pressed down and writhed against the hardness of him, as one large arm wrapped around my body, pushing me down, closer to him.

I was lost in the feel of him, his hands all over me as though he couldn't get enough and I wanted to devour him.

Outside it was dark and it was as though nothing existed except this moment.

His hand reached up to my hair and opened the clip, my curls tumbled out over him. His lips broke away from mine and for a moment, he just looked at me, his lips red and swollen and delicious.

I closed the space between us, I didn't want to be apart from him, my mouth belonged to his.

I searched his mouth, his tongue gently flicked against mine and I immediately felt warmth pool between my legs. With my eyes closed, I imagined the pressure I writhed against underneath me, was his mouth and a moan escaped my lips.

A deep, primal noise slipped from Aide's mouth as his entire body hardened and pulled me in harder so every part of me was pressed into him.

I wanted to rip my clothes off, I wanted to burn against him - *with him.*

A street lamp flickered outside, and I saw from the second of opening my eyes our living room light had been switched on.

I wanted to ignore it entirely - I wanted to stay here forever, but I forced my lips away from him, looked at my house and let out a large sigh.

My lips still tingled, begging to be reunited with Aides when I pulled myself from atop of him.

"Shit." I let out another breath and composed my clothing.

"Shit." He replied, his lustful eyes brighter.

CHAPTER SIXTEEN

Aide was all I could think about and with another decent night of sleep I felt a little more myself.

My phone practically begged me to text him good morning, but I fought against the urge and opened up social media to distract myself.

We were going out again in a couple days but it felt too far away, like I needed the distraction he brought, I was addicted to it.

As I clambered into my work t-shirt and a pair of tight denim jeans, I flicked on a little more makeup in hope that Aide might just nip into work today for a coffee.

Joey had agreed to keep the cafe open a little longer as me and Xander had convinced him that he was shutting too early and *losing business,* all so I could get a few extra hours in.

The weather wasn't too bad either, so to save on gas I decided to walk to and from work for the next few days, always passing through town and taunted by that stunning bracelet.

Aide was on my mind but I had decided that I didn't want to bring him up anymore around Xander, so when he asked what I got up to last night, instead of telling him about the amazing night I had, I lied - I said I did nothing.

Lying to Xander wasn't something I did often, in fact I couldn't remember the last time I actually lied to him.

Twisted the truth? *Maybe.*

Dodged the question? *Definitely.*

But lied to his face? *Never.*

When the morning rush had been satiated and I had a moment's break from banging coffee from the machine and tidying up the grease-covered plates, I headed over to the counter where Xander was standing waiting for the next customer.

The retro counter was cold as I leaned against it and caught Xanders eyes.

"We should do something tonight, just me and you." His eyes widened and a dimple formed as a smile curled his lips.

"We should." He stopped what he was doing, his attention drinking me in.

"I was thinking, could we go watch a film? Maybe I could be a better movie partner than your last?" I winked at him and pushed up my boobs underneath the ugly work t-shirt.

His eyes fell to my chest and even though they were covered in a cheap mustard yellow fabric, my breasts reacted to his gaze. I dropped my hands, ruffled my t-shirt and laughed it off.

"Well, I think anyone would be better than, what did you call her again?"

"I think her name was Holly - but I'm a fan of 'chick with the boobs' because that really was all she had going for her." I bitched, trying my hardest not to smile.

Xanders mouth dropped open and a smirk pulled at his cheeks.

"Ooo catty!" He laughed.

"Tell me I'm wrong?" I said, my eyebrows still raised and my arms open, palms up in a shrug.

"Well, I didn't notice the boobs." Xander blinked, as he held his hands up in surrender.

I hit him with the back of my hand across the counter.

"Yeah, of course you didn't!" He burst out laughing and the sound filled me with electricity.

"So what film do you fancy?" Xander asked, a moment after catching his breath.

"There's a new horror out, we could watch that?" My birthday was the week of halloween, so this time of year there was always a tonne of new horror releases.

"You don't like horrors?" Xander said, and whilst I don't particularly like scary movies, I really just wanted to spend some time with my best friend.

"Well, there's one that doesn't look too bad - plus you'll look after me." I nudged him again across the counter and he smiled.

"Sounds good to me," Xander replied, before a cough interrupted from behind us.

Dorris stood behind me, five foot tall and a cotton ball of hair on top of her head, with a disapproving brow raised and a leather like hand on her hip.

"Whenever you two are done flirting, I'd like another coffee." Her voice was serious but soft with old age.

My head turned quickly from her back to Xander to hide the smirk that threatened to burst open in a flood of laughter, as Xander pressed his lips together too.

"Sorry Doris, I'll get on it now," Xander said with a smile, as Doris just tutted to herself and turned back to the gang of gawking old crones in the corner.

As soon as she was out of earshot, the dam burst and I couldn't hold in the fit of laughter between the fingers that covered my mouth and Xander dipped below the counter out of sight to do the same.

We shut up an hour later than usual and it was steady enough that the day had flown by.

Xander pulled down the shutter on the cafe front, his broad back muscles flexed and his large arms made it look way easier than it actually was.

"So, I'll pick you up at about seven? There's a seven-thirty showing?" I asked, Xanders eyebrows raised in confusion, before smiling.

"I'll pick you up L."

"I don't mind driving Xan."

"And neither do I, I'll see you then. Oh, and let me know if you need me to pick you girls up anything on the way?" I smiled as he walked back towards where his black Clio was parked.

Aide hadn't come in for a coffee, and I hadn't heard from him all day but when I was with Xander I didn't think too much about it.

Now, walking home, just the thought of those intense grey eyes, and large tanned hands on my body had my breath shallow and a permanent smile plastered on my face.

As I reached home and unlocked the front door, I heard a huge crack as I opened it. My eyes shot to a large fissure that split the door from the frame and I immediately felt sick to my stomach.

There was so much that needed to be done in our home, so much I couldn't afford, whilst everything else was inside, it made it manageable. But a front door that didn't close properly was not an option.

I had been in such a good mood today, for a few hours I had even forgotten some of my worries, but this was like a bulldozer reminding me I'm moments away from falling apart.

Like another collision into the building that was my composure, my frail mother was asleep in my dad's armchair - a patchwork blanket covered her thin pale body and her face was dark and drained.

My lungs filled with a deep steadying breath.

The past few days she seemed to have looked a little better, but as I closed the door quietly behind me, trying not to worsen the widening crack, it became obvious she was doing worse, *far worse*.

I didn't think it was possible to see someone decline so rapidly from one day to the next, the colour of her life fading into a mix of dark blue bruises.

My stomach dropped and sickness hollowed it, as though I had been punched in my gut. I remember seeing my Dad this way.

My eyes watered, but I blinked the tears away. I told myself I needed to be strong, I needed to be strong for Kat. Because although Kat may have been the one taking care of mum all this time, I have felt the pain of this loss before, and it wasn't something you come out of unscathed.

I toed off my shoes and padded over to where my mother was curled up. Peeking from below the blanket was a photo, clutched in her thin hand.

My beautiful mother held one hand lovingly over her large belly bump and three smiles beamed towards the camera, happiness plastered on each of our faces.

*Are you ready Lana? One, two, three *click* Cheese!*

The moment's memory washed over me and my breath hitched as I stifled down the tears. Now pulling the blanket a little higher over my resting mother.

The soft sound of Kats voice told me she was on the phone to someone as I walked up the stairs towards her room.

I opened her door gently, and peered around the corner of it not wanting to interrupt.

Kat smiled and faced her phone towards me, a beautiful girl with raven hair and big brown eyes waved from the screen.

"Hey! You're home later than usual?" Kat said with Isha still on the line.

"Yeah well Joey needed me to stay longer this week, and you know how much he loves to threaten my job so I said I'd stay." I lied.

"Isha's coming over again tonight, if that's okay?" Her smile was as wide as her eyes.

"Of course, she's welcome anytime," I said a little louder so Isha could hear too. "I'm going to the cinema tonight if you guys will be okay?"

"We will be fine. So are you off again with the hot doctor?" I heard a giggle come from the phone.

"No, me and Xander are going to go watch that new scary film."

"But you hate horrors?" Kat looked at me, her face contorted in confusion and I sighed and rolled my eyes.

"I don't *hate* horrors, I just...I just want to go to the cinema and that's all that's on right now." I admit and Kats mouth tugs into a smile, her eyes a little too knowingly.

"Okay, well, have fun with Xan!" Her smirk deepens.

"I will! See you when I get home, and behave you two." I smirked back sarcastically and she just laughed in response.

Kat picked back up her conversation with Isha as I closed her door behind me and walked back across the landing to my room.

My hair was already up from work, but as I faced the mirror and pulled the hair tie from my curls, I remembered last night.

Aide unclipping my hair, the curls tumbling down over my skin that felt alive and completely on fire.

My eyes were closed, enjoying the memory of his hands on me and my body responded.

When my eyes opened and I looked back to my reflection, it was smiling back at me, a dark twisted smile with wild amber eyes staring into mine - a blink it was gone.

My body froze. I couldn't move, I didn't dare move.

My feet felt like lead and my body was fixed in place, fearful that if I moved the reflection wouldn't, and I'd be staring back at something that wasn't myself.

Kat burst through my door, and I jumped, my eyes not daring to look back towards the stranger in the mirror.

"That looks cute, but maybe you could try something a little-" She pulled out a low cut top from my wardrobe and walked over to me, the top now held over the thick jumper I had chosen earlier. "Sexier?" She smirked and my mouth fell open.

"I'm going out with Xander!" My eyes still wouldn't meet hers through the mirror, but I could tell she was still smiling.

"And who says you can't look less like a sack of potatoes, when you're out with your friend?" She made a good point, the jumper was comfy but far from flattering.

As quick as ripping off a band-aid, my eyes flicked up to my reflection, *nothing*. I took the green top from Kat, and placed it over my chest, she was right, *it did look better*.

"See! So much better." She beamed.

"Okay, I guess you're right, I'll go with that. But I'm still wearing a coat, it's freezing outside." I turned back to my closet and pulled out a long vintage leather coat that I had pulled from my mothers closet years ago when I couldn't afford a new one.

"You can, but you'll ruin it!" She tutted as she sauntered back to her own room and I looked back to the mirror, my head tilted and my eyes squinted. *Nothing.*

Xander texted me to let me know he was outside waiting. Isha and Kat pottered about the kitchen as I walked up to where my mum was now awake and watching TV.

"I'm going out with Xander, if you need me just get Kat to call, we can be back in minutes." I said as I placed a hand on her bony shoulder.

Contact with my mother still felt alien to me, and even a little awkward, but I was actively trying to fix the cracks that I had carved between us, one fracture at a time.

Daginas' hollow eyes smiled up at me, a smile slowly appeared on her face and looked like it exerted all her effort. Before her parted mouth could reply I leant forward and kissed her on the head.

"I love you mum." Her eyes welled up and it felt like some invisible boundary between us had begun to crumble, the weight of resentment now collapsing.

"I love you darling." Her voice was barely a breath. I pressed away the sob caught in my throat, and smiled down to her before I headed to the front door.

"Kat, if you need me, just call, and be careful with the front door, I will get someone to come fix it this weekend." Kat looked at me confused, but when I opened the door and pointed out the crack now splintering deeper into the wood, her face replied with a grimace.

The cinema was dead when me and Xander finally sat down, we might have been the only two people in there if another couple hadn't walked in at the start of the film and sat a few rows behind us.

Our local cinema wasn't exactly the high end scale ones like the ones in the city, but it had character. An art deco design and red curtains still hung to the sides of the screen, it was like stepping back into the twenties. Or at least how I imagined the twenties might look like after watching *The Great Gatsby*.

The screen room that smells like stale corn and tortilla chips was boiling hot, and I thought that it was a good job I had gone with Kat's choice of top instead of my own - as I might have just combusted.

Xander had bought popcorn from the kiosk for us to share, a mixture of salt and sweet, sweet for him, salted for me. My eyes tended to look more towards the popcorn than take notice of what was on screen, as I found it a fail-safe way of not jumping out of my skin every time something popped up on the big screen.

I noticed Xander kept checking on me, even though sitting down, my head only just reached his shoulders, I could still see the subtle shift of him, as his face peered towards mine.

My hand plunged into the popcorn and grabbed a handful, the only way to eat it was a fist at a time and I heard a breathy chuckle come from Xander.

I looked up to where he was smiling down at me.

"Not a fan of the film?" He whispered and his low voice sounded sexier than ever.

It took me a moment to think straight.

"The films, fine, the films okay yeah." I replied, my voice quiet and I tucked in a little lower in the seat, my legs pressed tighter together.

Xanders shifted closer down to me and I could feel his warm breath on my ear.

"So what just happened?" His quiet voice rumbled through me and I crossed my legs.

"You know, just blood, gore etc." I shook my head, his heat brushed against the curls that fell around my ear.

"Hmmm-" His response, a deep low vibration that called me closer to him. I schooled my face into a lazy smile and looked up, noticing he was closer than I expected.

"I mean they're all the same really aren't they?" I shrugged.

"Hmmm, maybe Holly wasn't that bad company after all." He smirked and I clipped his thigh with my hand, the hard contact made a slap sound louder than I'd anticipated and I flinched.

A loud 'shhhh' came from the couple a few rows back and my head dipped lower behind the seat, my face flushed as I looked back to Xander, one finger over his perfect lips and laughed.

Both now dipped lower and closer together in the seat, I rested against him, his skin warm through the navy sweater he was wearing.

A large muscular arm, lifted from underneath me, allowing me in closer as the arm rested over my shoulder, Xanders hand falling loosely over my chest.

I didn't care how hot it was in this room, I wasn't shifting an inch away from him.

My attention was now on the screen in front of me, and I watched with furrowed brows as a woman cut off her own hands and chanted something in a different language. *Bizarre.*

The woman's twisted face, manically began writing with the blood pouring from her hands still repeating the same unrecognisable words.

My brows furrowed, *what on earth had he brought me to watch?*

I looked up to Xander but he was gone, I was alone on the screen, no one around me, the screen silent save for the buzz of the film rolling on.

My arms reached for the seat below me, and I pushed myself up. Now stood I searched the dark room, which was near pitch black - *where had he gone?*

"This isn't funny Xan you know I don't like this." I rolled my eyes and walked to the aisleway, looking down through each row of the red velvet seats.

The light from the screen flickered, giving me a split second of sight between each flash.

"Xander, this is not funny." My tone was stern this time.

A hiss came from the screen behind me and as I looked towards it, I saw black smoke, billowing from beneath the screen.

The smoke was heavy and fell dense around my feet, which I could no longer see. The smell rising from it - *ash*.

The pit in my stomach hollowed out, and panic flashed across every nerve in my body, but I wouldn't still this time.

This time I would see, I wanted to see.

"What do you want!" I screamed, my voice trembled but I was determined. "Tell me what you want!" I looked around searching for the source of the mist. The smoke that was sentient, the air around me alive.

"What do you want!" I yelled so loudly my voice broke, and cracked.

The room was now completely packed with dense haze and I could feel the presence of the dark being between the shadows. Out of sight but my body recognised it.

I wanted to curl up, but I felt for the floor beneath my feet, grounding me where I was - *this was real.*

"She'sssss ready." A cold hiss whispered around the room and my head shot from one side to the other searching for its owner.

"She's not." A deep voice that reverberated against me replied harshly.

"Ready for what?" I screamed at the air around me. "Answer me!" My voice turned into a roar. The sound cut through the mist and it recoiled. My feet became visible again, and as I took a step closer to the darkness it retreated with every step.

"ANSWER ME! What do you want!" I didn't recognise my own voice, it was deep and darker - *ancient*.

Through the haze I saw two glowing silver eyes, flames of turquoise blue licked behind the iris.

"You." The primal voice replied, his voice cracked through the space between us sending the shadows towards me and I fell back.

My head hit the carpeted floor with a thud, and flung to face the aisle, where a low hiss sounded from the shadows.

Six blood-red eyes blinked in the darkness, slowly creeping closer towards me as a low rattling followed from their direction.

The hairs stood alert on my prickled skin. I couldn't see what the serpentine eyes belonged to, but I could see that they were close.

I shifted underneath myself, scooting myself back, but was not able to get to my feet quick enough. I tumbled backwards as I lost my footing, and rolled downwards towards the screen.

A large body stopped me, dripping in shadows, veiled by the mist that pulsated around him.

I looked up to see the two silver flaming eyes look down to where I was bunched up on the floor, my breath heavy.

The shadows began to move inwards, towards his body, as the skin beneath became visible now absorbing the darkness.

Each tendril that twisted around his torso left a mark on his skin, not a mark - they were tattoos.

I watched in both horror and fascination as the shadows one by one retreated into the man's large arms and chest, inking his skin with the intricate shapes of intertwining snakes, and letters.

My eyes drank in the sight with amazement as a man, with long silver hair, and tattooed skin, now held a hand down to me.

The haze still circled thick around us, but it was as though we were in an air lock, the air around us lighter, safer and I felt *calm*.

The large, tattooed hand reached out for me and I flinched back as I noticed the small flame that licked across his skin.

As though sensing my hesitation, the hand turned over slowly, the flame now larger and dancing in his palm.

His other hand passed over it and through the flame. It was almost hypnotic to look at.

I wasn't thinking straight. I reached for the hand and passed my palm through the flame. It tickled against my skin and felt warm, but it didn't burn.

It was comforting, not painful.

My head turned up towards the man, his eyes on fire with those same flames - his tanned face was still shrouded but from what I could see, it was angular with strong lines and full lips. He was beautiful.

I knew I had seen him before, maybe in my dreams and I no longer felt scared. The flaming hand grabbed a hold of mine and it was electric, my body felt alive in places I didn't know existed.

Part of me wanted to pull back but the other, dominant part of me wanted to get closer. His alluring energy had me like the storms have the seas, and the tide was coming in.

I could go wherever he was pulling me, I could forget about everything and just go with him. My mind was empty of worries and I searched for a reason but I found nothing but calm, peacefulness in its wake.

I could go with him and feel like this forever - powerless to the entrancing lure of him.

But I couldn't go, my sister would be alone. My mother. My mother was dying, and I couldn't leave my sister alone. I wouldn't leave my sister alone.

I snatched my hand back, immediately feeling the harsh cold air against it. My body feeling more like my own, I stumbled back, and managed to get to my feet.

One foot behind the other I backed away, passing row after row, stepping outside of the space between the haze and the smoke filled in around me.

My feet turned and I spun around, and ran towards the doors, the exit light a beacon in the darkness.

The doors burst open as I tumbled through them, but instead of falling into the lobby, I was back in the same screen, the film played and Xander turned to look at me from where he was sitting.

The couple from a few rows behind shot their disapproving faces over to me, a single finger over each mouth.

I looked down to the floor and back up around me in disbelief as I saw Xander now scoot across the chairs with his head dipped low as he walked over to me.

"Are you okay?" He whispered.

"What just happened? The last thing I remember, I was sitting with you watching a film and then-" I couldn't tell him.

"You said you needed the toilet L? You were only gone a second." His green eyes wide with concern.

"Not getting any sleep is really getting to me I guess." I lied to him again, twice in one day.

I was sure with every fibre of my being, that something was truly, medically wrong with me, but with everything going off right now with mum, it wasn't something I could handle knowing just yet.

I'm no doctor but I'd seen enough TV to know that having such visceral visions and hallucinations was never a good sign. Regardless of whether this was a mental or physical medical issue, it would have to wait, because I had no time to be ill with everything Kat was already going through.

The journey home was awkward and I didn't say much. My mind was too busy replaying the false memories and visions my sick mind had conjured up, and I couldn't help but think that illness probably ran in the family.

With my dad dying out of nowhere and now my mother, it made me feel sick to think I could be next. Not because I particularly cared about my own life, but because it would mean Kat being left completely alone.

She would have Xander I guess, and Isha, but she would need me. She would need her sister there when things are hard, when times are tough, when life hits her in the gut and offers no apologies. *She would need me.*

My skin shivered and I shook off the feeling of impending grief, letting it fall from me like a snake shedding its useless skin.

Feeling like this was useless, it wouldn't help, it wouldn't make me better so I pushed it away with the rest of my problems, and decided I would make an appointment at The Clinic next week.

When Xander dropped me off his face looked pained, and I felt bad, like I had ruined our night, and I had.

I wanted to ask him to come in, to share my bed with me and hold me all night, but I couldn't ask that from him so I just gave him a small smile and sighed.

"Sorry I freaked out on you and completely ruined our night."

"You didn't ruin our night L, but I do wish you would talk to me." He knew I was holding back but I just couldn't tell him. I couldn't be the person he felt sorry for, who he pitied.

"Honestly Xan, I just need some sleep. I'll be fine tomorrow." I nodded and his face forced a smile. He looked defeated.

"Why don't you let me sort cover for your shift tomorrow? You work yourself too hard L." His soft dark curls fell forward, over his kind eyes.

"I can't afford it Xan," I admitted, "After fixing the car this month it's totally screwed me." I hated the way the truth made me feel, but I couldn't lie to his face for a third time today.

His hand reached underneath my chin, and he looked deeply into my eyes. For a moment I was lost in the green and gold forest looking back at me.

"I'll take care of it, Joey never comes in on Fridays, so he won't even know." The kind smile on his face reminded me of when we were kids. "Because we both know Joey's way too cheap to actually have his CCTV recording when he's not there."

I laughed in response, knowing he was right - the only thing Joey had CCTV for was to see who he could potentially go and harass.

"Are you sure?" My face twisted.

"Of course, now go get some sleep." He leaned over and wrapped his arms around me, pulling me in closely.

A moment passed and I left his embrace before I stood on the curbside and watched him set back off, the autumn night pitch black around me.

The hairs on my neck stood up.

A shiver snaked its way across my spine as my focus was pulled to the dark space between the two houses across the road.

My teeth gritted, as a pair of red eyes blinked back at me, followed by four more.

J L Robinson

CHAPTER SEVENTEEN

The last time I took a day off from work, I was violently ill from the leftovers I'd reheated the night before, and ended up losing almost a stone in weight.

Today, having learnt now to never microwave rice again, I hadn't missed a day's work in over a year. So when my alarm went off at seven-am and I switched it off, pulled the sheets over my head and fell back asleep, it felt strange.

Even though I had slept almost ten hours, I still woke up feeling unrested. But deciding against staying in bed all day half-asleep, half-awake, I rolled out from under the soft quilt, opened my curtains and padded to the bathroom.

The bath tap gurgled as it trudged up the water from the house's aching pipes, finally spitting out lukewarm water.

The goldilocks zone of bath water had always eluded me, but we didn't exactly have money to waste, so I quickly ran it through to a warm enough temperature and filled the tub halfway before sinking into it.

With my favourite book beside me, I took in a large breath and dipped lower into the water, my head leaned back into the warm comforting suds that surrounded me.

With wet curls, I rested my head against the back of the bath and tried to ignore the crumbling tiles around me. I closed my eyes and imagined I was in some luxury bath in a high end hotel somewhere.

The kind of freestanding bath made completely of carved rock - or crystal even. The opulent smell of spiced soap and velvety bubbles tickling against my skin.

I smiled to myself before opening my eyes, still ignoring the disarray around me and opened my book. My wet fingers dampened the pages and caused them to ripple, but I didn't mind as I liked it when my books looked worn and loved.

I escaped into the story for at least an hour as the bath water turned cold around me. Before eventually draining the murky water, getting dressed and heading back downstairs.

The kitchen was tidy, and from the three plates still sitting on the draining board, I figured Isha must have stayed for tea last night.

I flicked the kettle on, before heading over the sofa where my mother rested her eyes. The patch work blanket placed across her, had fallen slightly off the sofa, so I scooped it up the soft fabric, and laid it back across her small body.

"Sorry mum, I didn't mean to wake you," I said softly as she stirred.

She opened her mouth to reply, but the words were nothing but a rattling breath. Dagina leaned toward her tank, the clear mask sitting on top of it.

Before she could strain herself any further, I pulled up the tank closer, lifted the mask to her face and carefully pulled the elastic over her head that held it in place.

After a few large inhales, Dagina's thin, blotted hand pulled the clear mask down and she coughed, clearing her throat of the thick phlegm I could hear in every breath.

"Don't worry darling, I was just about to get up and make a cup of tea." She shifted slowly onto her side, each bony arm trembled as she hoisted herself up.

"I've just put the kettle on. I'll sort it." I strode back over to the kitchen where it had just finished boiling. "Do you want anything to eat? Maybe some toast?"

When I couldn't make out her quiet response, I walked back over to the sofa and my mother shook her head with a smile that I could barely see through the clear mask.

"It's nice to see you having a morning off, you always work so hard." I heard my mother say, as I began pouring hot water into two mugs.

My back stiffened as an instinctual bite in the back of my throat wanted to say something, but I was done with the shaming. And whilst I wasn't completely over what happened to me as a child, I wasn't going to punish her anymore.

"Xander's covering for me, I just needed a real day off." I admitted, immediately felt a guilty for complaining to a woman who was literally dying.

"He's a good man," Dagina said between coughs.

"He is." I agreed as I drained out the teabags and leant down to the fridge for the milk.

Remembering that my mother had always liked one sugar in her tea, I dunked the spoon into the jar filled with the sweet sand, and stirred it into a large mug.

Dagina was now fully sat up on the sofa and had made room for me to sit next to her. A small hand tapped the empty leather seat and I placed the cups on the small coffee table before sitting down next to her.

She had switched on the TV to an old episode of *Will & Grace* that now played quietly in the background.

"How are you?" She asked as I took a sip from my tea and I almost choked on it.

I often wondered how my life might have been different if I had had a relationship like this with my mother growing up. How I might have been different.

"I'm okay, but how are you?" I turned the focus back to her because if anyone wasn't going to be alright it was going to be her.

She looked at herself, lifted her arms in a shrug and smiled.

"Well, I've been better, but somehow I feel I've been worse too." Her eyes creased with the smile that reached them. "So I'm okay darling."

She leant over slowly to the table and reached for the large mug of tea. I wanted to help, but she managed to lift it to her lips.

"But are you sure you're okay? You look-" Dagina paused as she ran her tired gaze over my own, "shattered," she finished.

"I'm fine honestly, I just think I need a good few nights of sleep." I smiled and took another sip of tea.

"You're not sleeping properly?" Daginas face dropped all expression and her eyes darkened.

"I've just had a few nights of broken sleep, just bad dreams I guess." My shoulders shrugged, but my mother's eyes still looked at me with concern.

"What kind of dreams are you having Lana?" She asked, her tone sharp, the clearest I've heard in a long time.

"Just weird dreams, honestly they make no sense to me but they seem to have stopped now, so it was probably just something I'd been eating." My eyes squinted in an effort to smile, as I attempted to reassure her. I couldn't help but notice the feeling of her concern, still felt strange to me.

"Who is in your dreams Lana? What do you see?" She croaked, her eyes still narrowed.

This was the most me and my mother had spoken, one on one, in over five years and suddenly I began to feel uneasy. The way she was looking at me, it was as though she was waiting for something she already knew the answer to.

An unsettling shiver snaked down my spine as I looked back into her eyes, those amber eyes. Her hair was identical to mine, just thinner and wiry with age, but I remembered the photograph, her hair was exactly like mine, *exactly* like my grandmothers.

Her head tilted, and her amber eyes looked straight through me, as though she searched for something on the other side.

My skin pebbled with goosebumps as I recalled the woman I saw in the dream, the woman I *thought* was me.

Her olive skin, her nose dusted with freckles, her hair tamed but still the same as mine and her eyes, her golden, amber eyes.

"I dreamed of...you." The words came out before I could stop them and my mothers breath hitched.

There was a knock at the door which disrupted my train of thought, pulling me back into the moment.

My mothers eyes had softened into a confused gaze as she shook her head and looked at the empty space around her wrist.

"What time is it?" She sounded confused. It was the first time I had noticed her go somewhere else in her mind, lost for a moment.

"It's eleven mum," I said as I walked over to the door and slowly opened it, careful of the fracture.

Two women dressed in blue scrubs stood outside the door, both holding a small bag. One was older than the other and they had quite clearly been here before, as she shouted through the doorway.

"Morning Dagina!" I moved to the side, as they strolled in and over to my mother. "Morning dear, you must be Lana." I smiled as I allowed the strangers to pass me.

"We're the community nurses in charge of your mothers palliative care," the younger one said and although I had already worked it out, it felt as though a thousand trains had just collided into me.

Palliative care. *End of life care.*

"Is there anything you need me to do?" I asked when I finally caught my breath.

"No dear, we have it covered from here." The older woman, small and round with a kind face, smiled sweetly at me before she knelt down in front of my mother.

I needed to get out of here, I needed fresh air.

The cold autumn wind swept across me the minute I walked out of the front door, and the icey bite of it against my skin was a well-needed reminder that this was real. *I was here.*

So many things had happened over the past few days that had my mind flipping in somersaults. I was completely overwhelmed with stress and feeling totally burnt out.

Exhausted and confused, I just walked and walked and walked.

I had no idea where I was going. I just kept going, one foot in front of the other the wind brushed against my bare arms.

The patter of rain sounded in front of me, and I wished for a second that I could drown in it.

My thoughts and imagination were running me ragged and I just wanted to feel something real.

I heard the rain before I felt it, droplets transformed into a downpour and before I knew it, I was standing in the centre of a storm. A storm that raged in my mind, pulling me apart and leaving me raw.

I wanted to scream into the storm and claw at every inch my own traitorous body that housed me, and prevented me from seeing the terrifying truth around me.

My eyes clamped shut and I just stood there. My face turned up towards the dark sky and the rain pelted against my face.

A trace of a warm, woody scent brushed against my senses. A spice filled mist, now soothed the internal hurricane that threatened to rip me apart from the inside out.

I drew in a large breath, the spicy aroma filled my body and I could almost taste it.

Another breath.

The ground beneath my feet felt hard.

My arms slackened, cold and wet.

With my eyes still shut, I took in another breath.

Warmth gathered against my pebbled skin, and I saw the sky brighten above me through my closed lids.

Another breath.

I opened my eyes, I was standing in the middle of the road, soaking wet. The sky had cleared, except for a few lingering, grey clouds that parted and drifted away into the horizon.

"Lana? What are you doing?" I turned towards the pathway, where both Kat and Isha were standing, with their brows raised. "Why are you wet?" Kat continued, and I looked down to where her gaze had fallen.

My top was soaked. Luckily it was an old, black, *Good Charlotte* band tee that hadn't turned completely see through in the rain.

"Mum's nurses came and I wanted to get out of the way. I just needed some fresh air."

"Lana, the nurses visit at eleven. It's three o'clock, how long have you been out here for?" She walked over to me and took off her grey school blazer that used to be mine and wrapped it around me.

My head shook, I must have looked as confused as I felt.

"Come on, let's go home." Kat smiled sweetly, her arm now wrapped around my waist.

When we arrived home, I was still shivering from the cold so I headed upstairs and stipped off the soaking clothes before putting on a warm pink fluffy dressing gown.

My phone was still sitting on my bedside table where I had left it this morning, and I hadn't even noticed I'd gone all day without it.

There was a text from Xander from hours ago.

Xander: Hope you're enjoying the day off and enjoying those books of yours ● *I've just picked something up for you I know you're going to love.*

The idea of any fuss being made for my birthday made me cringe, but there was no denying I was turning twenty-one tomorrow and, like it or not, this year I was going to celebrate with Xander and Kat before going out with Aide - or I'd risk being disowned as a best friend and a sister.

I opened up the message box and began typing a response.

Lana: Oh you have?

Xander: I have and I don't want to hear any complaints either.

He knew me so well.

Lana: ●●●
How was it today?

Xander: Steady, we barely even missed you.

Lana: Yeah right.

Xander: I think Doris was happy to have me all to herself in all honesty.

Lana: Oh, now that I can believe!

Xander: What are you up to tonight?

Lana: Honestly, I was just planning on reading and maybe watching a little TV with Kat and Mum, wbu?

Xander: You and your filthy books.
But an evening in sounds great. We're not opening until 10 tomorrow, so I'll be round for about 8 for your birthday breakfast!

Lana: ●

Xander: Good girl.

The corners of my mouth curled as my body flushed, heat now pooled in my stomach and I wondered for a moment, if Xander knew exactly what he was doing when he said that.

A ping came through on my notifications and I clicked on the message that dropped down.

Aide: I'm so looking forward to seeing you tomorrow.

The heat that had filled my stomach now burned, and my smirk grew even wider.

Lana: I can't wait.

The memory of Aide's taste was something I never wanted to forget. The seductive, yet sedative power he held against me, was completely addictive.

I thought of his hands wrapped around me, and the way he was able to lift me as though I was the weight and size of a feather.

I thought of the way I could open up to him and know he would absorb it all. Pulling at each of my stresses and worries so he could digest it himself, and let me be free of them for that moment.

Guilt poured over me and extinguished my burning desire when the honest, but frank truth hit me.

Aide was the only person I was ever truly myself with.

He was the only person I could open up to and willingly did so. He made me feel on fire, like I was the only thing that mattered and he was always there.

Xanders emerald eyes flashed in my mind - an internal contradiction arguing that he was the only man I could ever feel this way about.

There was absolutely no doubt in my mind I was in love with Xander, that I had been able to admit that to myself for a while now. But there was also no denying that he deserved better than me. He deserved someone who could open up to him, who wanted to.

Maybe we were like the old saying, 'two ships passing in the night'. And instead of heading for a collision, I avoided disaster by steering clear.

I stopped my thoughts before they spiralled further into self pity, catching them before they threatened to submerge me deeper into a stormy sea.

Instead, my thoughts drifted back to the blonde hair, grey eyed, insanely handsome doctor, and instantly my mind settled like a still lake.

CHAPTER EIGHTEEN

I was awoken to the sound of a blaring noise bellowed from outside of my quilt, and for a moment I didn't know where I was.

The bedding was snatched from me, and two faces beamed down at me. Between the two huge smiles were brightly coloured party blowers, each unravelling to release a loud horn.

My eyes flinched as I adjusted to the light and shuffled up in bed.

Xander leaned forward and before I knew it, he had wrapped elastic under my chin and placed something that felt a little too much like a party hat on my head.

"HAPPY BIRTHDAY!" They screeched in unison between blows on the horns, and I didnt know whether to duck for cover under the safety of my quilt, or snatch the horns right from their mouths.

I took in a large breath and smiled back up to the clowns now performing in front of me, both wearing their own party hats, they looked ridiculous.

"Come on we have a surprise," Kat said as she pulled my arm out from under the quilt, and my cheeks heated as I remembered I was only in the robe I'd fallen asleep in.

She didn't let go of my hand as she dragged me out of my room.

"Close your eyes," she said, with an obvious smile in her voice.

My eyes rolled underneath my lids, and I let out a little laugh at how silly this all felt.

Xander walked down the stairs with my hand held in his, as Kat steadied me from behind, each of her hands placed on my shoulders.

I felt for the last step as Xander reached the bottom before me.

"Don't open them yet." Kat giggled beside me, as both her and Xander let go of me.

"SURPRISE!" Three voices shouted, one softer and a lot quieter but just as enthusiastic.

I opened my eyes, lifting weary lids one at a time and my throat swelled as my eyes fell upon a memory I hadn't allowed myself to indulge in for a long time.

The whole living room had been draped in sheets, each hanging from the curtains, the drawers and the sofa.

Everywhere I looked had its own little marquee with fairy lights glowing from inside them.

Tears filled my eyes and it wasn't the reaction I expected myself to have today. I choked back a sob as two slim arms crashed around me.

"Happy Birthday Elly." Kat said, with her head resting on my chest for a moment. "Do you like it?" Her ocean eyes sparkled.

Not entirely sure my mouth would work properly, I swallowed down the sob and nodded with a shaking smile.

Two more arms, tanned and a lot larger, wrapped around us, and Xander planted a kiss on my head.

"Happy Birthday L." He smiled, and pulled something out from his back pocket. "You promised no complaints, so here. It's only something small so don't get your hopes up." Xander handed me a small, square box wrapped in brown paper and tied with a string bow.

My mother struggled to her feet, as we walked into the living room and shuffled towards me with her arms outstretched.

"Happy Birthday darling." Her arms could barely lift, and although it still felt strange, I embraced her.

"Thank you mum." I was surprised by how good it felt to be in her arms as I looked over her shoulder and noticed what was underneath the sheets that draped over the dining table.

"That's probably a safety hazard you know." I joked as I eyed up the croissants and pain-au-chocolats stacked up beneath it, with a single candle lit on top of the golden stack. "But seeing as it's my birthday-" The phrase felt alien in my mouth, "I get first dibs."

My feet shot over to the dining table and I ducked beneath the sheet, the small space now filled with the delicious smell of warm butter.

"Who wants a cup of tea?" I heard Xander ask, and I mumbled a yes through a mouthful of pain-au-chocolat.

After I piled a few extra pastries onto a plate, I walked back from under the makeshift tent and over to the larger one now draped across the sofa.

"Here," I offered my mother one of the golden brown pastries.

"I'm okay darling, you enjoy them." Her voice was quiet as she leaned back into the leather and Xander wandered in with Kat, two cups in each of their hands.

"Here we go," Xander said as he placed one of the mugs down in front of me and handed my mother the other.

"Thank you Xander."

"Anytime D, I put you in that extra bit of sugar I know you like." He replied and a small smirk reached her eyes.

"So, I was thinking-"Kat started as she lifted the old filing box that had our childhood photos in it and pulled out a video tape. "That we could watch some of these."

I took a sip from my mug and looked back to my sweet sister.

"That sounds like the perfect idea."

Kat and I huddled up on the sofa with mum, whilst Xander popped aVHS into the player and sat back down on the comfy green armchair.

The TV buzzed for a moment and grey and white noise freckled the screen before an image of my dad popped up. He was looking directly into the camera.

"Happy birthday Elly." His voice was as soft as silk, his proud eyes glittered at the camera. "Today you're six years old." He continued as he panned the camera over to a small girl with dark, curly hair sitting on the floor beneath a fortress of sheets, now playing with a doll.

"That means I'm a big girl now, daddy." The voice, my voice cuts me. Slicing through to my wounded inner child.

"You are a big girl darling," my dad's kind voice continued. "And now you have to be an extra big Elly." The camera pans again, this time turning to my mother, she looks in her early thirties and she's holding a newborn baby. She looks beautiful.

"I will be the biggest Elly. I promise daddy." My young voice spoke from behind the camera.

I remember this day, I remember toddling downstairs and catching my father hanging sheets where they hung now.

I remember screaming with excitement and diving into the comfy fortresses.

I remember the giggles escaping my little face, as my dad threw me over his shoulder and we raced around.

My eyes glossed and with a single blink I felt the track of tears that ran down my face.

The tape scratched and suddenly I was eight years old, a small honey blonde toddler with huge blue eyes sitting on my lap, cheeks puffed up and blowing out my candles as I watched and laughed.

I looked over to Kat who was leaning against mum, they both laughed at my raised brows.

Another flicker of grey and white across the screen.

My mother chased me and Kat wildly around a park, we both darted in different directions and screamed with laughter and my mum shouted after us.

"I'm going to get you!" I heard my dad laugh from behind the camera.

We sat for another hour watching the scenes from our life flick across the TV, memories filled with joy and I closed the space between Kat and I.

At some point my mother had fallen asleep, her hand rested on Kat's head and as I looked at my phone and realised it was almost nine.

I nodded to Xander and he followed me out of the living room, collecting each empty mug on the way out.

"I better get ready for work," I said reluctantly when really all I wanted was to stay here and do this with them all day.

He was wearing the same grey hoodie from yesterday, and as he lifted the sleeve to look at his watch, I couldn't help but think of how amazing it must smell.

"Shit, yes. I didn't notice the time! Are you going to open your present?" His mouth tugged into a smile as I fished the small box from my fluffy pocket.

The wrapping was simple but perfect, and I tore open the paper to find a small navy square jewellery box inside it.

I looked up to Xander whose green eyes sparkled. *There was no way.*

As I opened the box my mouth dropped in disbelief. Layed on top a black velvet cushion, was a simple, silver cuff with a gorgeous iridescent opal in its centre.

"Xander this is too much." My eyes flick from the bracelet to him and back again.

"Do you like it?" He asked, but from the smile plastered across his face, I figured my reaction was confirmation enough.

"Like it Xander? I love it! It's...it's beautiful." Never had I been given something so stunning, and the fact that there was no way he could have known I had been eyeing it up, made it all the more special.

"Almost as beautiful as you. Happy birthday Lana." My eyes filled with tears of pure joy as I flung my arms around his waist.

His arms tightened around me, pulling me in closer and I breathed him in as though I couldn't get close enough.

His jumper smelt like him, that perfect fresh, earthy scent, and I wanted to bury my face in it.

"So, I'll see you at work?" His hands now rested on my shoulders as I looked up to him.

"Right!" I said before giving him one last squeeze.

The front door groaned loud enough for me to hear as Xander left, and I still hadn't stopped smiling. The dressing gown I was wearing was now splayed out on my bedroom floor, and I danced around my room butt naked, wearing only the bracelet, fishing out my work uniform.

The mustard t-shirt didn't look quite as ugly today as I tucked it into a fitted pair of beige jeans.

With *Taylor Swift* now playing in the background, I finished off getting ready, applying a little mascara and lip gloss to the sound of *Midnight Rain.*

On my drive to Joeys, I plugged her new album into the car's aux - turning the volume up, with the windows wound down all the way down.

The fresh, autumn morning breeze wound around the hand that I snaked through the wind and I sang loudly along to the music. I felt on top of the world.

The gorgeous cuff adorned the wrist I used to jovially swing open Joey's front door and slid my eyes over to Xanders beautiful face flashing me a wide smile at me from behind the counter.

"Morning Doris!" I said an octave higher than usual, her tut at me being five minutes late, washed over me - today was going to be a great day.

My phone pinged intermittently throughout the day, old school friends and other people I haven't spoken a word to in years, wishing me a happy twenty-first.

As I scrolled down through the list of notifications, I saw the one person I was looking for. Doctor Flames.

Aide: Happy Birthday Lana ♥

My stomach was full of a thousand butterflies and I couldn't help the smirk that now graced my face.

I typed out a simple response - a single red heart and hit send.

"So did you like your surprise?" Xander asked as he wandered over to where I was standing behind the counter, with a smile in his eyes.

"It was perfect Xan." I played with the bracelet on my wrist. "How did you know about everything? The sheets, the bracelet?"

"Well your mum told me about how your dad would create a kingdom of fortresses in your living room and Kat had mentioned you always did it for her growing up so we thought you'd like it." He shrugged shyly with a smile.

"And this?" I looked down to the silver opal cuff.

"Well, I know you're not a jewellery kind of girl, but there was something about it." He closed the space between us and wrapped his hand around my wrist, "it's imperfectly perfect I guess and it reminded me of you."

"Xander Flynne, are you calling me imperfectly perfect?" My brows raised and I pretended that I didn't know whether to be flattered or offended.

"Perfection wouldn't come close enough to describe what I think of you Lana." His mouth curled into a smile that reached those beautiful, kind, green eyes and my breath caught at the back of my throat.

My heart was brimming and I felt so full of love. The warmth that filled my soul was like fire, welding together the iron cracks in my foundation, making me whole again.

My face felt rosy but I didn't want to brush it off, I wanted Xander to see how he made me feel and I wanted him to know I felt the same.

"Why don't you meet us out tonight? We could go for drinks together?" I leaned back against the counter.

"You want me to third wheel your date?" His brows pinched.

"I want you to come out for my birthday." My voice slowed and a pitch higher.

"But I thought you didn't like a fuss being made for you." Xander leaned forward, a hand rested on each side of the counter which I was leant against boxing, me in.

"Well I want the fuss, give me all the fuss you've got." He was inches away from me.

"And what will Aide think about that?" His head tilted and a single brow raised. *God he was stunning.*

"He's a nice guy Xan, and you two will get on!" Giving him my best attempt at Kats puppy dog eyes. "So you'll come?"

"If that's what you want, then I'm there." He said with a small sigh, followed quickly by a smile that cracked his fake, stern demeanour.

It took everything in me not to giggle and clap my hands like an absolute weirdo but it felt good, being chosen like this, being prioritised.

The day flew by, and the cafe had cleared out early enough for us to start the cleanup sooner than we should.

A smile had been tattooed on my face the entire day, and even as I took the grease covered plates and lipstick stained mugs into the back, there was a pep in my step.

My phone pinged loudly just as I was about to dunk the crumb-covered plates into the warm water. I pulled off the gloves I now wore for protection against any sneaky ceramic shards, and looked at my notifications.

Aide: Are you still good for six birthday girl?

Lana: I'm still good if you are!

Aide: Can't wait.

My mouth bit down a giggle and even I wanted to cringe at myself today. I was a kid in a candy shop, greedily eating up all the affection being served as though I had been starved of it for years.

Once I had finished the pots and cleaned the tables off, I walked over to where Xander was cashing up the till.

"So I'll see you about eight?" He looked up to where I stood opposite him across the counter.

"Mmm hmm," he mumbled as his lips pinched down on a wad of notes.

"You know you really shouldn't do that," I said as I eyed up the way his perfect lips pressed against the money between them. "Money is filthy." My brows raised as I saw a flicker of challenge in his eyes.

One hand freed the cash from his mouth, which now pulled upwards to one side, a dimple appeared and his eyes narrowed.

"I'm sure there's far filthier things that could occupy my mouth." His smile widened, and I was left stunned as he placed the notes between his lips again.

"Right well,I better-" My throat constricted and I stuttered.

"Get to your date," Xander finished for me. "I've got this, I'll see you later." His eyes large and innocent but that small dimple betrayed his attempt to act cool.

With my body still tense, I pulled off my apron and brushed off the invisible crumbs from my trousers.

"Yep, see you later!" I tried to sound as though he hadn't just completely rattled every lewd bone in my body.

CHAPTER NINETEEN

When I arrived home, the sheets were still strung up around the living room and Dagina was fast asleep on the sofa.

A small smile pulled at my mouth as the memory of the morning flushed my body with overwhelming love all over again.

Still feeling overjoyed from the perfect day I had had so far, I raced up the stairs as quietly as I could, up to my bedroom.

As I opened the door, there was a large, black box wrapped in a beautiful, silver bow, sitting on the edge of my bed.

I perched down on the edge of the bed beside it and lifted the box onto my legs.

Whatever was inside it felt pretty heavy, and as I searched the ribbon for a note or tag, I noticed there was nothing to give away who this gift was from.

As I pulled the silky bow from its knot and lifted the lid, the faint but familiar smell of spice and wood warmed my core. Laid on top of something wrapped in black tissue was a handwritten note.

Happy Birthday Lana. Here's a little something I thought you would like. Can't wait to see you. Aide

As though crazed, I tore the black tissue paper apart and beneath it, I saw the shine of dark purple silk, sparkle back at me.

The fabric was the softest thing I have ever felt, it was like silk but thinner and somehow it felt fluid.

I lifted the two straps up and out from the box, and before me, was the most beautiful dress I had ever seen.

It was simple, two delicate straps with gold spiral cuffs. The fine, aubergine fabric, gathered into a cowl neck before flowing down, straight to the floor in front of me.

The fabric glinted in the light, reflections of iridescent hues - purple, cobalt and silver shone back at me.

Practically tearing my clothes off, I raced to my mirror and held the dress up in front of me.

I felt a prickle at the backs of my eyes, and I pressed my mouth shut to stop the sob that was ready to spill from me.

I lifted the dress over my head and the fabric fell like a waterfall over me, effortlessly gliding over the curves of my body and down to just above the floor.

My eyes trailed my reflection, sliding up every inch of my body that the dress fell perfectly from.

The purple silk was fitted on around my chest, the draping offering just the smallest amount of lift to my breasts, the silk fitted to my stomach and hips, where it loosened slightly and fell to my ankles. A single slit carved up one leg, the open seam, appearing and disappearing within the fabric as it moved.

My hands adjusted the straps a little lower down my shoulders, and my fingers traced over the delicate gold spiral cuffs around the base of them.

With my hair still tied up and away from my face I turned to look at the back. Every inch of the dress fit my body perfectly, every curve and dip tailored too.

With one hand I pulled at the hair tie that confined my curls and with a small tug, my hair cascaded down and around me.

I had never felt so beautiful in my entire life.

My hands glided over the fabric, so light it felt as though I was touching my own skin. It was perfect.

My amber eyes caught my own in the reflection, they were glossed over as tears waited on the edge of my lash line. My reflection smiled and I felt the pull on my mouth.

As I blinked, a single tear of pure happiness ran down my face and fell to the floor.

Realising I still needed to shower, I slipped off the dress and laid it across my bed, stealing one more look at it, I skipped to the bathroom and turned the shower on.

There was a new bottle full of my favourite scented honey almond shower gel on the corner of the bath, I popped the lid open as I got into the steamy shower.

I glugged a generous amount of the golden soap into my hands and massaged the suds the whole way down my body. The foam swept across my stomach and around my breasts, my hands ran across each peak and perfectly-imperfect divot.

My skin felt smooth and taut as I ran a razor blade across my legs and underneath my arms.

My lungs filled with the luxurious scent that I had taken on as my own, before I rinsed the velvety suds off my skin.

For once, there would be absolutely no question as to what I was going to wear. There would be no sifting through my closet, no flipping through the clothing piles dotted dishevily around my room because there was only one option, and it was currently lying across my bed.

I blow dried my hair and added a little almond oil to the lengths to define my curls, as I decided to go with a half up half down look. I knew Aide liked it loose.

I took one more look in the mirror before I packed a small bag with lipgloss and my ID.

The door creaked from downstairs and I heard two giggling voices quietly chatting in the room beneath me.

As I walked down the stairs, each step was a groan that sounded my descent and Kat and Isha stood completely still at the foot of them, their mouths open as they looked me up and down.

It was silent as I made my way awkwardly down the staircase, and I couldn't help but break the stillness with a laugh as the two gawked at me - at the dress.

"Holy shit, Elly," Kat said, her mouth still wide open as she nudged Isha and she shook herself.

"You look-" Isha started but she shook her head again, her large brown eyes grew even wider.

"You look like an absolute goddess!" Kat finished for her, and I laughed again as I stepped off the last stair, and walked through them to the kitchen.

"Thank you, it was a gift from Aide." I said as I pulled a glass from the cupboard and filled it to the top with water.

"You look...I can't even deal with you right now, I have to borrow it." Kat said, her wide eyes still roaming every inch of the plum coloured dress.

I downed the glass of lukewarm water and smirked, my eyebrows raised in response as I finished the glass.

"What time is it?" I asked Kat who had just grabbed her phone out of the pocket in her straight leg jeans. But before answering me, she held her phone up to me, and with a sudden bright flash, my eyes now squinted, she took a photo.

"It's six, say cheese!" Followed by another flash.

"Right, I need to go, what are you doing for tea?" I asked as I walked over to the door, which was still broken, and toed on some small gold heels I had not worn in years.

"Isha's brought us food her mums cooked, do you want us to save you some?" Isha lifted a plastic bag full to the brim with plastic containers full of food.

"No I'm good, I'm going for Sushi remember." And with my hands, I gestured to the dress I was wearing. "We're going for drinks after, oh and Xander is going to meet us so don't stay up I might be late."

Kats face curled into that wry smile she loved to tease me with.

"Xanders going too? Like the three of you?" Her eyes widened.

"Not like that! He's meeting us after our date for drinks. Right I'm going!" I hadn't had a text from Aide, but I knew he was already waiting outside for me.

Leaning against his car in the same spot as usual, Aide stood up. He was wearing a black t-shirt that moulded perfectly to his large form, with a simple silver chain necklace that hung over it. The top was paired with loose fitting black trousers belted, low on his hips.

As graceful as physically possible in these heels, I walked over to where he now waited, his grey eyes seemed to sparkle and they were completely locked on me.

The dress moved as though it was part of me, each step it formed and reformed around each leg, fluid and non restrictive.

Aide's eyes dropped to my feet and lazily roamed up across my body and to my face, his lips parted.

It was as though he couldn't form words as I closed the space between us, and his eyes devoured every inch of me.

Before I could say anything, one large arm wrapped around my waist and pulled me flush, into his warm, hard body. The other hand curved around the nape of my neck and tugged my face towards his.

Aide's lips met mine with fire and passion and I melted into him. The muscled arm around my waist supported me upright, as his mouth roamed mine.

A whimper escaped me as my lips opened further for his, and he kissed me deeper, harder.

It was electric. My body formed to his, I needed to be close to him, I wanted every inch of my body touching his.

Heat filled every single cell I owned, setting my body ablaze under his touch as he pulled me in tighter.

"I want you." The words came out as a breath, between our hot mouths. "I want you Aide."

His arm loosened around me as he pulled back to look at me through narrowed eyes.

"You...you want me?" His voice wavered and I didn't know if I had upset him or he was still slightly breathless.

My hand lifted and raked it through his silky hair. Feeling their way through to the back of his neck. I tugged him closer, down to me and he obliged, his mouth parted and I placed my lips, throbbing, on the edge of his.

"I want you." I breathed and Aide's mouth crashed into mine, his arms wrapped around me and pulled me off the ground.

I wrapped my legs around his waist, with the dress falling around me and he turned with me in his arms. Pressing me against the car, my legs fell open around him as his body pushed hard against mine.

My hands gripped the back of his neck tightly, forcing him deeper into my mouth and my tongue slid against his, yearning for his taste.

His arms lifted me an inch higher as he tucked his hips under me, and I felt the hardness of him pressing through his trousers.

I would have let him take me right here, against the cold metal, and I wouldn't have cared. My body craved his own and I was famished.

But slowly, as Aide drew back, his deep kisses turned softer, small affectionate pecks on my mouth. He let me fall back slowly to my feet, each inch of me slid against his on my way back onto the ground.

He leant down towards me, and his lips dotted kisses on my face, down to my neck, where he slowly kissed the sensitive spot before he pulled himself away.

His lower lip was pulled under his teeth in a moment of restraint, and I realised we were still in front of my house.

A burst of laughter sprung from me and Aide's brows furrowed, before his own laughter followed. We were like teenagers, we were acting completely ridiculously, and I was entirely enchanted by him.

Aide's hand reached behind me and pulled the door handle.

"Come on, in a dress like that, it would be rude to keep you to myself." He opened the door, and I smiled as I slid into the passenger seat.

Aide closed my door slowly but firmly, before he made his way around the car and sat beside me.

My lips still tingled from the touch of his mouth, and the taste of him lingered on my tongue as we set off in the dark.

Aide's breathing was heavy but controlled, and I noticed him readjust himself as he lifted slightly out of his seat.

I thought of him hard against me, even through this dress, and I went to cross my legs, but his large hand reached over to my knee and he pulled it back down.

"If I wasn't clear enough, you look absolutely delicious."

"Well this dress was too beautiful not to wear. Thank you, by the way." I said as I looked down to where the dress clung perfectly to the outline of my legs.

"The dress wouldn't be half as beautiful without you being the one wearing it." He replied, and my face flushed with heat, but I didn't shy away from his compliment, instead I lifted my chin and took it all in.

Aide made me feel like I was the most beautiful thing ever to exist, and it filled me with a secure confidence I had always faked before.

Whenever I was around him I felt unbounded, completely free of my usual stress and anxiety. Walls that had taken years to construct, simply not needed, becoming brittle dust under his soothing touch.

Aide pulled up outside the doors of Barracuda, left the keys in the ignition, and hopped out of the car. He took a ticket from a small man who looked as though he wasn't old enough to drive, as he opened my door with his large hand outstretched to help me out.

As I lifted myself out of the car, my hand in Aides and my back ramrod straight, I felt like a movie star - everyone was staring at me.

Couples entering the restaurant stopped dead in their tracks, both looking me over from my head to my toes. A few smokers stood outside the restaurant, totally still as though time had stopped with ash falling from their cigarettes.

I looked to Aide who had closed the door behind me and had wrapped his arm around my waist, my arm looped into his.

We walked towards the door and I followed Aide's pace, slow and confident. Everyone's eyes were still completely fixed on us. No *on me.*

"It isn't the dress." Aide said as though he could read exactly what was on my mind. "It's you." Aide smiled down to me, as his arm that was wrapped around me, tugged me in closer.

The scent of fresh cucumber and dark soy sauce tantalised my senses as Aide pushed through the golden, honeycomb patterned doors and walked into the restaurant. The atmosphere was calm, but the dim lighting that glinted off the navy and gold interior, exuded elegance and sensuality.

Waiters dressed immaculately in freshly pressed white shirts, black tailored trousers and a black waist apron, passing us politely with plates of sashimi and nigiri rolls. I almost felt embarrassed that the closest I had come to this kind of sushi, was a packet of California Rolls from a supermarket meal deal. But when I was with Aide, it wasn't possible for me to feel anything but utter content.

As we walked up to a short man behind a mahogany desk wearing the same outfit as the waiters, only replacing the apron for a dark silk suit jacket, Aide dropped his hand down to mine, intertwining our fingers.

"Hi, we have a reservation under the name Vasiliás?" Aide towered above most people in the restaurant but he never acted arrogantly, he was always so kind and polite. He squeezed my hand a little tighter and heat flushed to where our skin met.

"Right this way Mr Vasiliás, Mrs Vasiliás," the host said, and I looked to Aide with my eyes wide trying my best not to crack into laughter.

The smartly dressed man led us to a round table large enough for four people in an area of the restaurant that seemed reserved for private, more intimate dinners. I pretended not to notice the eyes of other restaurant goers travelling the length of me, as Aide pulled out a chair and I sat down.

Aide sat himself down across the table and he immediately felt too far away, I wanted to crawl across the table and sit in his lap and I wasn't ashamed of it either.

Sitting up, Aide pulled the large mahogany chair around the table, lifting it as though it was the weight of a feather and sat down next to me. His hand landed hot on my thigh as he reached for the navy leather-bound menu laid on the table.

"So, what does my birthday girl want?" Aide asked, and my stomach clenched. *My* birthday girl. I grinned up at him as I scanned the open menu.

"I would be lying if I said I knew what any of this was." My smile turned to a small giggle as I looked around to other people's tables. "But those look amazing!" I was pointing to a couples table who had a small wooden board lined with a row of red sushi.

293

Aide's eyes tracked to where I was now eyeing up someone else's food, and he looked back down to me with a feline smirk that pulled one side of his mouth.

"How about I just order a mixture of things, then you can try whatever you like?" He said with a small squeeze on my leg, and those feline eyes dripped in self-confidence.

"That sounds perfect."

For a moment he just looked over me, his grey eyes slowly tracing the shape of my mouth before wandering back up to my eyes. His look was the tinder sparking against my skin, ready to ignite my desires - and I was willing to burn.

The waiter circled back around to us, and Aide ordered a bottle of wine named Koshu, before reeling off a bunch of different types of sushi plates.

"You know your stuff it seems," I said as my eyes flicked from his to the menu now leaving in the hands of the waiter.

Aide lowered himself in his chair, his hips shifted underneath him as he inched closer to me, and a low laugh purred from him. "Well let's see if you like it first." His slight smile turned devilish and I thought for one moment, I'm pretty sure that I'd love anything that this man wanted to put in my mouth.

His hand didn't leave my lap as the wine was brought out, taking a taste and confirming his approval with a nod before handing a glass to me.

"What do you think?" He asked, and I took a small sip, my eyes low over the rim of the glass.

"It's sharp, in a good way, like lemons." I said as I took another sip and nodded to the waiter who began to pour out another glass.

Aide's eyes never left me as I thanked the waiter, and reached for the other full glass, handing it to Aide. As I sat back in my chair, his head had dipped and his lower lip pulled beneath his teeth as he looked over the dress dripping across my body.

"Don't look at me like that," I said, my voice low, sensual and his eyes shot up to mine. "Unless you're going to do something about it." I finished and his face practically twisted into a smirk, his eyes narrowed and full of fire.

His chest expanded with a large breath, and I could see every contour of his muscles, held captive beneath his tight, black t-shirt.

His mouth parted and I wanted to taste him again. I was desperate to. I leaned forward, my hand reached over to his thigh and I closed the little space between us.

His eyes had softened and he looked at me through lowered lids, his mouth was still parted. I could practically sense his arousal.

"Ah ah ah." Aide tutted as I inched closer to his perfect mouth, "Lana, I have exercised every inch of control I have I can offer no more." His voice vibrated, each word a restrained carnality.

I leaned in closer, so only he could hear, my breath warm against his, and whispered. "I don't want control, I want chaos."

The voice didn't even sound like my own but I knew one thing, I didn't want him to hold back in the slightest. The moments in which he let go, was the time I felt most alive.

It was as though any self containing leash had snapped, and his mouth was on mine before I could take in another breath.

Nothing mattered - no one mattered. *No one but him.*

He kissed me deeply, each stroke of his lips firm against mine. His large hand roamed up my thigh, closer to where I ached for his touch and through the thin material I could feel the heat of him.

I shifted lower in my seat, forcing his hand closer between my legs and he groaned softly into my mouth. We were sitting close together, so no one could have seen his hand glide higher, but I don't think I would have stopped him even if we had an audience - I was lost in him.

My head pressed forward, hardening the kiss, and his free hand grabbed underneath my hair to the back of my neck, and I opened my mouth for him to go deeper.

His fingers were inches away from the heat that now pooled between my legs, and I shifted even closer to him, the tips of his fingers grazed against my centre through my dress, and I thought I might explode then and there.

I moaned softly into his kiss, a gentle plea that told him I needed him and he responded.

The inside of his fingers brushed against my centre, the fabric accommodating each finger now pressed hard between my legs. My face felt as though it was bright red and I bit my lip trying not to moan, as he rubbed against me in slow, hard circles.

His grey eyes narrowed, now drunk with desire and I saw him survey our surroundings through the small slits in his eyes, before pressing his fingers harder against me.

My hips writhed under his touch, and my breath was short and fast between our mouths as he muffled my moans with his lips. The pressure of him against me was delicious, and addictive, I wanted more and more as I pressed harder into where his fingers were circling against me.

Freeing one hand, I lifted the dress up, just enough that he was able to slide his hand underneath the slit discreetly, and I opened my legs for him.

I needed more, I was starving for his skin on mine. His eyes shot to where I had opened my legs, and another groan escaped him as his mouth still worked with mine.

The moment his hand touched my bare thigh I basically trembled beneath him, his hot skin glided up the inside of my thigh, and reached my soaked lace underwear.

We didn't need words, we understood each other on a purely animalistic level and he knew exactly what I wanted.

Using a finger to hook around my underwear, he slipped them to the side before using a thumb to press hard against my centre. My head tilted back in pleasure, I wanted to scream with utter bliss and red hot, burning desire now coursing through my veins.

My legs opened up another inch, practically begging him for more and as his warm mouth reached the sensitive area on my neck, he pushed his middle finger inside me.

Every muscle tensed around him and I had to bite down another moan as he pulled his finger out slowly, before pushing it back in. His thumb was still circling the outside as he pulled out, and pushed another finger in, my walls tightened around him and he growled pleasingly against my ear.

My face flushed with heat as my hips matched every one of his strokes inside of me, greedily moving faster.

Through lowered lashes, I caught him watching me whilst my hips rode his hand and he dragged his lower lip between his teeth.

My entire body felt alight and my breath was short as I rocked into him, his lowered eyes wandered every inch of my body.

My body ignited around him and as he clamped one hand softly over my mouth, I rode out each pulsing wave of ecstasy that washed over my body like an unruly ocean.

My moans turned into a whimper as he slowly pulled his fingers away from me and softened his hand around my mouth, gently wiping a thumb over my lips.

His face was dreamy and his lashes were low. He looked extranced by me and I felt as though we existed on another plane of reality, like we were literally in a world of our own.

That world soon came crashing down to an awkward reality when the waiter arrived, his face red, with two long wooden boards piled with rows of different styles of sushi.

My mouth curled and I wanted to laugh. Pleasure still coursed through my body as Aide sat up, his hand rested on my thigh and cooly nodded to the waiter.

"Thank you." He said as the man dressed in black and white placed the food down onto the table and practically ran off.

Aide looked at me, that perfect mouth curled into a smile. "Tuck in."

CHAPTER TWENTY

Everything Aide ordered was delicious, he knew exactly what I would like. Either that or maybe everything tasted good when your body was coming down from the best orgasm you've ever had in your life.

I ate until I couldn't possibly pass another spicy tuna roll through my lips, and Aide ordered us another bottle of wine to share.

"So did I do good?" His sparkling eyes focused on my lips as I took a sip from my glass of wine.

"You did perfect." I said as I leant forward and gently planted a kiss on his lips, feeling him smile beneath them.

"Would you like to stay here for a drink, or would you like to go somewhere else? I have a few bars in mind if you do." Aide straightened up and took another sip of wine.

"Well, I kind of asked Xander to meet us out for a drink? Would that be okay with you?" I asked tensely, hoping that Aide wouldn't feel like his company wasn't enough.

"Of course that's okay, what's a birthday without your best friend?" He finished off the wine in his glass and placed it down on the table before signalling to the waiter for the cheque.

I didn't realise I was holding my breath until he smiled reassuringly, and I felt relieved that any worry I might have had, wasn't necessary.

He smiled at me and placed that perfect hand on my knee again as I reached for my bag and pulled out my phone. I had kept it on silent and I didn't realise three hours had passed, without me even checking it.

There were three missed calls from Xander, and a string of unread text messages.

Xander: We still meeting for 8?

I'm at Barracuda but they won't let me inside without a reservation.

Missed call

If you come to the door they should let me in L.

Missed call

Missed call

I'm assuming you're face first in food and not just ignoring me so I'll meet you at champs?

Missed call
I'll see you there L

"Shit!" I said out loud as Aide placed his card on the bill that had been set down by the waiter.

"What is it?" He replied, his brows pinched.

"I told Xander to meet us at eight, but they wouldn't let him in. He's gone to the bar across the street."

"Do you want to call him?" Aide asked as the waiter approached the table with a card reader.

"It's only around the corner, I'll text him to let him know we'll not be long if that's okay?" I began typing out a text.

"Of course," he replied as he keyed in his details and slipped the waiter a fifty pound note.

My stomach dropped at the thought of Xander standing waiting outside, because I had basically forgotten

303

about him and I would definitely have to make it up to him later.

Aide's hand squeezed my thigh and instantly the pit in my stomach was filled with warmth.

"Are you ready?" He asked.

I grabbed my bag and placed my phone back inside it.

"Yep. Let's go!" He smiled, before standing to pull out my chair for me.

It was raining outside when we left the restaurant, but Champs was only a few minutes down the road. Figuring it was not worth the drive, Aide ran to his car and came back with a black blazer that he lifted over my head, to protect me from the rain.

With one of his large arms around my waist, he bundled under the jacket with me, and even though I was wearing four-inch heels, he still needed to dip down to my height.

We walked quickly across the road, the rain beaten off the black tarmac now splashed beneath our feet, and it felt like a romantic scene from one of the books that I liked to read. The comparison made me giggle and Aide looked down to me, his bright eyes pinched with a smile.

As we crossed onto the other side of the road, the hem of my dress was now slightly wet and we scurried into the bar with black doors.

Champs was the exact opposite kind of place to Barracuda - it was a sports bar, full of casually dressed middle aged men and students, so when everyone turned to look at me and Aide as we barged through the doors, it wasn't a surprise.

As my eyes scanned the room of jeans, hoodies and over washed t-shirts, I glanced over to the bar that stretched the length of the long room, and saw Xander perched on a stool, with a glass of amber liquid in his hand.

Aide shook off the black blazer, and droplets of rain fell from it as he threw it over his large forearm before placing his hand low on my back. We walked into the bar and I headed straight for Xander with Aide trailing after me.

"I'll get us a drink," Aide said as he looked for a spot between the bodies standing along the barside. "This end seems less busy - you go say Hi to Xander." He smiled and nodded in the direction to where Xander sat, and hadn't noticed us arriving.

"I'll just have a beer please." I smiled and walked over to Xander who was draining the last drop of his whiskey.

"Since when have you been a whisky drinker?" I said as I walked up to him and nudged him with my elbow.

He jumped and almost fell off the bar stool, before quickly putting down both hands to steady himself. As he looked at me I noticed his eyes tracked slowly, his gaze seemed distant. *How many has he had?*

Xanders green eyes lazily trailed the length of my body, his mouth fell open as he lingered for a moment on my hips, and I wrapped my arms around myself, feeling shy under his gaze.

"Hey, eyes up here you! I'm sorry we're late." I smiled down at him and he stood up clumsily from the stool.

"I need to talk to you." His hazy eyes darkened, as he stood slightly over me, his chiselled features, tense. "I need to tell you something." He drawled and grabbed both of my shoulders. Something in my stomach dropped.

"Hey Xander, sorry I kept her for so long." Aide cut through the awkward tension, carrying three bottles of beer, he passed me one and went to hand Xander another, who was still holding my shoulders, swaying.

"I need to talk to you now." Xander slurred, ignoring Aide. He was clearly drunk, but his eyes looked dark with worry.

"What's wrong? You're scaring me a little Xan." His expression pinched further.

306

"Xander?" The low voice spoke, deep from behind me and Aide placed a reassuring hand around my waist, Xanders eyes followed the movement.

Xander grabbed my hand, and pulled me towards him, away from Aide. The shock of his strength made my stumble, and I heard a low carnal noise spill from the man behind me.

I steadied myself and turned around to Aide, who was staring directly into Xanders eyes, his jaw clenched and his mouth slightly pinched.

The atmosphere rippled with tension, as I stood between the two large males.

"Hey!" I said sharply, looking at Xander who was still staring at Aide. "What's going on?" Xanders green eyes flicked to me and I tilted my head, my brows raised.

I had never seen Xander that way. I knew he was drunk, but I could feel the anger radiating from him. Xander was the one person I knew better than anyone, and at this moment, I didn't recognise him.

"Will you give me a minute?" I said softly to Aide as I smiled up at him, trying to loosen the tension that reverberated between them.

Aide's eyes still sharply focused on Xander, now dropped to where he was still clutching my hand and I noticed him bite down something, before he looked back at me.

As his gaze met mine I saw the tension he held, now soften a little, as he forced his lips into a smile.

"Of course, I'll just be over here if you need me." He said as his head dipped to me and his bright eyes soothed the pit in my stomach.

I turned to Xander and gently placed a hand over where his own was still clung to mine. "What's going on? What happened?" My voice broke as I now expected the worst, my emotional walls stacking brick by brick in preparation.

"He's not who you think he is." Xander said as he jutted his chin to where Aide stood a few metres away, his large build towered over the other men standing around the bar. "My mum has no idea who he is." Xander finished and looked back at me.

Joanne Flynne had worked at the clinic for as long as I had known Xander, and she had always made a point of knowing people's business, especially when they worked at the same place.

"He's probably just really private. Plus, he's not exactly the type to sit and have a coffee and gossip with the ladies in reception." I laughed but Xanders face stayed dead serious.

"She hasn't heard of him, because he doesn't work there. He's lying to you Lana." Xanders brows raised, and it was a plea for me to believe him, but it didn't feel true.

"What do you really know about him Lana?" Xander probed, his speech still slurring and my stomach opened up, nausea now creeping in.

"Why would he lie to me?" I asked him as well as myself, as I thought back to all the times I had been with him. I liked to think I had a pretty good judgement of people and I've never felt anything but pure, good intentions whenever I was with him.

I peered over my shoulder and as though he knew we were talking about him, he turned to me, and I forced a smile as his face sweetly smiled back.

"There must be some kind of confusion Xan."

Xander shook his head in frustration and let out a heavy sigh.

"He's not who he says he is, Lana. Why don't you believe me." I felt sick, his expression was the picture of devastation, but my body couldn't accept what he was saying. I knew Aide, he was a good man, he has been nothing but sweet and kind to me, and always there.

Always there. A shiver danced across my skin as I recalled all the times Aide had simply showed up, or happened to be in the same place I was and my breath paused for a moment.

What if what Xander was saying was true? What if Aide didn't work at The Clinic, and if he'd been lying to me about this, *what else was he lying about?* My skin froze over as goosebumps pebbled my arms.

A heated hand curled around my back, and I turned to see Aide standing behind me, staring down at Xander. My stomach twisted.

How is it possible to be so sure of someone, so happy with someone, and it not be real.

I turned to Aide and shifted away from his entracing touch, I wanted to see his face.

"Do you work at The Clinic, yes or no?" I said sharper than I intended, but my mind was whirling with worry and confusion.

The look in Aide's eyes told me everything - *he was lying.*

"Let me expl-" Aide started, but I stepped back and shook my head in disbelief.

"I told he was a fucking liar." Xander spat as he pulled me towards him. "Who are you? No ones even heard of you." I looked to Aide whose composure, for the first time, seemed to crack.

His grey eyes darkened, and his top lip twitched upwards. His broad shoulders seemed to widen as he stood up straight, towering above both of us and I noticed Xander stumble backwards.

Xander pulled my hand again in retreat, as though Aide might just combust then and there - I could feel the energy shift in the room as a familiar darkness brushed against my mind.

I felt vulnerable and it wasn't an emotion I handled well. Xander, was someone I knew that was undeniably a good person, with the best intentions, and he stood in front of me pleading with me that there was something not right about the man that I felt so connected to just moments before.

My mind told me to trust the man I had known forever, after all, he had only ever had my back and shown me love like no one else. But I knew my body, and I couldn't deny how I felt for Aide - he was intimately familiar and if I was honest, I felt most alive when I was with him.

A deep fracture split open inside me and as I looked between the two men, time seemed to still. My mind was spinning out of control and I needed to walk away - I needed some air before I became totally consumed.

My phone buzzed from inside my bag and the vibration pulled me back into the present, giving me a green light to remove and collect myself.

I fished out my phone and saw it was Kat who was calling. Sliding the button across, my stomach fell through the floor as I heard an uncontrollable wail, echoing down the phone.

"You have to come home Lana, it's mum." Her sweet voice was broken.

The world closed in around me, darkness glazing over my vision, as I dropped to the floor and sunk into a pit of unmanageable pain.

A deep voice called to me, like a beacon - a splinter of golden light pulling me from the darkest depth of my mind and I swam towards it.

Lana, come to me.

I raced towards the familiar voice, brightness splintering through the darkness.

There's no time left.

Another voice, a females voice.

You must come back.

Lana come to me.

The deep voice pulled me closer, heaving me towards the light.

"Lana, Lana?!" I opened my eyes and I was on the floor in Xanders arms, Aide was sitting in front of me and my phone was discarded beside us.

Everyone around us was watching, I must have fallen to the floor.

"I need to go home. Now." My voice, nothing but a breath, and my eyes felt damp.

"I'll take you." Aide said kindly, but as he moved towards me I scrambled away from him.

"I need to go with Xander." I said, my eyes full with tears, as I curled towards my best friend.

"I will take you both. Xander is in no state to drive." Aide said and I looked up to Xander whose eyes were furrowed in worry, but still hazy from the whiskey, and he nodded reluctantly at Aide.

Both men helped pull me from the floor as my body felt weak. My feet fumbled beneath me as we left the bar, one arm flung around each of the men, we stepped out into the lashing rain and headed to the car quickly.

The sound of Kats sobbing echoed through my mind and gutted my stomach from the inside out. I wanted to throw up - I just needed to get to her.

Aide raced towards the valet and quickly came back with his keys, unlocking the Mercedes before swinging open the passenger side door, where Xander helped me in.

My body didn't feel like my own, it was as though I was stuck in some middle space, between reality and the version of a world that threatened to rip me apart. My thoughts scrambled to the darkest places as Aide pulled over my seatbelt and shot off down the road.

The rain was heavy but Aide didn't falter. He drove with perfect precision and before I could fully come around, we were pulling up outside.

Before the car had even come to a full stop I had already unclipped the seatbelt and began to open the door.

"Thank you."

"Do you want me to come with you?" Aide replied, his eyes furrowed, he looked sad but I had no time. I needed to get to my sister. I looked to the man who had lied to me, and then to Xander who was sitting in the back seat.

Trustworthy, reliable Xander. The kindest man I have ever known, and the one man I know loves me as much as I love him.

"I'm sorry Aide. I just need to be with Xander and my family right now." I leapt out of the car, and as I shut the door behind me, Xander was immediately beside me.

With my breath still caught in my lungs, and nausea still snaking around in my stomach, Xander and I rushed towards the fractured front door of my home.

As soon as we opened the door, the fracture split wide open. A loud crack followed by a crash sounded, as the door fell completely off its frame. Dismissing the noise, I ran towards where Kat was sitting sobbing on the floor with my mothers hand in hers, her beautiful eyes swollen with sadness.

A large man that I recognised, with black hair speckled with grey and wearing a white coat, was kneeling with a hand on Kat's shoulder and to her other side Isha was sitting with Kats other hand in hers.

Kat looked up to where I bounded towards her, my knees dropped to the ground where she knelt and I forced myself to look towards the sofa.

Kat's arms wrapped around me, her small body shaking with each sob and as my eyes slowly looked up at the hand she was holding, down the pale arm, I saw my mother, drained and colourless.

Her slow breath rattled into the clear mask across her hollow face and her eyes looked lost, as though part of her had already gone.

The sand had fallen through the hourglass and her time was up.

My throat filled and burned, but I needed to be strong, I couldn't fall apart now, not when Kat needs me the most.

My hand reached for my mothers, her skin felt waxy and cold and my stomach twisted.

She coughed, the sound of blood filled her failing lungs as her eyes blinked slowly, dipping in and out of consciousness.

"She doesn't have much time." The doctor said, and I caught a glimpse at his name tag, Shivay Ashah - Isha's father now stood beside us, his voice calm and collected. "The nurses have done everything they can to make her comfortable, but I would prepare yourselves now."

Kats breath hitched, before a loud bawl escaped her and I pulled her close into my body. My shaking hand stroked gently through her hair as I steadied my breathing and stopped myself from completely collapsing alongside her.

"We were cooking tea, and she fell, and Isha called her dad because we didn't know what to do." Katerina stuttered between sobs.

"Shhh, you did the right thing," I said as my hands continued to stroke her hair, my eyes on my mothers chest, barely lifting. "You always do."

My mother coughed again, the blood from her lung blotted against the clear oxygen mask, and my entire body cringed at the pain she must be suffering.

"I have given her something for the pain, she should be as comfortable as she can be." Shivays calm voice said from behind me, and I bit down my sob and nodded. *It was time.*

Years wasted, every memory tarnished, every effort pummelled by my own bitterness and now it was too late.

Too late to create new memories, too late to make up for all the times I had missed out on, too late to have a mother.

But I had always had a mother. She may not have been perfect, but she was mine.

My eyes burned as another rattle came from her chest and she coughed up more blood, her dark eyes slowly opened and focused on us.

A shaking hand, frail and blue, lifted towards her face and pulled down the mask, just far enough that her mouth was free.

"My darling girls," My mum's voice grated against her throat, and Kat took in a sharp breath. "I'm afraid that it is my time to leave." Her voice cracked with each word as she drew in a large inhale.

I wanted to stop her, I didn't want her to say it, I didn't want her to be in pain.

Kats hand gripped our mothers harder.

"I am so sorry that I must go, but I am so proud of you-" A blood filled cough filled her throat and stopped her mid sentence. "And I love you, both of you, with everything I have."

"Mum please stay." Kat pleaded as her head fell into her hands and my heart shattered.

"It's okay Katerina, it's okay." I looked towards my mothers amber eyes, our eyes.

"It's okay." I pressed a smile to my mother as Kat inched closer and rested her head on our mothers shoulder. I smiled even though I wanted to fall apart. If

317

this was the last moment I would ever have with my mother, I would make sure it was one filled with nothing but pure, vulnerable, honest love.

My eyes burned but I swallowed down the tears.

"I'm so sorry for the burden I have passed to you, my dear Lana. I am no better than my own mother but I hope you can forgive me." My mothers eyes welled up and a tear tracked down her pale speckled face.

It didn't matter, I would make things work, I always had. I could pick up more hours, find another job, I could make it work for me and Kat.

"We will be okay mum, it is okay." I reassured her as her eyes heavied, her lids fighting to stay open.

"I know you love him." Her voice was now a whisper. "And for that I am so sorry."

My mind scrambled to make sense, sorry for what?

"In my bedside cabinet, I have left something for you-" Cough. "It explains everything." Another cough and I could hear the thick, claret liquid pooling at the back of her mouth.

"Mum, please rest. Please. It's okay." My eyes filled with tears of acid that burned and begged to be released. My mouth pressed together tightly and my jaw clamped down. I would not cry, I would smile. I would smile for her, and for Kat.

My brows pinched over my solemn eyes, and I nestled closer into Kat who was still weeping, but had calmed slightly, with my mothers frail hand stroking the top of her head.

I placed my head in the small space next to Kat, careful not to add pressure to my mothers body, which was fading fast with each breath.

"It's okay." I whispered to both of them, the heat from our bodies wrapped around each other, and as I thought back to when we would all curl up together on the sofa, on this sofa, I let my tears fall.

They came like a quiet ocean, gentle but free flowing across the planes of my face and I smiled, embracing each one of them.

We laid there with her, and I didn't know how much time had passed as both Kat and I held each other warm in my mothers last embrace.

The rattle that ricocheted from within her body, began to quieten and her chest now slowed, each breath becoming shorter as her lungs could take in no more.

A faint breath drifted from my mothers body, a final goodbye in the wind and I felt the entire world around me darken, the air violently punched out of my lungs.

Everything was black and I existed in a space in between. I was familiar with this space now - it was the far recesses of my mind that I reached to when I wasn't able to cope.

I felt something crawl against my skin, a soft brush against my mind before it fell through my body dissolving into me. The taste of iron burned in my throat and my dry eyes stung.

The atmosphere was pitch black so I didn't know my eyes were still open until I clamped them shut. A familiar smell of spice and ash tickled my nose as I swallowed down the sharp metallic taste.

Waves of emotion pulsed through me, a lifetime of love and hate and sadness. Each swell was a reminder of both my brittleness and my endurance but I let them wash over me. Caressing and embracing each sentiment instead of retreating deeper into the dark fissures of my mind.

With each slow determined breath I clawed at control, I was a phoenix rising from the ashes of my own despair, I felt strong.

CHAPTER TWENTY ONE

A week had passed since the night my mother died, the night I thought I might shatter into a thousand shards of ice and disintegrate along with her. The same night where my kind-hearted, selfless sister fell apart and wept in my arms for hours as the ambulance took away my mothers lifeless body.

The funeral was eight days away, and I would be the one making sure things run smoothly so Kat could grieve, we had always processed emotions differently and this had completely crushed her.

She didn't leave the house for the first few days, and I couldn't get her to eat - if it wasn't for Isha I think she would still be sitting on the floor of my mothers room sobbing into the carpets.

I don't want to say I was coping fine, because in truth, I wasn't. But there were so many things that needed sorting, and I was the only person to do it, so it was a welcomed distraction.

The day after my mum died I received a phone call from a company named EF Insurance. Apparently, according to the insurance advisor, my mum had a long standing policy with the company, that stated in the event of her death the mortgage would be paid off in full and a sum of one-hundred thousand pounds would be paid out to her two surviving daughters.

I had never heard of the company, or even known my mum had sorted anything like that out, but the call left me feeling a thousand tonne lighter after years of financial stress falling on my shoulders.

Drawer by drawer I uncovered the past, letters, photos, niknaks I haven't seen in years - but I needed to sort through my mothers stuff so I was able to contact the companies she had bank accounts with, or anyone else who may have needed to know of her passing.

My mother had no family left, and no friends to inform of the date of her service. It would be a small service but it didn't matter, I would make it perfect for her.

When I reached the drawers upstairs, I sifted through them top to bottom, each one filled with colourful clothing and weirdly wonderful accessories to match.

A smile tugged at my mouth as my hands pulled out a denim dungarees, unfolding it to reveal years of paint splatters and smudges where my mother had wiped her hands no doubt.

I pressed the denim into my chest and smiled as my eyes welled.

"What you doing?" I toddled into the garage, the bare brick walls lined with rows of brightly painted canvas. I looked up to my mother who was like a giant covered in denim dungarees and watched as she closed one eye and held the paintbrush in front of the piece she was working on. Turning it back and forth before dipping it into a pot of thick yellow paint and streaking it across the centre.

I stood on my tiptoes to try to get a better look at what she was painting this time and held onto the fold out table with a rainbow of paint pots beside me.

My mother looked down at where I stood, three foot tall, beside her.

"What do you see my darling?"

I raised a little higher onto my toes and stretched my tiny body to peak upwards at the easel.

"Sunshine." I smiled, "It looks like sunshine."

My mothers smile reached her eyes as she dunked the fraying paintbrush into another pot and swilled it round. The sweet scent filled my little nose.

"How about now?" She said as she flicked forward the paintbrush, and multi colored specks dotted across the canvas.

As she pulled the paintbrush back, the remaining paint sprayed across my face and I took in a large breath as my face twisted into a smile.

My mothers hand shot up to her gasping face, not realising her own hand was covered in its own layer of thick purple paint.

A fit of laughter burst from me as I looked up to my mum, her face now smeared in purple paint, my own now freckled with a candy store of colours. She pulled her hand away and turned it over to reveal the paint now spread across her face, her shock turned to a wry grin.

Laughter bellowed from my mum's mouth as she wiped her hands on the denim, scooped me up and tossed me over her shoulder, covering us both in the goopy stuff.

A single tear fell from my eye and cooled the place it tracked along, as it fell to the dungarees still held tightly against my chest.

Warmth swept across me as I folded it back up and placed it back in the drawer.

The top was slightly jammed and needed a forceful tug to free it, as I managed to open it I stumbled and almost fell back.

There was a small letter, placed on the top of a pile of random things you'd find in a drawer that has it all, with my name handwritten across the front.

In my bedside cabinet, I have left something for you. It explains everything.

The memory of my mothers final words hit me like a hurricane and filled me with guilt. *How could I forget this?*

My hand tingled as I reached for the envelope, but what my hand pulled out from the draw, was not a piece of paper, but the small linen bag beside it.

The bag was heavy and something *clinked* inside it. I looked at the letter still sitting in the drawer, and then back to the small bag that my hands didn't seem to want to part with.

Whatever was inside it felt *weird*. As though I could feel a pull from beneath the fabric and whatever was hidden recognised me.

My hand warmed as the bag became heavier, and the sound of metal inside was almost seductive. Each clink, a seductive purr that begged me to expose it.

I needed to open it, I needed to see what called me.

A shiver both hot and cold danced across my skin as I pulled the drawstring and tipped the bag upside down into my burning palm.

A dark gold chain fell into my palm, and a thrum so quiet, it was barely audible, sang from it. I rubbed a finger through the chain and the noise became louder, each note reverberated against my pebbled skin.

With another swipe over the gold, I exposed a pendant, the thrumming stopped and time stood still.

I looked down to the dark tarnished medallion, with its simple redstone in its centre. *My mothers necklace.*

The unopened letter caught my eye, and I managed to resist the strange pull that the necklace had on my attention for a moment long enough to pick it up.

The envelope was sealed, a simple black wax seal glued it shut and I broke it open.

Anxiety filled me, freezing me in a bath of ice as I prepared myself to process whatever words couldn't be said in person. A moment passed as I just looked at the broken seal, the handwriting through the folded paper now becoming slightly visible.

With a deep breath I pulled the letter out, and unfolded the paper.

My darling Lana,

For what I am about to tell you I hope that you can forgive me and I know in saying this I am asking for something in which I myself could never give.

There is a story in our family, one that has plagued the defixio women for as long as time and it is rooted in greed and self pity that even I myself succumbed too.

Before my mother died she told me a story of her mother, and her grandmother before her, but it was no fairy tale

- it was a story of tragedy and greed that would soon tarnish everything I had loved.

A long time ago, a woman of our family name made a very stupid decision, a decision that we all still pay for.

She fell in love with a man who could not reciprocate the way she felt, and so, she began to meddle with dark magic. Desperately trying to make him return her love, she unwittingly summoned a dark entity, a malevolent and mischievous being of fire and ash.

He granted her her wish, and provided her with the right blood invocation that would make the man she desired fall entirely in love with her.

But what she didn't know was that dark entity, that demon, wanted her for himself. And so he granted her wish, but entwined his own terms into the curse she desired.

A year had passed and they were madly in love, she had even fallen pregnant and they had welcomed their first child.

Her life was everything she wished for, until the man she loved more than anything in her life fell terribly ill, his body rotted from the inside out with an illness that he had shown no signs of.

Only days later, he was dead. A shell of himself in her lap.

As you know, grief is an ugly monster that can eat away and break apart the strongest of souls, and so she couldn't cope.

In the dead of night, whilst her daughter slept, she ran to the field in which she had summoned the demon the year prior.

But this is where her story ends, her body was found with both forearms sliced open, and although we assumed she thought she would join her love in the afterlife, she had already sold her soul to the lord of the underworld.

Before my mother died and your father became ill, she told me of the curse that has tormented our family ever since that dark day, an ancient hex that states a Defixio woman may never love without tragic loss and my dear Lana, this is where it will fall to you.

The first daughter of the Defixio women must carry the weight of our ancestors' sin, and when I die the curse will pass to you.

I am so sorry I couldn't give you more time. I'm sorry I couldn't give you a small part of life, before bearing this terrible burden.

I was not the mother you and Katerina deserved, and for that I will be forever ashamed. Even as my body deteriorates, too weak and too cowardly to break your heart and let you down once again, I know that you need to know the truth.

I have left you my necklace, it has been passed down from each in our line, and it is said to promise the wearer protection so please wear it, wear it every day.

A lifetime in hell wouldn't be punishment enough for what I have put you through my darling girl, but this is something you can only face without me, and my time is almost up.

I love you Elly.

I stared at the piece of paper I held in my hand and for the first time ever, I felt nothing.

J L Robinson

CHAPTER TWENTY TWO

After spending an entire day going through files and hoards of paperwork, I was relieved when Xander had text to say that he was coming over to cook tea for us.

With everything that has to be sorted following a death, it leaves little room to begin to process your own personal grief, and for the past week Xander had been the glue that kept me temporarily stuck together.

When I made my way back downstairs and into the kitchen living room, I found Kat laid on the sofa, wrapped up in my mothers patchwork blanket and soundly asleep.

She needed the rest, Kat was having a harder time dealing with it, after all it was the first death she had experienced having been too young to really understand what happened to dad, but I could tell with each day, her darkness brightened a little.

I switched off the TV that was playing the same reruns we must have watched a hundred times, and pulled the blanket up around her before heading into the kitchen.

As I leant down to reach for the stack of dinner plates nestled in the bottom cupboards, I heard a metallic clatter come from my pocket, a gentle *clink* followed by a high pitched thrum.

The noise was almost too high to hear, resonating around my ears as if I could hear the waves on which the sound travelled through the air - each one a heartbeat that tickled against my skin and whispered into my ear.

The pocket of my jogging bottoms became heavy and I winced as the sound became higher, louder, stronger.

My hand instinctively reached into my pocket, and pulled out the necklace. The metal felt hot and heavier than it should be.

I wrapped my hand around the chain and the noise stopped.

I shook my head, I truly was losing my mind, but I took some comfort in the fact that I hadn't been seeing things or woken up by terrifying nightmares recently - *swings and roundabouts I guess.*

I opened the drawer in front of me and slammed the necklace inside it, pushing it shut as soon as the metal clanged against the rest of the random stuff piled into it.

That necklace had always weirded me out, but now it was a reminder of my mum and I felt conflicted, knowing I should be grateful for the last gift I would get from her. But whether it was stress, grief or the two combined, something about it felt dark, as though the pain the wearer had suffered, somehow fed it and filled it with life. A seed of despair sown in rotten soil.

My head turned to the front door as I heard a knock, followed by the familiar footsteps that belonged to the one person keeping me together right now.

"Hey," Xander said quietly, noticing Kat was still asleep on the sofa.

I smiled back as he toed off his vans and walked towards the kitchen with two white plastic bags hanging from each hand.

The smell of fried food made my mouth water as he placed the takeaway bags on the kitchen side and began to unpack the clear boxes filled with sticky rice, dark noodles and sweet fried chicken.

When Xander was around the air felt lighter and it became easier to breathe, to think clearly.

Warmth washed over my skin as he looked over his shoulder to where I was standing, gathering the cutlery before he turned to lean back, against the counter, opening his arms to me.

I practically melted against his form as I put down the knives and forks, and settled into his warm body, his scent was a calming walk in a forest of fresh pine.

His large arms wrapped tightly around me as my head lay flat on his chest. The sound of his steady heart settling mine.

Xander had been here every day since my mother had passed away. Sometimes to help sort through the stacks of paperwork and sometimes to distract Kat with a game of chess but every day he came and he held me.

His embrace was firm but tender, he knew what I needed and in his arms I was able to relinquish my responsibilities for just that moment, allowing his strength to bolster me.

The hard lines of his body pressed into my soft curves and we fitted together like lock and key - like we belonged together, and I was over denying it.

I had come to understand that life was too short to dismiss the way I felt about Xander, and I was sure with every bone in my body that this was a love that was undoubtedly mutual. That he was in love with me, just as much as I was with him. That he wanted me just as much as I wanted him.

I didn't need those words of confirmation, because his body had always spoken loudly enough and now I was listening.

My hands stroked up his chest as I pulled my head away from him and looked up at those bright green sparkling eyes. His mouth pressed into a soft smile before he leaned down to kiss my head, but before he could, I lifted my chin, and his warm lips met mine softly.

His mouth pressed against mine as I took in a large breath, taking in every part of him, his warmth, scent, and love.

His lips didn't pull back, instead his hands reached up from around my waist and stroked up to the back of my neck. Warmth trailing behind where his fingers had touched.

As his hands reached under my hair, his lips pressed firmly against mine and I parted my lips slightly, allowing his mouth deeper. He obliged and my eyes burned with tears. He loved me the way I loved him, and the realisation was a waterfall of emotions, but I did not drown, I flowed into his stream, becoming part of him and him part of me.

Our kiss was like nothing I had felt before, instead of lust and desire, it was earthy and grounded - a foundation that felt like home.

A hand cupped my face as his thumb gently wiped away a tear. I smiled beneath his lips and I felt him do the same.

A sob left my mouth, not one of sadness but of relief, of all encompassing, completely unmistakable love.

His head lifted away from mine, my lips felt instantly cold without his, as his eyes washed over my face and wiped at the dampness on my cheeks.

"What about Aide?" Xander asked, his brows pinched over his wide, green eyes.

I hadn't told Xander yet with everything that had happened, but I hadn't even spoken to Aide since that night - I guessed it was pretty clear how I felt about Xander, and he must have assumed as much, since he hasn't reached out to me since either.

"Aide is lovely, he's a great guy, but Xander he isn't you." I confessed and hot lips pressed into mine. Tears now not my own, pressed against my skin as he wrapped me inside him warm, safe and treasured.

As we parted, completely overcome with both relief and delight, I took in a huge inhale. As I looked up to the man I had loved for years, my face still wet with our combined tears, my mouth pulled into a smile of pure joy.

His own lips followed, mirroring my emotion and at the same
time, now completely in sync, we began laughing.

I wasn't entirely sure of what we were even laughing about, perhaps it was the ridiculousness of it all, of how long had we waited to do this, to admit this to one another - but I knew it was the first time in a long time that I have felt truly happy and I let the laughter flow freely from me as I fell back into his chest.

A head of messy blonde hair peered over the green couch, with a querying eyebrow raised in our direction, and Kats sweet face peered over to us, looking more rested than she had all week.

"Morning!" I joked as I started to lay the table, placing a plate on each side.

"Wait what? What time is it?" Kat rubbed her eyes, her honey hair, wild, but no less beautiful.

"She's having you on Kat." Xander smiled as he pulled out the plastic tubs of food, and placed them down the centre of the mahogany table. "You hungry?" He asked, lifting a tub of noodles in her direction.

I had never known Kat to turn down food from her favourite Chinese takeaway, and she wasn't about to start now. My heart grew in size as she padded over to the table, whilst Xander pulled out her chair and placed the noodles on top of her plate.

The three of us tucked in and piled food onto our plates, Kat went for seconds and spooned huge amounts of sticky rice and fried chicken onto her plate.

Xander placed his hand softly on my knee underneath the table, lovingly rubbing a thumb back and forth, as he used his free hand to fork the food in his mouth.

As I looked across the table, to the empty place where my mother sat I felt gutted, the wind taken from me. But as the warmth of Xanders hand caressed me, I looked to where Kats face had softened into a small smile as she twisted the noodles onto her fork, I smiled too.

After we had gorged on far more food than any of us actually needed, Xander and I began clearing the table, whilst Kat tidied up the food cartons, piling in any leftovers into a single tub.

"Hey, how would you feel about staying tonight?" I asked Xander, feeling a little shyer than usual as I dunked the plates into hot soapy water.

"You want me to stay over? Like with you?" Xander replied with a small smirk that betrayed his surprise, and I pretended not to notice as I placed a clean plate onto the draining board.

"I just think it would be nice, we could watch a film together - you and Kat could play a game of chess too maybe?" I submerged another plate as I tried to school my face from showing how nervous I felt.

"I'd like that." Xanders arm affectionately nudged against mine.

"It's about time." Kats voice said and I looked over my shoulder to the table, my hands still wet now hovered over the sink.

My sister's face had a wry grin plastered across it as she flicked her eyes between me and Xander, before lingering on the little space between us.

"Sooooo? Who's going to fess up?" Her brows raised above her suspicious eyes as she looked at me and Xander, waiting on a response.

After a few seconds of her scrutiny, I turned back towards the sink and a small giggle left my mouth, quickly followed by another nudge from Xander before he began giggling too.

"I see how it is then, I'm stuck with you two love birds for the night then am I?" She laughed as she tried her hardest to sound serious.

"Well you could always invite Isha round." It wasn't a confirmation or a denial, but one thing I knew about my sister was that she was never the one to miss what was right in front of her.

With the kitchen-dining room now as clean as it was going to get, the three of us sank onto the sofa, and flicked through Netflix to find a film we would all enjoy.

Usually this was a recipe for disaster, and was probably the reason we had always simply rewatched the same things anytime we were together - I liked romcoms and Kat preferred darker stuff - which always seemed strange and triggering to me.

There was a knock on the front door and the sound felt unfamiliar, the hard wooden door had been replaced with a more modern, far cheaper sounding plastic style door.

Isha walked in, her beautiful black hair wrapped up in a messy bun atop of her head, dressed head-to-toe in cream fluffy pyjamas.

"Hey! We were just about to choose a film," Kat said as she sat up from the sofa and moved over to where Isha flicked off her converse, already swapping them for fluffy slippers that matched her outfit.

Kats arms wrapped around her, and I snuggled closer into Xander as they hand-in-hand, walked back over to where we were sitting.

"There's room on here," I said, my head now tipping towards the small space on the edge of the sofa.

"No, you two can keep it, we wouldn't want to get in the way," Kat joked as she sat down onto my dad's favourite chair and Isha climbed on next to her, now pulling a blanket over the two of them.

Isha's brow raised as she looked over to where I was now fully pressed into Xanders chest, still flicking through the list of recently added films.

"Oh yeah, cough up." Kat said and Isha rolled her large brown eyes, before pulling out a small purse from her pyjama pocket.

My head shot up from Xanders chest to look for his reaction as Isha passed over a twenty pound note. *Was it really that obvious?*

We spent a further twenty minutes arguing over films before settling on *Love Actually* - after all, it was now November, which basically meant it was Christmas anyways.

I had watched that film so many times, yet somehow every time I saw the scene where Karen opens her present and sees it's not the necklace she found in Snape's coat pocket earlier that week, I still felt sick.

It was Ishas first time watching it, so we all practically gawked at her when we knew that this scene was coming up, and her reaction did not disappoint.

"What a dick!" She swore at the screen and we all burst into laughter.

By the time the film had finished, Kat and Isha were fast asleep, and I don't know whether it was the carbs or the warm hot chest I was resting on but I could have stayed lying on Xander like that forever.

Today felt like the first time I had really had a chance to just stop for a moment and my body clearly needed it, I was completely exhausted.

"Hey, shall we get you to bed?" Xanders voice was soft as he reached a hand under my chin.

Not having the energy to even reply, I rubbed my eyes and nodded.

Two large arms reached underneath me, and with little to no exertion, I was in Xanders arms, my head still resting against his tensed chest.

He took the stairs slowly, careful with me in his arms and as he got to the top of the landing where my bedroom door was, used one elbow and his back to open it quietly.

Placing me down on the bed, the mattress sunk beneath me as he pulled over the quilts. In my half-asleep, half-awake haze I heard him shuffle out of his clothes before sliding into bed next to me.

His skin felt warm against mine as he moulded himself around me, his large arms pulled me in closer and I drifted into welcomed darkness.

Ω

My eyes burned as they were forced open into the darkness, to the sound of an ear splitting scream and my body was instantly paralysed with fear.

My chest felt on fire as I blinked and tried to clear my hazy eyes, to see something, *to see anything.*

My arms felt heavy as though something unseen weighted down against them, something cold and stiff.

I was completely gripped in fright as a foreboding sense of familiarity, brushed against my senses.

The taste of metal stung the back of my throat as a sickly mixture of spice, fire and ash forced its way through my nose, the sharpness of it making my eyes water.

A chilling crackle whispered against my ear, and my hot skin shivered to life. The sound was quickly followed by a piercing ringing that thrummed against my head so hard, I thought my ears might bleed.

My fingers twitched and I realised I could now move my hands but as I tried to lift them to protect my ear drums from splitting, I found something forcing them down.

The blackness around me was a sea of darkness and I was deep in its waters, but as I willed my eyes to see, the void around me opened up.

My bloodshot eyes burned and my nose still stung from the acrid scent that surrounded me, as the world around me began to take form.

My eyes fell to the field of grey, dying grasslands that now surrounded me, the hot soil underneath my blistering knees burned my bare skin.

My arms prickled under the weight that was beginning to cut off my circulation, but as I looked down to pull them free, I was met with the terrifying scene I had dreamt of once before.

The body of a man, his once tanned skin now lacked the colour of life and a head of dark curly hair covered his flaccid head.

This was a dream, I knew it was a dream because I had seen it before, I just needed to wake up.

I squeezed my eyes shut.

This is a dream Lana, this is not real. It is not real. It is not real. It is not real.

I repeated to myself over and over again with my eyes clamped shut.

It is not real. It is not real. It is not real. It is not real. It is not real.

"Oh, but it is." A dark voice replied. Dripping in power, it responded to my thoughts as though spoken out loud and my entire body froze.

My eyes shot open, and staring back at me only inches away from my face, were two sinister flaming eyes, manically looking into mine.

The breath I tried to draw in wouldn't come, only my body could tremble as I looked into a face hiding in the darkness that had now returned.

A twisted face mostly shrouded in blue flames and black tendrils of smoke covered his features, the heat from him licked against my skin, and the only parts I could see of its haunting face were those terrifying silver irises and a wicked smile now curled up unnaturally wide.

"This is what is to come, it is your past, present and your future." The mouth purred without moving before dissipating into a mist of smoke that whipped against my skin with the force of wind.

"Take a look." The voice echoed from around me, and my entire body was trembling as I looked down to the body in my arms.

A tendril of darkness on the wind blew the dark curls from the face underneath it, and my entire stomach felt as though it had fallen through the earth and down into the pits of hell.

His unseeing eyes were clouded over, but still distinctly green, lifeless emeralds cracked and fogged forever. A burning knife twisted my stomach as my tearing eyes ran across his hollow face. That mouth, the one I had only just felt so lovingly against mine, now colourless and slack, void of any worldly existence.

My burning stomach twisted and my limbs shook uncontrollably as I saw the love of my life, the one man who had loved me unconditionally, lying dead in my arms.

I opened my mouth to scream but no sound escaped me, just the burning in my throat and ache in my empty lungs.

Darkness surrounded me and my arms came free, his body melting into a dark slick pool of oil around me.

Echoing around me was a vile laughter so deep that I could feel it through my bones.

I could see nothing as I clawed into the darkness. My hands reached out into the open for the dark entity, threatening to rip it from its very being.

I stumbled to my feet, my knees sore from the blistering heat beneath me as I tore at the air around me.

That's enough Hades. That is enough.

A familiar female voice reverberated around me, it was a calm voice, a voice I recognised as I would my own family, but it did not belong to anyone I knew.

My head shot around searching the darkness, feeling the presence of multiple things, but my senses felt confused, overloaded.

My emotions were a hurricane I couldn't stop, an echo of anger, pain, grief and *love*.

I screamed into the pit and this time sound ripped from me, tearing its way from my body and chased after the retreating darkness.

This time I did not awake from *a dream*, no, I understood that when I opened my eyes and I was looking towards my bedside lamp, with Xanders warm body still pressed against me, that this was something real. This was the demon my mother wrote of, and I knew his name.

CHAPTER TWENTY THREE

The morning sun was already rising when I left Xander in bed and had quietly padded to my mothers room.

Filing through the draws I found the letter she had left me and my eyes scanned over the words.

She told me of the curse that has plagued our family ever since that dark day, an ancient hex that states a Defixio woman may never love without tragic loss and my dear Lana this is where it will fall to you.

Everything clicked into place.

My grandmother's secret that had torn their relationship apart, the same secret my mother had kept from me.

My dad died weeks after my grandmother herself died, when she had passed the curse onto my mother. The curse which I knew, deep in my bones, had passed to me.

Suddenly the dreams that had tortured me made sense, the woman, the hex, the man dead in her arms.

Blood falling from her wrists.

The man in her arms, the one who was dead in mine.

That demon, the same one who had twisted itself within my mind, the one of sickly spice, ash and shrouded in flames. The one who was named Hades.

Hades, an ancient god of the underworld. I had heard of this name from films and fairytales but this wasn't a character from a cartoon or a children's story. It was a dark, malevolent entity, feeding on pain, starving from a millennia of jealousy and greed.

As fast as my feet would take me, I ran down the stairs, each step closer to the siren call singing from the kitchen drawer, the ringing becoming louder.

I pulled the drawer right from the hinges and slammed it down on the table.

The necklace, glinting in the sun, called to me, a whisper that begged me to claim it and I answered.

I unclipped the dark clasp and wrapped it around my neck, the clip closed itself as the necklace settled around my neck, the heat from the pendant tickled against my skin as the whispers that came from it, suddenly stopped.

A shiver rippled across my body and my chin rose in response, an invitation to the surge of energy that now snaked across my being and settled around me like a second skin.

My lungs filled with the air around me as I took in a huge breath and leaned against the kitchen side. With my head slightly foggy, drunk on the feeling that warmed my core I closed my eyes.

"Morning!" My eyes shot open as Kat stood in front of me and she stumbled back a step, her blue eyes narrowed. "Jees Elly, you look wired. How many coffees have you had?"

I blinked the sharp sting out of my eyes, and shook the morning haze from my face.

"Oh my god, you're wearing mum's necklace," Kat's eyes glossed with tears as her mouth twitched into a small sad smile and ran towards me.

My open arms caught her embrace and we stayed held together for a moment, just the two of us in our home.

The sound of heavy footsteps creaked against the stairs as Xander made his way downstairs, followed by Isha, still wearing her fluffy pyjamas.

The sight of Xander made my stomach drop, his wide eyes smiled at me and that small dimple might have just shattered my soul as he walked over to me and kissed me on the cheek.

The memory of his dead body cold in my lap twisted my insides, and I had to remind myself this was something I had to stop, a premonition I could prevent from becoming real.

I steadied myself on the kitchen side as Kat left my arms, not realising she was supporting me, and as I looked to the three people around the room, I knew nothing would ever be the same.

It felt like one tragic thing after the next with my life, and I was surprised that somehow I was still standing at all, how I hadn't yet crumbled under the weight of a lifetime of pain, was a miracle.

"Anyone for an omelette?" Kat offered as Isha, still a little sleepy, nodded.

"If you girls have no plans this morning, why don't we see if there's something on at the cinema?" Xander asked, his voice sounded hoarse as he flicked the kettle on and handed over a frying pan to Kat.

"Oh I'd love-" Kat started but I cut her off.

"Actually Xan, I have quite a bit of stuff to finish sorting, so I think I'll be busy most of the day." A crack formed in my heart.

His brows raised and a cough rattled from his chest.

"You okay Xan? Sounds like you're coming down with something." The crack in my heart splintered off, and I held a hand over my aching chest as he cleared his throat.

"I'm fine, just a little morning cough." He smiled palely. "Okay well, I'll check for some other screenings later in the week if you fancy it?"

"I'll let you know Xan." I couldn't hide the sadness from my voice and his eyes searched mine, his brows furrowed around his darkened eyes.

"Okay, sure." He replied as he walked a little closer to where I was standing. "Is everything okay?" He asked quietly, closer to my ear.

"Everythings fine, I just have a lot to deal with." I pushed past him as I walked out of the kitchen and up the stairs, tears threatened to fall and I didn't want anyone to see me cry.

There was a soft knock on my bedroom door and I wiped away the tears staining my cheeks.

"Lana?" Xanders voice came through the door. "Can I come in?"

How could I tell him? What was I supposed to do? My mind spun and I felt sick, searching for a way out of this, one where I could have everything I wanted. But I knew deep down that joy wasn't ever meant for me, it never had been.

I wiped my runny nose with the back of my hand and blinked away any excess gloss on my eyes before opening my bedroom door.

Xander stood in the doorway, almost taking up the entire length of it, the look of worry etched on his face.

"Lana, I'm here, I can help with whatever you need." His soft voice was a reminder of the love I would never have.

I shook my head, trying to fight the tears as his hand reached for mine, but I pulled back.

"I think this is a mistake." My voice cracked and I looked down at the floor. I couldn't face him, I couldn't look into those eyes and lie to him like I needed too. "I think last night was a mistake Xander."

With my eyes still fixed to the floor, I saw his trembling hand reach again for me, but I retreated a step back into my room.

"Lana-" His voice broke. "Lana look at me." I could hear the heartbreak as my heart splintered alongside his. "Lana I love you." I heard a sob fall from his mouth before I saw the tear fall to the floor.

I couldn't look at him. Not like this, I couldn't do it.

Knowing there was only one way he survived this, only one way he would survive me, I would need to break whatever bond we had, sever it to where it would never be able to be repaired.

"Well I don't love you." I forced my eyes to meet his and bit down the waterfall of tears waiting behind my eyes. "I couldn't ever love you like that." The words shook from my mouth with forced venom. "Xander, this was a mistake."

My body trembled as I tried to lift my chin to his face, his broken eyes now completely welled over with tears as they streamed down his face and across his quaking mouth.

He took in a shallow breath, and just nodded as the tears fell to the floor and it took everything in me to school my face and not let my own flood of tears fall.

"I understand, well I guess I'll see you later then, L." Xanders voice cracked as he tried to compose himself. "Please let me know if I can do anything, I'm still here, however you want me, I'm still here." I watched the tears fall from his eyes as he nodded and turned away. The cracks in my heart splintered their way through my entire chest when I saw him wipe his face as he walked towards the stairs and I closed the door.

My body collapsed against the door and I fell to the floor.

I wanted to scream but all I could do was sob, the place where my heart belonged ached as though I had ripped the organ straight out from beneath my ribs. I had torn it away from the person it belonged to and in doing so I had split my own chest open, leaving a cold hollow cavity in its place.

Hours passed and I didn't move, my body too exhausted from the ragged breaths I managed, as I let out every tear I had held in.

My soul felt truly crushed, I had beaten it to a pulp for a final time and I didn't know if I wanted to survive this even if I could.

As I closed my eyes and hoped for a moment of solace, a single second of reassurance that I had done the right thing, the necklace on my chest began to heat.

I looked down to the gold pendant, the ruby now glowing on my chest, the metal was hot against my skin as I pressed a hand against the pendant.

My eyes rolled to the back of my head and I was in the field again, Xanders body across my lap.

Cloudy green eyes.

Blood falling from my wrists.

The darkness was closing in.

I pulled my hand away from the chain and instantly my eyes were staring at my bed, my back still slumped against my bedroom door.

I took a deep breath, steading myself and my mind as I placed my hand over the pendant again.

I was there, in the darkness again, I didn't need to look down to feel the cold weight across my lap as I pulled my hand from the burning necklace.

It was the painful reminder of the future I had stopped, a terrifying possibility of what my love would do to Xander, and although what I saw would break me for good, I let out a breath, a moment of ease, because I had made sure that it never would.

J L Robinson

CHAPTER TWENTY FOUR

Xander had texted me every day since last week, and I knew ignoring him would never get any easier. It didn't feel right. The feeling sliced me open and gutted me raw every time I swiped to delete the notification, not able to stomach whatever it said.

Even Kat had asked about him and I had managed to pass it off as us both being busy for now, but she knew something was up, I just didn't know what to tell her.

"Will Xander be coming today?" Kat asked quietly as she straightened out her black dress and checked herself out in my bedroom mirror. I took in a large breath.

"I'm not sure he's going to be able to Kat. And I think you should wear something colourful, mum hated black," I said, pulling a dark green dress from my wardrobe and passing it over to her.

Kat undressed and slid on the dress with ease and it looked perfect on her.

It was our mothers funeral today, and I was feeling surprisingly better than I thought I would, Kat seemed better too. Having dealt with the details pretty much myself, I had allowed Kat to rest and grieve. So when she woke up today, without the evidence of a full night of tears, I assumed she was feeling better - but I guess she also didn't really know what to expect today either.

As I slid through one hanger after the next and looked through the few dresses I have, many of them too old or too small, I passed the iridescent purple dress that Aide had bought me for my birthday.

For a second my eyes roamed the shimmering fabric, the feel of the satin reminded me of how I felt wearing it. But I wouldn't allow myself to reminisce on self indulgent memories, not today, and I slid straight past it.

Finally finding a navy dress, that was long enough to be fairly modest and colourful enough without being over the top, I pulled it from my closet, and held it up against my form.

"What do you think?" I asked Kat, who still faced the mirror and plucked at the dress she was wearing.

"I think it's perfect." She replied, before she walked towards the door. "See you downstairs in five? I'm going to wait for Isha if that's okay?" I smiled, nodded and I walked over to the mirror with the dress still held over me.

We drove ourselves to the Church, which was a little further than thirty minutes away, and Isha's parents followed behind us.

It was sweet that they wanted to come, even though they didn't know her, it made my heart full that Kat had people in her life that wanted her to feel loved and supported besides me.

As the car drove up the long, winding path through the pristine grounds of the church, we passed row upon row of stones marking the dates of people's deaths.

It should have felt morbid, but there was something comforting about a graveyard, a solidifying reminder that you were still alive.

My mind wandered to Xander, and how much I wanted him here. It felt completely wrong to go through this without him, to go any day without him.

But the large, stone reminders of mortality that surrounded us served as a caution to any lingering regret I was torturing myself with.

If it meant living my entire life without his love, just to keep him from taking his place in this field, I would. I would do that for Xander. *I would do anything for Xander.*

I slowed as we reached the church, it was a small grey-brick building, with tiles the colour of autumn leaves on the roof.

The church grounds rolled across the hills beyond where I could see, and I thought to myself how old this place must be.

As we parked up and got out of the car, Isha's parents followed close behind.

My mothers coffin was being brought from the funeral home, and this would be the first time in two weeks since she had been back with us.

Although the weather was lovely, and the sun shone down on us, it was mid-November, so the air was almost freezing as we stood outside and awaited the arrival of the hurst.

I wrapped an arm around my sister and Isha held tightly onto the other, as the three of us watched a long, black car wind up towards us.

The ferryman of death sailed silently towards us in a shiny black BMW. The only sounds were the crackle of the gravel under it's tyres, and crow caws in the distance.

I took in a large breath of the fresh autumn air, as the hearse rolled closer. My arm pulled Kat a little closer it turned, and the beautiful mahogany coffin with golden hardware, came into sight.

Tears pricked at my eyes as I heard Kats breath hitch whilst we looked through the glass windows, to the inside of the car.

My mother had never liked black, in fact I don't think I ever saw her even wearing it - instead, she would always opt for something far brighter and more offensive to the eyes.

That was the reason I had decided that the flowers must be equally as offensive, and they did not disappoint. Surrounding the coffin were hundreds of multicoloured roses, petals of vibrant yellow, fuschia, purple and turquoise so bright that it reminded me of the mediterranean oceans.

They were gaudy, and far too flamboyant, but they were perfectly my mother.

Four men walked the beautiful, floral covered coffin into the church as Kat and I, hand-in-hand, walked slowly behind them.

She was holding up so well, her head held high and proud, though her bottom lip trembled a little as we passed the rows of church benches.

Every pew was empty, but at the ends of each row were a bunch of technicoloured roses to match that on the mahogany box now being placed at the front of the church
.

Kat tugged on my hand and her large eyes smiled, causing the tears that swell in her eyes to fall over her thick row of lashes.

"It's perfect, Elly." Her sweet smile was every confirmation I needed, but her words meant so much to me. After all, she was the only person I could truly, *safely*, love entirely.

We took our seats on the front row, with Isha and her parents sitting closely behind us. The four men who had helped to carry my mother in, respectfully nodded once to the coffin, and then made their way out of the church, closing the large wooden doors with a clunk behind them.

"Shall we begin?" Said the short, balding man who was dressed in all black except for the white collar around his neckline.

"Please." I managed, unsure of whether my voice would work through the restraint I currently held against my tears.

He nodded and opened up a black leather bound book, flicking through the pages until he settled on one.

"We are here today to celebrate the life of a Dagina Defixio, a woman of colourful eccentricity, and a kind heart." He spoke sincerely as he read through the notes I had sent over to him a few days earlier. "But before I go on, would either of you like to tell a story about your mother - something that you will always remember her for?"

My stomach flipped and twisted into a knot of anxiety. I had many stories of my mother, but the majority of them were blackened through the years, by my own spiteful heart. The truth was, I wasn't ready to stand and talk about her yet because I wouldn't be able to hold myself entirely together.

Knowing what she went through and why she became how she did, I could no longer be mad at her, but the bitter aftertaste still lingered on the tip of my tongue, not yet digested entirely.

"I would like to," Kat said quietly as she turned to me, "if that's okay?"

My mouth trembled as I schooled it into a smile and nodded, before wiping away the tear that fell down my face.

She placed a hand on my mothers coffin and lifted her chin, proudly embracing the tears that fell down her rosy cheeks.

"Mum, to me, you were the most kind hearted, gentle person I've ever met. You taught me to be strong, not only for myself but for others. To always be generous and to never forget the people we have lost." She took a moment and closed her teary eyes before she wiped her nose and continued. "I cannot remember our dad, but you made sure that I knew him just as well as anyone who had spent a lifetime with him, did."

My eyes burned and I wiped the back of my hand across my damp cheeks as I looked to where Kat stood, her hand still placed on the dark wood surrounded in roses.

"She would tell me stories of how they met, and how he loved it when the seasons changed and the leaves turned orange, because that was her favourite colour." She paused for a moment. "My mother made sure I had a father, even when I didn't, and that is what I will forever hold onto, her memories - *her stories*. Thank you, for everything." She finished as she lowered her head to the coffin and placed a gentle kiss on the wood.

Tears that already flowed, now poured from my eyes and I couldn't feel prouder of who she was, than I did in that moment. For everything we had faced, everything we had been through, she was still the kindest, most compassionate person I had ever known and I was in awe of her.

Kat gracefully walked back towards our bench and I pulled her under my arm, planting a soft kiss on her golden head of hair, as the vicar took up his folder again and began sifting.

"Actually, I would like to say something too?" My voice trembled as I sat up, and Kats face beamed up at me. "If we have time?"

"Of course, please." The vicar replied, gesturing his hand to the spot on the floor beside him, welcoming me to step into.

With a breath that reached the pit of my stomach and settled it temporarily, I walked across the stone floor, next to where my mother was rested.

I gripped my hand into a fist and willed the shake in it to stop as I peeled my fingers open, and placed them softly on the coffin next to where I stood.

As I looked over into the empty benches, to where Isha sat with her parents, and Kat gave me a smile that told me *you can do this*, I couldn't stop the selfish longing for one other person that wasn't here by my side. This was the longest I had gone my entire adult life without seeing Xander, and I wondered what he would be doing right now.

I wondered if he was at home, or maybe he was on shift at Joeys, probably talking to some gorgeous girl that's pretending she likes coffee just so she can tell him how beautiful his eyes are. *Ugh.*

I shook my head, annoyed that I was thinking about him - *I needed to stop thinking about him.*

"I'm similar to my mother in more ways than not." I started with my eyes focused on the floor. "I hold pieces of her everywhere. I have her eyes, her hair, her...fire." My hand reached to my chest where her necklace lay. "And it has taken me too long to appreciate those things. I wasted a lot of time, took too many things for granted and I know that it is time that I will never get back." My chest filled with an aching sorrow, that same feeling I had anytime I thought back on just how much I chose not to see. "But in the end I knew one thing-"

I was cut off mid sentence as the heavy wooden doors to the church clunked, and began opening.

It was brighter outside than it was in the small church, and it took a moment for my eyes to adjust to the crack of bright sun blaring through the doors, outlining the silhouette of someone small, walking towards us.

My gaze roamed to the shoes that tapped against the stone floor as the man approached.

His dark blue suit loosely fell from his slight frame and my eyes washed over him, not completely free of the specks of light still distorting my vision.

His pace was slow as the man clearly struggled to walk, making me wonder who this stranger might be. But as my eyes finally reached his face, I realised it wasn't a stranger at all.

His bronzed skin had paled to dull ochre and the skin around those perfect emerald eyes, had darkened. His beautiful face was now gaunt, angular and hollow as he taxed his mouth into a smile, his small dimple appeared.

My heart stopped dead in my chest as my body froze, completely stilled in a paralysing fear as Xander walked towards me. A small breeze could have knocked my unsteady knees from beneath me as my body cracked open from the inside, shattering every shred of hope left in me.

I felt my heartbreak physically, I felt it explode in my chest and burn through my breathless lungs as the reality of what I was seeing, *what I had done,* seared across my skin.

It didn't matter if I had turned Xander away. It didn't matter that I watched his own heart break when I told him that I could never love him the way he loved me. It didn't matter because it was a *lie.*

The truth was it was too late, I was already completely in love with the man now metres away from me and he was dying. *Because of me.*

"Xander, you need to leave!" I sobbed, unable to stop the torrent of tears now coursing across my face as I saw, with each step closer, just how ill he had become. "Xander please!"

I saw Kats eyes dart to me, raised in confusion before she looked at Xander and gasped loudly, but I didn't have time to think, I just needed to get out of here, *get away from him.*

Distance may be the only thing that could save him so my legs ran as quick as they could, each step felt out of body. I couldn't even feel the ground hitting my feet as I raced straight past Xander and out, into the church grounds.

The icy chill burned my skin as I kept running out into the fields of death and stone. The weather had turned grey and rain had begun to speckle from the dark skies above, before my legs finally gave out and I crashed to my knees.

The ground was soft and wet beneath me, and I just wanted it to swallow me whole, to take me away from here. The rain poured harder and the smell of wet grass filled my nose, a smell that usually, I would love but everything felt wrong, the air around me felt too thick and sickly.

The necklace around my neck thrummed against my skin, a call for me to close my hand around the red and gold pendant hanging on my collarbone.

But I had seen before what the necklace had tried to show me - the pale man lying in my lap, a vision of history once again repeating its gruesome past and I closed my eyes to shut out the image.

The rain lashed against my face and I welcomed the pain as the tears and rain joined, now raging rivers that cascaded down my sore face.

My lungs ached as I refused to breathe in when suddenly a soft hand reached for my shoulder, and I turned to see Xander, stumbling to the wet ground next to me.

He had found me in a maze of gravestones, his brittle body had come for me.

His mouth parted as rain whipped against him, and just as a small sound cracked from his pale mouth, he collapsed in front of me.

"XANDERRR!" I screamed into the rain but it was swept away on the storm that now whirled around us, the darkness pulled closer as I heaved his limp body onto my lap.

His dark curls were now soaked, and fell across his sunken face as I lifted him closer to my shaking body.

I thought I had felt pain before, but this was an agonisingly unbearable storm that ripped at my insides, tearing my soul apart and I felt hollow.

With Xanders head completely limp in my arms, my gut tore open and I screamed again with the small trace of life left in me. I howled into the darkness that gathered around me, a thick, inky mist that began circling around us.

"COME OUT YOU COWARD!" I yelled, my head whipping around, searching through the tendrils of darkness now licking against my skin. "What do you want, have we not paid enough? Have you not had your fill of despair and depression to satiate you?" The black mist began to rumble around me, a crackle of power brushed against my skin and the sickly smell of spice filled my nose and I fell into Xanders cold body.

"Must you now feast on mine too?" I yelled through each furious sob. I felt completely defeated. "Well take it! Take it all! I beg you, take it all." This was not something I could survive, even if I tried, and if I was honest to myself, I didn't want to try.

My ears cracked as the energy around me shifted and the ground began to hiss. The heavy raindrops that hit the floor sizzled and evaporated as the thunder clapped and I saw the large form that writhed within the shadows, step out.

There was no denying that the being that crawled from the darkness, was not human and never had been.

The air seemed to crackle and thrum around him, as two bright, silver flaming eyes became visible through the haze, followed by his huge half naked form. His long hair was the same colour of his eyes and it moved as though he was under water. The shadows retreated to reveal his tanned arms, covered in inky curls that shifted and danced along his skin, settling into those familiar tattoos I had seen once before.

I felt sick as a purely primal, instinctive part of me felt drawn to the attractive form this demon took. I was completely terrified and overwhelmingly captivated by the man standing in front of where I knelt, but his face, and far more intimate areas were kept veiled by the shifting shadows.

I couldn't see his features, except for his intense burning eyes, but I could sense him somehow, and there was something softer about him than I expected. I didn't feel horror or even alarm as he drifted closer, the air bending and contorting around him seemed to brush warmly against my skin.

"I didn't want it to be this way Lana." A voice spoke so deep it was almost an echo, reverberating off every surrounding surface, sounding as though it came from nowhere and everywhere all at once. Whilst his mouth was still veiled, I knew who the voice belonged to.

Xanders heavy body grew stiff in my arms but no matter how much I wanted to cry and wanted to scream, the tears would not come - it was as though every drop of sorrow had been spent and I was left with nothing to feel.

"Bring him back! You can take me, take me! He does not deserve this." I begged the dark being standing seven feet above me, and the blue flames surrounding his silhouette seemed to burn brighter.

"Hades take me!" I shouted and the males form shivered.

His large body knelt in front of me, and he was still far taller than I was on my own knees but I could see into those terrifying eyes easier now and they almost looked...beautiful.

"I can indeed offer you a deal, sweet Lana." His voice dripped like black treacle. "A promise to bring him back, but I need you to promise something in return." He purred.

"Anything, I promise anything." I sobbed. I would give up myself a thousand times over if it meant saving the people I love.

"I will bring back the one you say you love, and if, when he does return, he does indeed still love you, still *want* you, then your soul and your family will be free of me, forever." He stepped back up to his feet and the darkness moved with him. "But if he does not love you as you say he does, then you must come with me willingly." His voice turned darker as the tattoos danced along his bare skin.

I knew better than to fall for a trickster's scheme, I would not make the same mistake my ancestor did all those years ago.

"And that is it? No secret clauses? No added terms?" I spat back, finding some form of will left in me.

He nodded with a growl.

"That is it Lana." His voice crept along my skin and traced to places I ignored.

"Then I agree." I said as I looked him directly in the eyes, and they burned brighter.

There was nothing I was more certain of in this life than the love Xander has for me, and the demon was a fool to doubt it. A fool that had just cost himself the shackles he had placed on my family a long time ago.

"Just bring him back to me." I looked down to Xanders pale body, still lifeless in my arms.

"As you wish, my love." His voice faded into the dark mist, as his form disappeared and the grey skies above began to break, and clear.

The smell of autumn reached my senses again, wet grass and fresh air.

"Lana! Xander!" I heard Katerina calling from close by.

"Kat, I'm over here! Call an ambulance, quickly!" I shouted and Kat appeared a moment later, her face turning sheet-white as her eyes fell upon Xanders lifeless body.

She fumbled quickly into her small bag, and pulled out her phone, tapping the screen three times before lifting it to her ear.

"Please! I need an ambulance now!" She yelled before turning back to where I sat with Xander, her small hand over her mouth in complete disbelief.

Sirens blared and lights flashed as the ambulance arrived and pulled Xanders body from my lap. My legs felt completely numb and I couldn't stand as they shut the doors, and sped off from the church grounds.

Kat knelt down next to me, her dress was caked in mud and my head was spinning out of control. Any words were impossible to form in my mouth.

Two large warm arms lifted me from the ground, and I turned to see it was Ishas father, Shivay, now lifting me to my feet.

"We need to get you home." His comforting voice said, as he held me steady, all the way back to his car, helping me into the back seat, a moment before the actuality of it all flooded me and everything went black.

CHAPTER TWENTY FIVE

I had woken up on the sofa in our living room and I had no idea what time or even what day it was. But I was still dressed in the same dress I had worn to the church, still completely crusted in mud.

Using the back of my hand, I rubbed my eyes as my head pounded, and the memories of Xander laid dead on my lap, caused me to shoot upright.

"Xander?! Xander!!" I shouted as I stumbled to my feet, my head still feeling somewhat hazy, and the necklace around my neck hung heavy.

"Hey, lay down Elly, it's okay." Kats sweet voice came closer as she rounded the sofa with a small towel in her hand, and placed it on my forehead. The coolness soothed my pulsing head.

"Where's Xander Kat? Is he okay?" I said as I began to sob, and Kat placed her hand over mine.

"Xander is at the hospital, Shivay followed after he had dropped us off and Isha has already texted me to say that Xan is okay. He will be fine." She pressed the towel against my forehead again, and I released a weep of complete relief.

"What happened, Elly?" Kats eyes searched mine and I wondered for a moment how I could possibly tell her the truth. I decided that I couldn't.

"I was just overwhelmed, I just needed a moment of fresh air when Xander found me, he fell and I don't know what happened." The lie sounded convincing enough, after all which sounded more realistic, the truth certainly didn't.

"Well he'll be okay. Shivay contacted Joanne already, and they are at the hospital too." Kat said as she picked out her phone from her pyjama bottoms and I shifted forward to stand.

"Well what are we doing here? Let's go." I replied, trying to stand but my legs wobbled as Kat caught my arm.

"Elly, he will be fine. You passed out and you need to rest. Xander has his mother with him and she has promised to call as soon as it's okay to visit." I released a breath, he was okay. He was okay.

The next day I sat anxiously by my phone, and had already texted Xander three times, but nothing delivered. The last thing I heard from anyone, was from Isha via Kat, that Xander was being released with nothing more than a little concussion, and I was itching to see him.

I restlessly paced the kitchen and living room all morning, feeling too sick to be able to eat anything, whilst Kat just stared at me as she ate a large bowl of cereal.

A loud knock at the door startled me, and I couldn't stop my mouth from pulling into a wide smile as I ran over to answer it. Twisting the key and practically snatching the door off its hinges, I felt so ready to stare into those emerald eyes forever - my stomach was a kaleidoscope of butterflies, each one eager to see him.

As I pulled the door open and stepped forward to embrace the man I loved, a very confused looking girl with raven hair and large brown eyes looked up to me. I stumbled back as Isha walked in with a wry smile spread across her face.

I let out the choked breath I was holding, and turned disappointedly to close the door when it jammed open, and as I looked down, I saw a foot now jarring open the door, *black vans*.

My heart leapt as I watched the door open, and standing in front of me, taking up almost the entire door frame, was Xander.

The colour had returned to his perfect skin, which was no longer hollow or sunken. In fact, he looked even better than I'd ever seen him before and I didn't think that was possible. His fresh scent hit me before I crashed into his body, my arms wrapped around him as his wrapped around me and swung me out onto the front of the house.

His chest was warm, and in his large arms I was weightless as he placed me to the ground and looked down at me, his gorgeous smile decorated with that single dimple, spread widely across his face.

Before he could open his mouth to say a word, I ran my hands high up to the back of his neck, and hoisted myself up to his mouth. His warm lips felt firm under mine as I met his mouth deeply.

I was lost for a moment in his embrace, before he abruptly pulled back and my lips cooled, instantly mourning his mouth on mine.

"L," Xander said, his brows furrowed as he looked down to me and inched himself away from me.

The space between us felt cold and I was confused. I know what I said to Xander was wrong, and that I had hurt him, *a lot* - but he had to know, he was the only one I had ever wanted.

"Hey-" He said with an awkward laugh. I tried again to close the space between us again, to show him what he meant to me.

"Lana, stop." He said as I reached for his lips as he placed a hand on each of my shoulders to stop me. "Lana,

I'm sorry, I love you. I love you so much, but it's just-" I felt the world fall from beneath my feet. "It's just not like that."

My hand grasped at my chest for air, as my palm fell upon the necklace, it began to thrum and vibrate beneath my burning fingers.

Everything was black.

The darkness cleared out into an open field and I was standing in a dark purple dress, with golden bracelets lined up each arm.

Through the cypress trees that surrounded me, I could see a blonde woman in an ocean blue dress, and a large male between her legs. His dark curly hair swept over his face, as he was on his knees, devouring every inch of her.

I had seen this before, and I thought it was a dream, but as I stepped closer, I saw the familiar outline of the man I was staring at.

He lifted his face away from the woman for a brief moment, and my stomach twisted into a thousand knots. As he smiled up to her with complete adoration, my gaze fell to the single dimple that graced his cheek.

"Do you now understand Lana?" A deep voice came from behind me and my skin recoiled. "This is the man who your ancestor cursed." My skin shivered and I refused to turn to look at the demon I knew stood behind me.

He had come to collect his bargain.

"He never did love you, his soul was cursed too. Your souls were bound before you were even born. Your ancestor, my sweet Persephone, made her choice a long time ago, but this time I thought you might make another." I turned, I wanted to scold him, to question him.

But when I turned to where the voice echoed from, there was nobody there, no darkness, nothing.

Who was Persephone and why did she do this to Xander? No - *not Xander.*

I looked at my wrists, still clinking with the bracelets as I reached a hand behind, to my hair. It felt soft and it curled just like mine, but it was kept better, shinier, and it was pinned half up.

My hand reached for my chest, and I was relieved to find the familiarity of the necklace that still sat on my chest, but as I looked down, I noticed the dress that I was wearing looked old, and not just worn or aged, it looked ancient - *like it belonged to a different time.*

Suddenly I remembered the dream, the sobbing woman who had my eyes, who looked exactly like me and moved as though we were one.

The realisation hit me like a force so strong it could fell a forest.

I didn't just look like the woman in my dreams.

I was the woman. And they weren't dreams, they were memories.

Three deep tuts came from behind me and I swung around quick enough to find Hades, towering above me. A dark crack in reality hovered beside him, swirling in on itself as wisps as dark smoke leaked from inside it.

"When he died and the curse Persephone placed on Adonis' soul was broken, I knew that your Xander, as he is named now, would not truly love you." His voice dripped in arrogant satisfaction, and I wanted to claw at that face I could barely see.

"How did you know? That it wasn't still real?" I yelled, anger rising in me.

"Because I know who you love." The sound rippled against me and my body tightened.

The crack swirling next to him grew darker. A splintered chasm, ripping open the world. I stared into its abyss and felt something stare back. My necklace began glowing and scorched against my skin and I ripped it from my neck before it could burn me.

"It is time." Hades held out a hand and my body involuntarily jerked forwards towards him, still clutching the necklace in my hand.

The bargain must have taken over the will of my own limbs, as my free hand reached for his and he gently wrapped his fingers over mine.

A shiver shot across my body and circled back to the hand he held tightly. It was painful, a sharp *zap* of electricity, but I didn't let go.

The abyss grew larger and the air around us became darker, the mist that had thickened completely surrounded us.

Fire, ash and sweet spice drifted on the warm air that the mist carried and I clasped my eyes shut as we stepped into the darkness.

The world around me spun, and I felt as though I belonged to the wind whipping around me. Like I was nothing and everything all at once. My head spun violently and I felt out of control. Sickness rose to the top of my mouth with the taste of iron on its trail, before my foot landed on something solid.

Something felt cold beneath my bare skin, and I opened my eyes as the mist that surrounded us began to fade. I was standing on a stone floor, ornately decorated with small golden mosaic tiles.

I remembered the hand holding mine and snatched it away as I stumbled back, falling to my bare ass on the floor. *I was completely naked.*

Hades' colossal form was still wrapped in shadows as he walked away from the dark gateway we had just passed through, and his silver hair seemed to get shorter.

The flames that licked at his bare skin, began to die down and he almost began to look normal. *If normal meant seven foot tall and completely ripped of course.*

I shook my head and used my arms to cover my bare skin as the demon stalked closer.

He rolled his head and loosened his shoulders as though shaking off something that lingered on his skin, and the shadows that veiled the few parts I hadn't seen of him, began to fade along his skin, settling into intricate tattoos.

The outline of his manhood became visible and my eyes shot away, looking anywhere but there.

I landed on his eyes, no longer blazing with fire, but a beautiful shade of grey - fractured slate, sparkling like diamonds. I clasped a hand over my mouth but quickly regretted the skin that I had left exposed, and pulled my knees up towards me as I recognised the face which had always remained hidden, *until now.*

Blonde curls fell from where his silver hair had flamed a moment before, and his large tanned hand raked it back, away from his face. His high cheek bones pulled with a feline smile that now tugged at his lips - lips that I was far too familiar with.

The air was thick with the heady scent of spice and wood as Aide stepped out from the little mist left in the room and the crack behind him closed.

Every inch of his body was corded with muscles and proudly on display, as he knelt down to where I sat on the cold floor.

I kicked a foot out to him but he caught my ankle.

"Stay away from me! You tricked me!" I yelled, as a low laugh rumbled from his large body and I couldn't deny the pool of warmth that now ran to the base of my stomach with his touch.

I looked at the wrist that gripped my ankle and saw a single gold band glowing around it. There was another on his other wrist.

He must have watched me eye them up, as without moving his mouth, his voice filled my head.

"You have your own." He said looking down to my wrists, where I now saw two golden bands glowing as though sunlight itself was tattooed onto my skin. A soothing heat emitting from the warm, yellow glow.

My hand still gripped the necklace that I had torn from my neck, and it burned into my skin, the sound of flesh sizzled against metal, before my palm quickly released it.

The necklace clanged as it hit the ground and began to distort. The dark gold metal warped and twisted into a pool of living gold.

It was melting, the floor was melting the necklace.

The metal began ringing, calling to me - a desire for it to be close to me and I reached for it, I needed it.

But the metal was now nothing but a golden pool that swirled on the floor, the molten gold rising from the ground, splitting and circling back on itself - forging something new.

I couldn't take my eyes off it, as the song it sang became louder and my draw to it pulled harder.

The metal twisted and curled as it cooled. Fine wisps of bronze-gold began entwining around a small circlet as the molten gold hardened and the ringing in my ear was loud enough to make me wince. A crimson stone shone at its centre, set within the shape of an eye. The ear splitting sound became louder as the metal cooled and turned bronze, still hovering above where I had dropped it.

My skin set on fire as wisps of dark shadows wrapped around me, the feeling more pleasant, than painful. Passing through my legs and over my breasts, I noticed they were covering my modesty, no, they were forming clothing.

A long, black dress made from a satin so smooth it felt like water, now flowed from my body, just as I heard a harsh *clang* reverbarate from the floor beside me.

My eyes shot to the crown inches from my hand, and I felt it, begging me to touch it, to claim it. I looked to

Aide and fire blazed behind his wide eyes, he looked terrified as he ran towards me, reaching for it.

My fingers clasped the hot metal and my skin burned. Aide shouted something, but I couldn't hear anything over the siren's song that pleaded to me from within the blazing metal, as I placed the crown on top of my head.

HADES

Twenty years to an immortal is nothing, but a single minute without her by side, was too painful to bear.

So much time has passed since I made that fucking bargain, one I was still paying for and now, he had done this again.

My brother's greed is much like our fathers, his ambition to have it all, to control everything, rots him.

"Zeus is the only one that could have taken her soul Cerb. He means to disrupt the veil." I spat, pacing the stone floors of the Hall of Praesidium.

"My lord, for what reason would he do this?" Cerb asked, her blood-red eyes pinched in confusion. She was always the voice of reason, but this time I was certain - she was missing something.

"He knows who she is. Who she really is." I looked at Cerb, who was in her human form.

"How could he know? You and I are the only ones who know. And I would cease to exist before I would betray my Queen." She flipped a strand of her straight, waist length, black hair away from her slender shoulder.

Smoke billowed from her nose as her chestnut skin began to glow. Her red eyes brightened, with a ring of silver now flaming around the iris.

"Cerberus. Not now." I ordered, knowing full well I couldn't stop the primal rage that came with questioning her bond to our Queen.

"We have no choice. We cannot wait this time." I said, and I felt my shadows shift uncomfortably on my skin.

"If what you say is true, if Zeus has torn both Adonis' and our Queen's soul, and plans fate to reunite them, there is nothing you can do now to stop it." Her red lips scolded me.

That bargain I made long ago, when she was first snatched from me and born as Persephone, still haunted me. Part of me had wondered, if I had time, would she have chosen me.

"I will go." The darkness slipped from the tattoos on my arms, a dense haze now forming a crack in the air.

"You will not have long. You know you cannot leave this realm unguarded for long."

But we didn't have any other choice.

"Hades," Cerb called as I padded over to the large golden doors of the hall, "she must come willingly, her mortal body will not survive if she doesn't." I nodded as I stepped through the chasm. A second later, my foot landed on grey stone as my shadows wrapped around me, dressing me in a fitted black top and blue denim.

The black fissure closed behind me, and as I looked up, through a glass door with the strange image of a cup smiling back at me, I saw her.

Acknowledgments

It's safe to say that without Booktok, this book wouldn't exist. The story started off as a screenplay, an original project that I needed to work on for my coursework - and somehow, years later, and mountains of encouragement from the best online community of people I have ever met, we have a book.

So this is for Booktok, for those that want to read, write and live in another world for a few hours. For those that have a story to tell but are too scared to start, and for those that have given me the confidence to put this out in the world. You really are the best.

Brontey, and Polly - you have been a lifeline through writing this, and your feedback as my first readers, chapter by chapter, have helped form and enrich this story - I cannot thank you enough.

Bookclub! To all my friends in my book club and beta readers, you have no idea how much it meant to me that you took the time to read the book and give me open, honest feedback, that I could use to strengthen the story.

I could babble and babble with acknowledgements because the honest truth is, every single person in my life, online and offline, has been so supportive of this journey over the past few months, and I can't think about you all without tearing up.

So thank you, I hope you love it, and I can't wait to continue this journey.

Printed in Great Britain
by Amazon

12497167R00223